SAY I D, Sunshine

TAYLOR WILSON-WEST

Paperback ISBN: 979-8-9883969-0-1

eBook ISBN: 979-8-9883969-1-8

Cover Designer Indie Editorial, LLC

Cover Illustrations by Roze Stojovska

Edited by Freedom Editorial

Proofreading and Final Pass Editing by Type-A-Tweaks, Trinity McIntosh

Formatting by Taylor Wilson-West

SAY I DO, Sunshine

To my little cheer corner and all of the plus size girlies who have ever felt unlovable.

Author's Note

Thank you, beloved reader, for taking a chance on my debut contemporary romance. Thank you for taking the time to read what I hope you will enjoy.

Some of the content may not be for everyone, and I respect that. Something you should consider before going into this read: My female lead is a fat woman who loves her body and doesn't apologize for it. However, there is language used to belittle her pertaining to her weight (Not from the male lead). If this makes you uncomfortable in any way, I advise you not to read this story.

Nevertheless, if you love a strong female who doesn't let the words or opinions from others drag her down, this is for you. If you love a grumpy woman who doesn't believe in her happily ever after, but meets a ray of sunshine who makes her believe, this is for you.

<3

All my love, Taylor Wilson-West

Bellamy

Save the Date

I didn't know why I let Ronnie drag me out to places like this. Places where the sweaty bodies of men and women grinded on anyone they set their sights on. I mean, yeah, dancing was fun. Ronnie and I danced all the time back in my little house where we had to shove the couch against the far wall to have even a sliver of room to move.

Lights swung over the dance floor, creating flashes of sweaty bodies. You never knew who you were dancing with until you moved to a table, or just away from the frenzy of bodies. Away from all the grinding laced with sexual tension.

We'd been to Dusk 'Til Dawn a few times. Ronnie way more than me. She was my best friend, my party animal. Up all night with new stories to tell. Her blonde hair was almost white, especially in the dark club. We pulsed and moved to the heavy beats flowing around us from invisible speakers in the walls. Her hands on my round hips were warm, and when I looked into her dark blue eyes, she gave me a cheeky wink.

I didn't like to be touched. It was something my therapist and I had been working on. I didn't trust people not to hurt me, and logically, I knew it was a little extreme, but you don't grow up in a home like mine and survive without some baggage. Given the fact that my mother had taken every opportunity to pinch, squish, and embarrass me about the weight around my hips, thighs, and arms. Public shamings I could still recall with clarity that had started around the time I was eight.

Ronnie knew I hated physical affection, but I let her get away with it. She was just...different. She always had been. First, she basically bullied me into being her friend. Not that I was shy by any means. I just didn't *people* very well. It was a curse I inherited from my father.

The first day I set foot into economics class junior year, Ronnie had plopped into the seat beside me with dark sunglasses covering her eyes. I knew I wanted nothing to do with her, but she had other plans. About halfway through the professor's introduction, she ripped off her glasses and spoke to me. Her voice wasn't as annoying as I had thought it would be. Less glitter and rainbows, more depth and intelligence.

"Is he going to be this boring all semester?" she had asked. "Also, your eyes are so pretty. Like more green than gold, but in these horrendous lights, they seem brown."

When I didn't answer her weird ramblings, she'd answered herself, "At least he's pretty to look at."

That he was. He was young—a lot younger than any of the other professors I'd had there on campus. Not that I particularly cared; I didn't have time for dating. I was a few credits away from graduating. I was going to finish my degree and get the hell out of California as per my arrangement with my parents. In order to obtain my trust fund, I had to get my bachelors degree in "something useful". I would never understand my parents' complete hatred for me. It seemed everything I had ever done was wrong. So when the time finally came, I left as quickly as I could.

Fast forward almost two years and here we were, two college graduates working for the same wedding planning company.

"You aren't allowed to think about her tonight, Bell!" Ronnie leaned in to scream at me over the music. I gave her a fake smile as if Olivia was who I was thinking about, and we continued to dance for another song before she started pulling me toward the bar.

Once free of the crowd and a few lewd comments thrown

at us, we were firmly planted on two bar stools. Elbows on the illuminated bar, Ronnie crossed her long legs while mine dangled over the floor like a child on an amusement ride.

"Two peppermint twists, please!" Ronnie shouted at the beautiful bartender as she turned around and propped her elbows up on the silver bar to look out over the crowd. The bartender's hair was shaved on one side, braided on the other in a long rope down her back, her dark bronze skin glowing against the soft blue lights of the bar. She gave us a wink and set about making our drinks.

"You know I hate that shit," I grumbled under my breath, but not low enough Ronnie couldn't hear it. Holiday flavored drinks were her kryptonite even though they were essentially the same vodka flavored drinks that would normally be three dollars cheaper if ordered without the holiday flair.

"I know," Ronnie snickered. "But we need your buzz to continue! This is a heartbreak date, babe!"

The bartender placed our drinks on the bar, the soft, bluish-white light casting a pale light on the pink liquid. I had no idea what was in this, other than the cheap vodka I could smell, and I'd probably regret it in the morning, but I grabbed the drink and took a sip. The mint and alcohol burned a path straight down my throat and into my stomach.

I pushed the glass away from me, barely holding back my grimace. "That shit is awful!"

Ronnie downed hers as if it were a shot—which it most definitely was not—before grabbing mine and downing it too. She shrugged. "I paid for it. Someone had to drink it."

I rolled my eyes so hard it was a wonder they stayed in my head. The bartender came back around and this time I ordered a shot of their best tequila. Nothing said heartbreak quite like Patrón.

It went down smoothly, and I sighed at the buzz starting in my head. It wasn't like I was *that* upset. The sex had been mediocre, she was the messiest roommate ever, and on top of that, we'd had little in common. Sure, we had dated for nearly a year. Like I said, I didn't *people* well. I guess it was mainly the shock that came with learning you had been with a woman who cheated multiple times and you never noticed. It didn't bother me much that she'd moved on. If I hadn't been so wrapped up in my work, I probably would have noticed sooner. As it stood, she was now happily living her best life, while I was stuck with the mortgage we signed for. I was just glad she didn't want half of the measly earnings we would get if we'd sold it after our split.

God, when was the last time I'd had a good fuck? It was awful—*I* was awful—that sex was the first thing that came to mind when I thought of our relationship. Depressing as it may be, I still longed for exceptional sex.

"Hey, sexy thing. Wanna dance?" I faced the not attractive, but not totally *unattractive*, man talking to Ronnie. His fake blond hair was slicked back as if he'd been running his hands through it, and sweat dampened his brow.

"Run along, playboy," Ronnie sing-songed. "I'm here with a date." She threaded her arm through mine as much as she could without pulling me out of my seat.

"Oh, it's like that." He ran his tongue over his top lip, which I guess he thought would be enticing, before opening his damn mouth. "I like to watch."

We burst out laughing, and Ronnie slapped my knee. His smile faltered a little before he turned on his heel and walked away. We laughed for another few minutes, giggling like children at the audacity of this stranger. We had been dodging slimy men and their wandering hands all night. It was no wonder I found myself more attracted to women than men. Most men were gross creatures, and I was sick of letting them ruin my me time. This wasn't exactly what I imagined as a fun time, however, it made Ronnie happy and I loved seeing her happy.

It wasn't that I didn't think Ronnie was attractive. I just knew she wasn't into women. Though we never talked about her sexuality, most of her one-nighters turned out to be dudes. Me on the other hand, I wasn't into labels. I liked who I liked.

Plus, Ronnie was the only one who had stuck by me even when I didn't want her to. Like a sister without the biological mess of my family.

"Ma'am." Someone tapped my shoulder.

I snapped, annoyed, "Look, I really just need a good, hard fuck, and honestly, you don't seem like you have the proper equipment to handle those needs. So pleeeease..."

My brain shut off as I got a good look at the gorgeous man standing before me. He was tall, damn near six and a half feet. A giant compared to my five-foot frame, especially sitting on the stool. His fiery red hair was messy, but artfully arranged in a way that screamed "I know hair products". His green eyes widened before his cupid shaped lips tipped up in a smirk.

"Fuck off," I muttered, finally finishing my thought.

"You dropped your clutch." His deep voice sent shivers down my spine and a warm wave over my skin. Maybe it was the alcohol coursing through my veins, but I felt it all the way down to my tingly bits. Sure enough, my little black clutch was in his hand. It must have fallen when Ronnie slapped my knee, and I hadn't noticed.

"Thank you," I grumbled, unsure of how to approach the man in front of me since I insulted his manhood. Even though, looking at him, I was ninety-nine percent sure this man knew how to fuck with whatever he was packing.

I slowly reached out for the clutch, as if he might bite back. Our fingers brushed as I took the purse from him—and maybe I was hoping for it—but a spark ignited in my system. At the last minute, he held on and leaned forward, so close I could smell his intoxicating cologne and feel his hot breath on my ear.

"Just so we're clear, I always please my woman. Big dick or not."

He drew back just far enough I could see the dusting of light brown freckles over his nose and cheeks before he stood to his full height and smiled down at me. His grin told me all I needed to know about my face before he walked past us heading for the VIP ribbon. I watched his form like the good little masochist I was, and he looked back before ducking inside.

"What. Was. That?" Ronnie was standing, leaning back, trying and failing to get another glimpse of the beautiful mystery man. She fanned herself with the napkin from her drink as if she could pass out from his looks alone.

"I have no idea," I breathed out.

Ronnie's eyes widened. I tried following the trail where the mystery man went, but she pulled me off the seat and through the exit. The cool air of late October brushed my dark curls away from my face.

"Why are we leaving?" I asked, breathless from the exertion. Or maybe it was the entrancing smell of the hot stranger mixed with the alcohol talking. She didn't answer. Instead, she continued to pull me along, into an idling car that had a bright pink sign in the front passenger window. I realized Ronnie had ordered a car to take us back to my house while I was distracted by the puzzling man.

The man in the driver's seat was blessedly quiet—thank God, because I loathed the talkers. He drove us out of the city and back into the little town outside of Charleston, South Carolina that existed without really existing. Tourism wasn't strong here, and when we did have out-of-towners, it was because of an event we threw.

He didn't say anything as we rolled onto Main Street where the shops were all closed and the lights adorning the street glowed a faint yellow. Ronnie thanked the driver as we stepped out on the sidewalk in front of the florist Ronnie and I loved to use for our events. We never stopped at either of our places with car services. Call us paranoid, but do you ever really know?

Once the car was out of sight, the two of us raced across the street. The old colorful buildings of the French Quarter looked leeched of color in the dark night as we made our way back to where my little house sat.

Even though we had grown up in California, we both loved the atmosphere of our sleepy little town. Some of the older buildings had been renovated and painted bright colors, giving the whole town the kind of character we had been looking for.

The real beauty of the French Quarter though was the little brick paths that often led to some magical place. In this case, we followed the winding bricks to my home. Tucked away on a sleepy little street, my house sat between large leatherwood ferns and any flowers I could get to grow. Hydrangea bushes, peonies, lavender, I had a bit of it all. No matter the season, I always had something blooming. Currently, the ferns were the only thriving plants. It reminded me of the forest, especially when it rained. I loved sitting on my little front stoop and watching the rain droplets hit the green leaves, rolling down to soak into the earth.

Ronnie unlocked the bright green door with her key I had given her for emergencies only—which she instead used for whatever suited her best. And right now, it was to fall into my bed face first and promptly pass out.

I chuckled, draping a blanket over her form. After returning to the front door to double check the lock, I fed Smokie, my fluffy gray Maine Coon who demanded attention from anyone who entered the house. I huffed out a breath as I sat on the couch, ready for her to jump into my lap so I could stroke her soft fur before putting myself to bed.

After Smokie had enough petting,she sauntered off in the direction of my bedroom as I shut off the lamp by the couch. I followed her and changed into my pajamas, then pulled the comforter back gently, although I was fairly certain I could have swiped it out from under Ronnie and she wouldn't have budged.

I settled in as Smokie made her biscuits before laying down and softly purring between us. I closed my eyes and willed my mind to quiet.

Try as I might, I couldn't get the cute redhead out of my thoughts.

Bellamy

The following Monday was full of flower selections, cake tastings, and all the other hoopla brides go through. Sure, Ronnie and I may have been the best wedding planners in the South Carolina area, and loved our job most of the time, but that didn't mean we were always excited about it. There were only so many floral combinations, color swatches, and cake flavors we could stomach before finally giving into whatever our current bride's vision was. We let them have the illusion of control even though they almost always ended up wanting what Ronnie and I put together in the first place.

Business had been at an all time high since our Southern Homes article ran a few months back. Being the top duo at Fixin' To I Do was an honor I never thought Ronnie and I would achieve. It wasn't that I didn't believe in us, I just had to unlearn everything I learned growing up after we left California.

Holly-Jay, the proud owner of Fixin' To I Do, scooped us up at the first wedding we ever planned back in California, giving me another perfect opportunity to get away from my parents. Most importantly, Ronnie had been all too excited for the adventure.

When we first heard Holly-Jay's company name, Ronnie and I had thought it was a little cheesy, but it suited her perfectly. Her soft southern accent made the clients swoon.

Before Ronnie and I came to work for her she only had an assistant. Now she had three teams and two assistants. Ronnie and I did everything ourselves, so we had no need for an assistant. We were Fixin' To I Do's dream team, so Holly-Jay usually left us alone more often than not.

We had been working for Holly-Jay almost two years now, and to be honest, she didn't show up much which suited us just fine. We got to lead brides toward their dream weddings, and our paychecks hit the bank without much fuss.

It was as close to freedom as I could imagine.

"Veronica, Bellamy," Holly-Jay called from her office. We both knew she was up to something the minute she waltzed in today.

All too eager to get away from the happy couple, we excused ourselves and directed them to the room with swaths of fabric, hoping by the time we got back they would have come to their senses and hear out our plan. The bride would be lamenting over the different shades of blue she wanted to use in her wedding for a while anyway if her flower choice told us anything.

"You rang," Ronnie beamed.

Holly-Jay smiled with her teeth—at first I had thought it was a cheesy thing, but later learned it was just her face. She was pretty, with long, strawberry blonde hair and bright blue eyes. Her little nose made her look like a pixie, and her stature matched. She was a little taller than me, but where I had curves, Holly-Jay had tight muscles. Her dewy pale skin made her look younger than she was.

"We have—well, sort of—a celebrity wedding to plan." Her baby blues bounced between me and Ronnie as we took the seats opposite her white desk. She was dressed in a dark navy dress with a white cashmere sweater draped around her slender shoulders.

"We just got two more brides this month. Can't Maxine and Tracy take this one?" I asked. Not that I wasn't up for the challenge, but I could imagine celebrities weren't exactly the easiest people to work with. I really didn't want to deal with all of the attitude that came with someone who was used to getting everything they want.

"This particular bride asked for you two specifically. I'll

give your current brides to Maxine and Tracy so you can focus solely on this one." She was using her sweet voice, which never boded well for us. It also hadn't escaped me that she hadn't told us which celebrity had asked for us.

As if reading my mind, Ronnie blurted out, "Who is this celeb?"

I held my breath, thinking of all the awful women who might be planning a wedding.

I wasn't into celebrities much though, so I couldn't place the name when Holly-Jay said, "Haven Macemore."

Ronnie must have known exactly who that was because she had already started to jump around the office, fists bumping in the air. Her white blonde hair flew in all directions, sticking to her bright red lipstick. Her black slacks that made her already long legs look impossibly longer flared at the bottom, exposing the chunky heels she wore today.

"Bell! Haven Macemore! She sings, like, my most favorite song ever." Her hands squeezed my shoulders since I had yet to move from my chair. I could feel the buzzing anticipation in her fingers.

"And when is the wedding?" I asked. I couldn't deprive my best friend of her most-favorite-song-ever celebrity crush. Her fingers squeezed my shoulders again, and I was suddenly glad she kept them short, or I feared I would be sporting bloody marks in the shape of her fingernails.

"One month," Holly-Jay muttered. Ronnie squealed again as I gaped at our boss. One month? I guess when you're a celebrity, you don't have to worry about money, and it was going to cost her a pretty penny to get everything in on time.

"I'm assuming they have a venue?" I asked, willing my nerves to settle. Now was not the time for a panic attack.

Holly-Jay nodded with another one of her all-teeth smiles. "They have special permits for the fountain in the French Quarter."

The fountain? The mayor never let anyone use the fountain. It was old; probably one of the oldest things in the Quarter with its original copper and surrounded by cobblestones that had seen better days. How would we even get chairs to sit on the cobblestone streets comfortably? Exactly how many guests did Miss Macemore have in mind? I couldn't imagine this would be a small affair.

"I will email you all the details I already have." Holly-Jay had either read my mind, or my face—I'd been told it was quite expressive. "Also, Kelly and I have been talking..." She paused, giving us both a devious grin as if she didn't just drop a whole wedding on us with roughly thirty days to plan. Holly-Jay often hopped from subject to subject with little to no warning, so this wasn't uncommon, but ripples of tension crept up my shoulders. "With her encouragement, we have decided to open another shop in Tennessee, and we think you two would be the perfect pair to run it."

It was Ronnie's turn to gape. I swear her jaw dropped all the way to the floor. Neither of us spoke, too stunned to form words. Holly-Jay had never even hinted at another location. Kelly either for that matter. Even though Kelly didn't run any operations for Fixin' To I Do anymore, she was still Holly-Jay's partner in life which they made official two years ago in the most beautiful ceremony I had ever seen.

Thank you, Kelly!

"I will call Maxine and Tracy to cover your brides." She shuffled the loose papers on her desk to find her phone. "Tracy should be around to take over. Now, check your emails ladies! You have a celebrity to meet."

She was already here? Holly-Jay must have known before today that the singer was coming. Sneaky hussy, she had made sure we couldn't say no.

I could tell Holly-Jay knew we didn't have the words to convey our feelings on a new place, especially since she was offering it to us to maintain. Gratitude swelled in my chest, along with a big ol' ball of anxiety.

We read our emails across the hall in our shared office.

Private security offered by two military veterans, wedding location, tentative itinerary, the whole nine. By the looks of it, I was certain Holly-Jay had been planning for much longer than the short notice she provided us with. There was one function that I couldn't wrap my head around though.

"Holly-Jay!" I called, making my way back to her office. "This email says we're planning a benefit concert?"

"Oh yeah! It's for the history society. That was the agreement so they could use the fountain."

I tried to reign in my annoyance. "We aren't party planners anymore."

Holly-Jay smiled at me with one of her signature get-away-with-murder smiles. "I know, I know. Please Bell? Do this for us, for me?"

Sighing, I gave in and nodded my head. She clapped her hands together and let out a tiny squeak. I couldn't help the small grin that graced my lips as I walked out of her office.

I didn't even know this airport existed. Granted it *was* small; barely two office buildings wide with three chairs in the lobby. The tarmac was alarmingly close to the building, and

I couldn't help the nervous jitter to my leg as we sat awaiting Haven's arrival.

Of course before we hit the airport, Ronnie had to change, so we had made a quick detour back to the apartment she barely even used anymore. All for her to throw clothes from her closet onto the floor insisting she had nothing to wear. I finally got her settled into a white pantsuit that clung to her thighs and flared at her knees with slits down to her feet, exposing her freshly waxed and exfoliated white legs. The top was similar with squared shoulder pads and oversized split flares which cascaded to her wrist. Her dark red bralette peaked through the buttons on the blazer, but it was tasteful and oh-so fabulous on her.

She had also insisted I changed, but since we weren't even close to the same size, I turned her down. Stopping at my place would only delay the inevitable. The black swing dress I wore to work suited me just fine to meet Haven. I did, however, let Ronnie put me in a pair of pink chunky heels that connected around my ankle. *"Just for a pop of color,"* she had said. She hated that most of my wardrobe was black, but it had been my go-to color ever since I could remember.

The small private plane landed with a screech. We waited at the sliding glass doors until the passenger entry swung open and the stairs descended. Ronnie grabbed my hand

and squeezed. Turning her head to face me, she smiled.

"I can't believe we're going to meet Haven Macemore!" she squealed as quietly as what was possible for her.

I chuckled under my breath, giving her a smile before we strode hand in hand for the stairs. The plane looked nice; a bright white outside, most likely with cream colored seats inside. I didn't get the chance to look. Blacked out SUV's pulled up to the stairs, warning lights flashing. Of course Charleston would send their very best to make sure Haven was protected. But didn't celebrities have their own security detail? Two more cars followed not far behind. I guess that answers that.

The two cars closest to the plane unloaded, four very large men checking the area, including the inside of the plane, filing back out behind a beautiful raven haired woman. I cast a glance at Ronnie, but her eyes were zeroed in on her.

I guessed that was Haven. Her slim figure was covered by ripped jeans and a bright red sweater. Pearls circled her neck, and when her eyes landed on us, she gave a demure smile that would make any pageant mom swoon.

Ronnie and I took a few steps in her direction, knowing we were expected to greet her. I was so focused on Haven I didn't see the black fuel line that ran from the plane to the building. I tripped in those chunky heels, and try as she might, Ronnie just couldn't prevent me from hip checking the closest blacked-out car. I couldn't grip anything as my body careened over the hood and rolled, heading face first for the concrete.

"Bell!" Ronnie shouted as I fell. I could only imagine what I looked like. Arms flailing, legs tangled around each other. The concrete wasn't as forgiving as I hoped, but thankfully I landed on my side. My shoulder took most of the hit, scraping up my arm in the process.

I gently rolled to my back, closing my eyes and willing everyone to pretend they didn't just see me fall on my ass. Inhaling deeply a few times, I breathed through the intrusive thoughts, trying to quiet their voices. There would be no room for negative thoughts like those of my parents. At least not at that moment since all that was running through my body was pain and embarrassment.

A shadow fell over my face, and behind my eyelids I prayed it was Ronnie coming to help her girl out. Shielding my eyes from the sun, I stole a peek at my would-be savior. Unfortunately, the glare was too bright and I had to slam my eyes shut, jerking my head against the car behind me. I grumbled, bringing a hand to the back of my head when I heard the figure speak.

"Are you alright, miss?" a deep voice murmured, full of humor.

My eyes popped open again. I knew that voice—had been dreaming about that voice for the past two nights.

Sure enough, Mr. Handsome from the bar was in front of me.

Instead of the same perfectly styled hair, he had a black ball cap on backward, making his eyes appear brighter and his freckles stand out a little more. Sweet baby Jesus, could someone die from embarrassment? Because if not, I was about to be the first. That's right, I was about to shrivel up and die on the tarmac of an airport I never knew existed. Would Ronnie send my body back to California? Or would she just leave me here to rot in my humiliation?

No longer in the jeans and T-shirt I'd met him in, he wore black tactical pants with all kinds of things hanging off his hips, an unlabeled black vest, and I wondered who this mystery man really was. I sent up a prayer that he couldn't see my face through my curls.

"Bellamy! Oh, my god! Are you okay?" Ronnie's heels came into view, but I couldn't look up at her. If I did, I knew he'd see me. And then what? Recognize the half-drunk woman who told him he didn't have the proper equipment to service her needs?

How was this my life?

I prayed God would let the ground swallow me whole, right here and now. Maybe it would be peaceful, you know? To get rid of the burn of embarrassment and just sleep.

"Bellamy?" she said, a little softer this time. I guess she thought I was crying, and I guess the old me would have been in that moment. But the new me wouldn't give this man the satisfaction.

"I'm fine. Just didn't see the line." I stubbornly refused to lift my face, but if Ronnie knew I was okay, she could stop making a scene and introduce herself to Haven who was now leaning over the car to see what all the fuss was about.

From the corner of my eye, I noticed Mr. Handsome smirk before placing his hand on the hot concrete to my right. "I've got Miss Bellamy. Please escort Miss Macemore to the SUV in front of the building. We'll be along shortly."

The rest of the men, also head to toe in black, grumbled their acknowledgement and I watched Ronnie hesitate before Haven wrapped an arm through hers and they walked to the sliding doors. Slowly, I turned my head in the direction of the impossible coincidence that my mystery Mr. Handsome was here, beside me, within touching distance.

"Can you stand?" he asked, his voice impossibly soft.

I nodded before planting my hands in front of my body

and getting to my knees, which unfortunately left me face to face with Mr. Handsome's crotch. I felt my body flush and knew my cheeks were redder than a tomato.

Quickly, I used the hood of the police car to hoist myself up before he could comment or offer another hand. I didn't want him to touch me again. I didn't want the icky feeling of unwanted hands on my body.

Worse, I didn't want to feel that spark again. If I did, it would mean I was actually attracted to someone. Someone who didn't know me and all the issues that came with my life.

"Thanks," I said as he helped brush some of the little pebbles off my dress. His hand swiped a path down the side that had taken the brunt of the fall before his calloused fingers wrapped so gently around my wrist.

"Stop touching me!" I all but shouted into his face.

"You're bleeding." His eyes flicked up to mine, and I had the urge to hide my face again since he had basically just caught the start of an anxiety attack. Instead I glanced at my arm, scraped in a few places, the blood already starting to dry.

"I'll live," I said with a shrug, looking back up into his perfect face.

"Now, what kind of gentleman would I be if I didn't at least clean it up for you?" he asked, his eyes never leaving mine. "That is, if you'll let me?" His jaw looked even sharper in the daylight, and I almost wished I could cut myself on it.

When I didn't answer his question, he guided me behind the closest unmarked SUV without touching me, though I noticed the heat of his hand hovering over my lower back. Opening the door to the trunk, he found a first aid kit. After pulling out some cleaning pads and a few large bandaids, he placed them on the carpeted floorboard, doused a cotton ball with alcohol, and looked up at me, a silent question in his eyes

I nodded reluctantly. I couldn't tell if the hiss under my breath came from the sting as he lightly brushed the cotton across the shallow cuts, or the contact I was allowing him. It wasn't much, but it felt like a storm brewing under my skin.

Electricity danced along my skin as our eyes met, and we stared at each other a beat too long for my brain to compute whatever silent conversation he was trying to convey. Pulling my bottom lip between my teeth, I severed the connection between us and filled my lungs with air to recenter myself. He got back to work on the cuts, and when he seemed satisfied they were clean, he placed the bandaids on.

For another uncomfortable moment, we stood in

unmoving silence as his hand rubbed slight circles over the bandages. Our eyes locked once more, and he leaned in, much like Friday when he was handing me my clutch.

"What do you think, Bellamy?" he asked, his voice dripping with pure sex. I had never heard anything like it before, at least not directed at me. "Have I satisfied you yet?"

Just like that, the moment was over. I pulled my arm from his grasp, stomping off, heading for the building where Ronnie was hopefully waiting for me. His laugh followed me all the way through the building until the sliding door cut him off.

Bellamy

As I made my way to the front doors, I could hear Ronnie and Haven talking animatedly, Ronnie's voice lifting higher the more excited she became. I stopped, drawing in another steadying breath to steel my nerves and hopefully not embarrass myself further before stepping into the room. They were already talking about linens, colors, and what styles of dresses she was into.

"Oh, Bellamy!" Haven cried, throwing herself past Ronnie to get to me. "I sure do hope you're alright!" Her southern twang surprised me more than her little arms that suddenly wrapped around my shoulders. I had thought for sure she would be one of those modern house wives we used to see on TV—snarky and full of hate.

"I'm fine, thank you," I replied, trying to keep the obvious discomfort out of my voice. "Shall we get you to your room? I'm sure you've had a long flight."

She leaned back to observe the bandages. I slowly turned

the arm Mr. Handsome had made quick work of, letting her see that everything was taken care of as she said, "Oh, hunny, I'm fine. Why don't us girls go have a drink?"

I could see Ronnie over Haven's head nodding furiously, but honestly, all I wanted to do was go home. I didn't want to have a drink, and I really didn't want to stick around with Mr. Handsome.

"Come on, we could talk about the wedding! After all, we only have a month to plan." Her voice turned dreamy, and I couldn't help my eyeroll. Marriage seemed silly to me. It was most likely because of the terrible relationships I'd been in over the years. Plus, watching my parents marriage deteriorate and become nothing more than a contract was enough to have me convinced true love didn't exist.

The irony didn't escape me that planning weddings was what I was good at, but it just seemed to fit, especially with Ronnie by my side.

"We can take her to that little restaurant you like, Bell," Ronnie continued in encouragement. I knew she really wanted to go, and again, I didn't have the heart to tell her no. Any excuse to see Billy, she knew I wouldn't resist.

"She said she wanted a drink, Ronnie." Before I could turn, Haven wrapped her arms around my middle, pinning my arms to my sides. Anxiety blew through my system. This was twice now she had invaded my space.

"I don't care, really. I'm just so thankful y'all agreed to plan my wedding. This is going to be the best day ever!" She made sure to squeeze me tight before letting go, and I had to hold in a wince at how strong she was for such a tiny woman.

The drive over to Billy's Chicken Pit was mostly filled with chatter from Ronnie and Haven. I let my mind wander to the front of the SUV where my redheaded mystery sat. He was probably the prettiest man I had ever seen until he opened his mouth. Granted, I couldn't be too mad considering what *I* had said to him upon our first meeting.

Ugh. Why did life have to be so damn difficult? Couldn't he have been just another pretty boy with a terrible attitude and a "give you the world" complex? God must have been really upset with me and the way I left my parents back home if this was his idea of a good time.

But they deserved my wrath, mostly because of the pain I had to endure growing up with them. I didn't fit in with their life—I never had. With their money and influence, they wanted me to become a person of high society. To marry a rich man and have babies for him. To stay home and cook and clean, to be invisible.

I was never good enough, never smart enough, and my career to them was nothing more than a glorified party planner.

What they didn't understand was that a wedding was huge for every little girl or boy who had dreamed of their most perfect day. It was something I could give someone without having to offer a piece of my soul to go along with it.

It made me feel less alienated. Less unwanted, especially if this wedding hit big. Plus, a store of our own sounded like heaven, and I was already picking out colors in my head. What would our theme be? Holly-Jay had designed her space to look as elegant as possible. But knowing Ronnie, I would bet money we would go with something a little more edgy. More modern.

Before I could get too carried away, the SUV rolled to a stop in front of the door to Billy's. Billy was the first person I had met when we moved here. I had gone out without Ronnie for the first time to get a few things from the store since we had barely anything when we moved. He had found me with a map looking like a tourist, starving, and alone in the pouring down rain. Of course I hadn't had a rain jacket or an umbrella, so I was soaked to the bone and shivering when he approached me and asked if I needed help.

I couldn't read a map, and had hoped my phone would help until it shut off and wouldn't turn back on. I was a broke college graduate then and I'd known in my gut my parents had shut it off. Retaliation for leaving them and their toxic environment.

Billy had helped me into his restaurant and filled the old fireplace with logs to burn while he cooked me the best chicken I had ever tasted. He was kind and full of life, much like I wished my own father had been.

We had talked about everything like it was nothing until I finished, and he'd walked me back to the apartment Ronnie and I shared then. He'd made me promise to call him if I ever needed anything and placed a takeout menu with his phone number on it in my hands before waiting for me to get inside.

The old wooden door screeched on its hinges as our group made our way inside. His restaurant was a little hole in the wall; a building with a small dining room and a private area for entertaining. I heard Billy's boisterous laughter from across the room. He was a tall fellow with graying hair and a matching beard that looked freshly groomed, his potbelly covered by his signature white apron that read "I can cook cock five hundred ways". It never seemed to fail at being funny no matter how many times I saw it.

He stood over a table of customers, talking away. When his dark brown eyes met mine, he flagged me over with one of his meaty arms. I smiled and tilted my head toward

Ronnie, Haven.

"Hey, Pop!" I said, making sure to pop the '*p*' a little. "My friends and I would like a table."

After excusing himself from the customers, Billy wound through the packed tables to wrap me in a hug. He was probably the only person I let get away with touching me besides Ronnie. He just felt like home—it was hard to explain. But I had been coming back at least twice a week to see him and find out what kind of trouble his grandkids had gotten him into. You could get caught talking to him for hours and not notice the time slip by.

"There's my Kitten." He released me and immediately spotted the bandages, eyeing me without question. I knew he would be all ears if I had something to tell him. And that story was not one I wanted to relive just yet.

Just thinking of the red-haired man had my cheeks heating, and as if I summoned him with my thoughts, he walked through the door. My mind couldn't rationalize my body's reaction—the kind of reactions I simply didn't have with people, not even with my ex.

Billy looked me over and smiled at Ronnie, then his brows dipped at Haven before settling on me again. "Since when did you become friends with country singer superstars?" he whispered, but not soft enough that Haven didn't hear.

She chuckled and held out her hand. "I'm Haven Macemore. Nice to meet you."

"Oh, sweetheart, I know who you are," he said with his megawatt smile, covered with gray and white whiskers from his trimmed mustache. "My grandkids are gonna flip when they find out you're in town."

"Pop, she's getting married. We won't have time for that," I chided, not wanting Haven to think that was why I brought her here. Billy had the best food around, and I had a feeling she liked to eat.

"Alright, alright." He raised his hands in surrender. "I'll let you ladies dine in the back, away from all the pryin' eyes." He glanced around the room, and sure enough, people had stopped their conversations in favor of staring at Haven.

She laughed and waved as Billy led us back to the kitchen where he'd let me sit while he cooked for me that first time. The fireplace sat empty now, not needing the heat because of the bustle in the kitchen.

I eyed Mr. Handsome as I walked our little entourage to the back. He was talking stiffly with the other man who had driven us over, never once smiling like he did at the club as he stood by the door statically.

The other man nodded and left, and a weight lifted off my chest at his departure.

I sat at the table facing the swinging doors that lead back to the main dining room. Every time they opened, I got a glimpse of him. It was intriguing, in a frustrating sort of way.

The table back here was much smaller than out in the dining room, but it made for better conversations. Billy could work and I could talk—it was our thing. I rarely ate in the dining room with the other patrons. Not that I didn't want to. It was just nice to catch up with Billy since no one would bother him in here.

Sometimes his grandkids—who weren't much younger than my twenty six years—would be back here, too. They were the apple of his eye. None of them could know how much he loved them, and I envied them a little. Billy was the best grandfather, and I could imagine he was the best father, too. His son died sometime while overseas. We didn't talk about him much, and the kids didn't either. His son's picture, decked out in uniform, stayed in its place of honor in his office. It was the closest I had ever gotten to know about it. It wasn't a subject I pushed because Billy never pushed for my background either. He let me talk about whatever I wanted, when I needed to.

After he placed four sweet teas on the table, he smiled and told us he would be right back. I knew he was gearing up to provide us a master chef quality meal when all I really wanted was some greasy fried chicken and loaded potato skins.

"Billy, nothing too fancy!" I hollered in his direction. "And there's only three of us."

He scoffed and said, "I want her to come back!"

I couldn't help but laugh because he meant it. He didn't care that she was famous, he also didn't care if she promoted his restaurant. He did alright for himself here, and it really showed in his food. All he wanted was to make sure we had stuffed bellies by the time we walked out of the door.

"He's harmless." I gave him a wink before turning back to Haven, who sat across from me, "Most of the time."

I heard his laugh as we continued light conversation.

Haven told us about her vision for her big day, and honestly it wasn't what I expected at all. I mean here she was, a super star, and all she wanted was a low profile wedding. She didn't have any color preferences, and she hadn't even started looking at dresses.

On top of that, she only had a guest list of maybe fifty people. Mostly family, I guessed. She spoke of a sister for her Matron of Honor, and a best friend for Maid of Honor. But no bridesmaids.

Lucky for Ronnie and I, we could definitely work with that, especially on such short notice. With the wedding in a little over thirty days, that put us at the first weekend of December. A winter wedding, so it would be cold, but bearable.

"Have you taken engagement photos?" Ronnie asked Haven.

"Oh goodness, should I have?" The look of horror that crossed her face had me almost spitting tea out of my mouth.

"No." I had to hold in my laugh. "Honestly, you don't need them. We can just do bridals."

"We have the perfect photographer for you!" Ronnie smiled and grabbed her tablet from her tote she liked to call a purse. "He's amazing, and I think you two will become fast friends. I know we did!"

I had to agree. Xavier-Michael was the premier photographer in South Carolina, even though he mostly stuck to weddings, engagements, and bridal shots. It was his way of capturing everlasting moments. He was a people person much like Ronnie, and I couldn't fault him for wanting to experience all types of people. We had planned a Greek wedding the year before, and those pictures were legendary.

It wasn't long after our second wedding with Xavier that we knew he would be the perfect asset to us. Now, he mainly contracted with Ronnie and I. We kept his photography business, New Leaf Photography, busy throughout the year, and he was mostly booked solid for the next two years.

He rounded out our friend group that met every month for game night. It was our only time to speak completely work free.

"Oh my goodness! This is his work?" Haven exclaimed, her eyes darting between Ronnie and I as she continued to flip through the portfolio we had built from our previous clients. I was pretty sure he already had a wedding that same day. Maxine and Tracy would be handling that bridezilla, thank God. But I knew he wouldn't want to miss the opportunity to photograph a celebrity wedding, so I had texted him earlier, letting him know he might need to finally hire help to which he immediately turned me down. He just didn't know what was coming his way.

I eyed Haven's ring. It was simple: A solitary, emerald cut diamond, crystal clear with a few more around the band on either side. It had my thoughts traveling to the ring I could have had if it weren't for my conniving parents. My grandmother had wanted me to have it, something my mother never got over. So once I left, she kept it along with all the other things I was promised.

Billy had come and gone, placing dishes of mashed

potatoes, collard greens, macaroni and cheese, and fried chicken in front of us. Our table had already devoured two baskets of his yeast rolls before he dished us up. I could smell the bread cooling near the oven, and I hoped he would bring at least one more basket back. Haven and Ronnie both praised Billy's food, and what we didn't eat he placed in to-go containers and sent them with us.

Billy kissed my cheek after walking us to the car. "Don't go lettin' this one boss you around, alright?" He stuck his thumb out, gesturing toward Haven. "I'll jerk a knot in her tail if she gets outta line, you hear?"

I couldn't help the chuckle from escaping my lips before throwing my arms around his neck.

"I love you a bushel and a peck," he whispered just for me. After almost two years, Billy had become my own stand-in parent, and I couldn't have felt any better knowing he would always be in my corner.

"And a hug around the neck," I finished before sliding into the SUV. The mysterious redhead sat in the front seat, never speaking a word.

We dropped Haven off at Bedknobs & Broomsticks, the local bed and breakfast she insisted on staying at. Once she was set and in her room, Ronnie and I headed back to my house. We had plans to make, and fast.

Bellamy

The next morning, I woke to a glaring alarm and an empty house. Ronnie probably slipped out to change and shower. I made myself a quick breakfast of fruit and a bagel smothered in peanut butter and chocolate chips.

God, peanut butter and chocolate is the best combination.

After devouring my breakfast, I slipped out of my T-shirt and into a pair of black jeans that clung to my curves and hit my ankles. Grazing over my bras, I chose the one that made the girls sit nice and pretty, which always gave the illusion that my stomach was smaller. Not that it really mattered, it was just a fact. I loved my wide hips, soft stomach, and large breasts, and no one could convince me otherwise.

Finishing it off with a V-cut, dark red blouse, I made my way to the bathroom. I applied my minimal makeup and winged eyeliner, glossing over my lips with a dark nude matte lipstick. I fluffed my curls, careful of the piercings that lined my ears, and headed to the door where I slipped into my tried and true black flats.

Throwing open the door, I inhaled the scents of morning. Dew coated the little forest in my front yard, glistening in the rising sun. Pulling my phone from my back pocket, I sent a quick text to Ronnie and Xavier, letting them know to meet me at the shop. Xavier texted back immediately telling me he would be late; still editing a few photos from our last wedding.

On my walk, I made sure to stop by my favorite flower shop, Thorns & Petals, where Misty was just opening up. Ronnie and I discovered Thorns & Petals shortly after our move. Misty could get us anything we needed, and her prices didn't cost an arm and a leg. Buckets of poinsettias propped the doors open so she could cart out the sidewalk flowers, their blossoms in deep hues of yellow, red, and oranges.

Misty gestured me over, and I made my way to grab the other side of her cart before it toppled sideways. She pushed as I pulled to bring the cart over the hump at her door, settling it against the shop windows.

"Lord, I'm getting too old for this," she said, pretending to wipe sweat from her brow. "Thank you Bell." She snapped her fingers like she just remembered something important.

"Glad you stopped by! I have that sample arrangement for you inside."

I followed her into the maze of flowers and greenery. Thorns & Petals was the best place for anything a gardener could desire. Misty had actually helped me plant the hydrangeas in my front yard when I bought the house.

We walked back through the swinging door that led to her work station. The floor and tables were usually covered in stem clippings and flower petals, but today it was all clean save for the small work table right in the center of the room.

The sample bouquet of flowers sat in a milk glass with large white gerbera daisies, sprigs of fern, and a touch of baby's breath. It was beautiful, elegant, and clean—just like the bride this coming weekend wanted. I snapped a few pictures and sent them off to the bride as well as Maxine and Tracy for confirmation.

"Misty, this is beautiful. As always."

She blushed and pulled my attention to the front of the store where some morning patrons waited with a few stems of carnations and roses to purchase for whatever lucky partner they would be gifted too.

Maxine and the bride texted back that the flowers were a go. Thank goodness—this was the last thing I needed to transfer over to Maxine and Tracy for the bride this weekend. No way Ronnie and I could attend that event with Haven just now coming into town.

"The flowers are approved. We'll need seventeen for centerpieces and a few for the gift tables," I said, glancing over the notes in my phone for the bride this weekend.

"You got it, girly. Now scoot off. I've got money to take." She winked at the men near the register and they smiled back at her as I passed the front doors.

The sidewalk was a little busier now that the sleepy town was awake, and I took my time heading for Fixin' To I Do, taking in the shops sitting out signs on the sidewalk advertising discounts with cute little messages, breathing in the roasting coffee. The glass windows were being cleaned and prepped for the art that would be all over for the holiday season.

It was another reason why I loved it here. Everyone got into the holiday spirit. Even the maintenance crew would be hanging wreaths of garland over the lampposts and lights in the bare trees that line the sidewalk, giving the appearance of wonder and promises of snow although we only got a dusting every year. The small drug store on the corner of the shop's street had old school lettering you would see at an apothecary back in the day, and the couple that owned it sometimes dressed that way too, bringing old school dresses and suits back to life.

Olde Elixir Parlor was probably one of my favorite places that had absolutely nothing to do with weddings. I threw up my hand at the window as I passed. The shop owner's wife, Georgie, smiled and offered me a wave as I continued to work.

The outside of our shop was painted a charming yellow with light blue trim, the sign displaying calligraphy lettering in shades of white across the bottom saying *"Fixin' To I Do"*. Pictures of our previous weddings were exhibited in the windows along with Holly-Jay's very own wedding gown.

The front door stuck sometimes so I had to pull a little harder the second time I tried the handle. It must have loosened it the first time because I pulled it entirely too hard and tripped over my own damn foot.

I braced myself to hit the hard concrete but two arms caught me around the middle before I made impact. On instinct, I took a deep breath, steadying my heart, taking mental notes of where I should have been hurting, but wasn't.

Men's cologne and a hint of mint enveloped my senses, and it was intoxicating. As the stranger lifted me up, I caught a small glimpse of red hair.

Mystery man again? Add that to the other *two* times I

had fallen over myself in his presence, he might have been starting to wonder if I could even function as a human being. I guess I should have been happy he didn't let me fall, but I was more irritated that he had to see me in yet another embarrassing moment. When had I become such a walking disaster?

"You don't have to swoon to get my attention." He chuckled while steadying me on my feet before removing his hands from my shoulders. The cool air hit the spots his hands left, and I found myself wanting his warmth back. The thought stunned me for a moment before his words registered.

"I didn't swoon," I grumbled once I got out of my tangled thoughts. I reached for the door, but before my hand could close around the handle, his large hand wrapped around mine.

"Let me." He smirked. "I'd hate for the door to spank you a second time."

I could think of a spanking I wouldn't mind having. No, Bellamy, NO. I shut that train of thought down real fast. Taking a deep breath, I motioned for him to open the door. His back brushed against my front as he stepped in front of me to pull the door open.

I flexed my hands and walked through without thanking

him. There was a current of something traveling between us, but I didn't want to think about that right now. What I wanted to know was why I let him touch me again without going absolutely berserk like my normal response to practical strangers.

Walking straight through the waiting area, tasting room, and little kitchen, I found Holly-Jay typing away on her computer.

"Why is he here?" I asked, impatience running through my veins. I wasn't usually such a bitch, but the man irked me, and I didn't even know his damn name.

"Who is this *he*?" Holly-Jay looked up from her computer, a saucy smirk graced her features.

"Gosh, Sis. Not even a hello for your little brother?" His voice startled me—I didn't realize he had followed me back here.

Wait, did he say *brother?*

I was so screwed. Holly-Jay would have to fire me now.

Or maybe I could just quit. If she found out what I had said to him...I couldn't imagine the embarrassment.

Holly-Jay looked up then and squealed, "I'm so glad you're home!" She launched herself at him, wrapping her arms around him in a hug, which I couldn't imagine was all that soft considering the gear he was wearing.

He patted her back and smiled. When she let him go, I mentally kicked myself for not noticing sooner. Even though she had more blonde in her hair, the shade of orange was the same. So was the tilt of their eyes.

But that was where the similarities ended. He was tall—much taller than Holly-Jay. His eyes were deep green where Holly-Jay's were bright blue.

"I got in early a few days ago," he said with a shrug and a wink my way.

Astonished, I asked, "What?" at the same time Holly-Jay said, "Well, you should have called."

She turned to me, confusion written on her face. My feet felt rooted to the floor, but I couldn't look away from the two of them.

"Bellamy, why don't you go ahead and get set up in the screening room?" Her voice was soft, but her gaze still held a bit of wariness, like her confusion over my outburst would suddenly reveal itself.

I nodded, not taking my eyes off my boss's brother until I was safely in the screening room next door. I sunk into a chair, willing my nerves to quit firing off in every direction. It pinched like little bursts of pinpricks lighting up inside my head.

I took two deep breaths, closing my eyes and finding

my center. When I opened them again, they landed on a blank deep green wall. It reminded me of his eyes, and I wondered if Holly-Jay had painted it this color specifically to remember him.

"I brought donuts!" Ronnie's voice carried through to the back room where I had set out all of the pictures and swatches that we had come up with last night for Haven's wedding. We had three theme options: a winter wonderland complete with fake snow, Christmas complete with reindeer, and mulled wine complete with a wine tower.

Each had their own color scheme that we had perfected last night. Since Haven didn't have a dress, we didn't want to pick a theme without her.

The country star followed behind Ronnie as they made their way to the screen room. Haven eyed the light gray walls of the room shyly. When her eyes focused on the emerald green wall adorned with her options, they went wide. I had arranged the options neatly in groups so there would be no confusion on what went with what.

I placed a large copy of one of Xavier's fountain pictures right in the middle so she could get an idea of what each of the options would look like. She didn't say anything as she approached each. It was the bare bones of what we would build on for her big day.

Ronnie bumped my shoulder, her sign of thanks for getting this together while she did who knew what.

Holly-Jay and her brother entered the room not long after. "Bellamy, Veronica. This is a great start." She crossed the room to where Haven stood, offering suggestions and moving pictures around for a better view.

Mr. Handsome immediately went for the box of donuts. Ronnie's head whipped toward mine when she saw him, eyes dancing with glee, smiling so wide I thought her cheeks would burst. "Oh, this ought to be fun." she said while rubbing her hands together, which didn't bode well for me.

"I'm going to do my best to forget he's even here." I pinned her with my serious glare.

"To pretend who isn't here?" He was suddenly beside us, and it unnerved me that he had moved so quietly.

"Could you mind your own business?" I snapped as softly as I could, praying Holly-Jay and Haven were too engrossed in their chattering to hear my tone.

"Considering you are my business, I need to know these things." Glaze from the donut stuck to the corner of his mouth and I had the sudden urge to wipe it off with my hand upside his head.

"I am not your business. Haven is. And for the record, it's

you I want to pretend isn't here." My snark didn't seem to bother him at all. Actually, the look in his eyes made me think he was looking forward to it.

"Too bad, Sunshine." He stuffed the rest of the donut into his mouth and chewed slowly. I watched his Adam's apple bob as he swallowed, and had to suppress the urge to vomit. "I've been asked to watch over Haven, and as it seems you and Haven will be spending a lot of time together, that makes you my responsibility as well."

He retreated to the corner of the room, a perfect vantage of the whole space, including the door. Ronnie looked between the two of us before whistling. "You two just need to hate fuck."

My mouth swung open as I turned away from where he-who-is-too-handsome had taken up residence. "Ronnie!"

I couldn't deny I would enjoy it. It had been a while since I felt the touch of a man, but that one? No, I couldn't, that would be...crossing a line.

Right?

My boss's brother, the veteran in charge of keeping our bride safe? No, I couldn't do it. I shouldn't have wanted to. But I would be lying if I didn't admit that I could feel myself get all hot and bothered at the thought.

"Bellamy, I think we have an idea," Holly-Jay called over her shoulder. I watched her rearrange the pictures and get rid of the ones Haven didn't like. "What about this?"

Haven's eyes widened, and I caught the faint glint of water gathered in her eyes. She loved it. I had to admit, I would have chosen the burgundy and white pairing. They had settled on a mix between mulled wine and winter wonderland, keeping both the fake snow and wine tower. This wedding would be perfect even if I did have to deal with Mr. Handsome.

Aaron

B ellamy was gorgeous, with dark brown hair in spiral curls just a little past her shoulders and impossibly dark lashes that framed the most gorgeous set of hazel eyes I had ever seen. I couldn't see them in the club before, but twice now she had looked up at me with contempt, and I couldn't get her out of my head.

She was a disaster walking. Catching her at the door, I almost asked how her arm was doing. I just couldn't think. My arms around her body, smelling the sweet scent of vanilla and coconut, something entirely her... My mind had gone blank as I held her soft body against mine.

She wanted to pretend I wasn't here, but I definitely noticed her little glances when she thought I wasn't paying attention. My eyes kept drifting to her ample backside. I could tell when I had wrapped her up in my arms that she had a soft stomach and the kind of hips made for holding.

Then I started to imagine what those hips would feel like

naked and under me. I had to shut that shit down as soon as I could or I would have a hard dick during this entire meeting, and even though my pants were black, it would be pretty fucking obvious.

Too obvious for the spitfire that scolded a stranger in a club. I could only imagine what would come out of her mouth if she knew my thoughts were consumed with her.

I watched the four women as they fussed over a few minor details for what felt like hours. Good thing the blonde had brought donuts. I was starving, and in my anticipation to see Bellamy, I had forgotten to eat breakfast after my run.

Holly-Jay rearranged some photos and they all stepped back to admire the work they created as a team. It reminded me of how my own team operated as a unit. Where one lacked, the other stood strong. I missed the hell out of them. They'd had my back on more occasions than one. They'd saved my damn life.

It was odd to see in this type of setting. Wedding planning seemed too tedious. A show of wealth that most didn't even have, or an excuse to shove your happiness in guests faces. If there ever came a time I found the right woman, I would skip all the fanfare and go straight to the court house.

My eyes seemed to gravitate toward the short, dark haired woman with a sharp tongue on their own, keeping her in my sights even though I was supposed to be watching the darker haired celebrity.

I could do this. While I was chanting in my head, *I could do this, I could do this, I could do this,* a picture fell to the floor, and of-fucking-course Bellamy had to be the one to bend over to pick it up. She bent at the waist, leaving her ass straight up in the air, looking plump and delicious.

Those dark jeans clung to her every curve—her thighs stuck together, the material stretching tightly around them, and damn if I didn't imagine what they would feel like wrapped around my face.

Maybe I couldn't do this.

I'd had a rough time assimilating back into civi life since leaving the Marines. Everything I had ever worked for, gone with one decision. I wasn't upset about it, I knew it was the right call for me. Holly-Jay was all I had left, and if anything happened to her while I was away... I didn't think I'd survive it.

"We're heading to the dress shop," the blonde girl said, whose name I believed was Veronica, pulling me from my thoughts. The other three women were already out the door by the time I snapped out of my daydream. I nodded and followed her out of the room to where Bellamy and Haven already had their coats on and waited for Veronica.

Holly-Jay turned to face me. "I'm so happy you're home, Aaron." Her eyes went glassy and I crushed her to my chest, not wanting to see her cry again. She sniffled and put on her brightest smile. "Ladies, you're in the best hands! If you need anything I'm just a phone call away."

"Are you ladies ready?" I asked, heading for the door to make sure there wasn't a crowd. Townies knew Haven was here, but most of them would wait until her benefit concert later next week to approach her.

I spun the keys around my finger, catching them in my palm. Bellamy made a dash for the front door of the shop, holding it open for the women ahead of me and letting it slam closed when I tried to walk through. I laughed, silently thanking the man upstairs for military issue boots.

Bellamy took the lead toward the black, unmarked SUV I had dropped off for us to use last night with one of my best friends, Finn. I unlocked it using the key fob. The lights popped on and the doors clicked.

Bellamy's hand raised to grip the back handle, but I wanted her up front with me. "It will be cramped in the back, why don't you sit up front?" I didn't say her name, but I knew she would know I was speaking to her.

Her friend seemed to pick up on my suggestion and said, "Yeah, Bell. Go ahead. I'll sit with Haven." I could hear the mock innocence in her tone, and I didn't need to see her face to know Bellamy was shooting daggers at her friend with her eyes. If looks could kill, the blonde would most likely be a pile of ash on the ground.

"Let me grab that for you." I mocked a bow and tugged on the passenger door handle, slightly nudging Bellamy out of my way so I didn't end up whacking her with it.

She cursed under her breath and I smirked at her. "If I sit here, I cannot be held accountable for my actions," she sassed.

"I am most interested in seeing what those actions entail." I leaned closer to her, hopeful that she would lean a little closer to me so I could breathe her in again.

Her tiny fist punched into my stomach and I *umphed*. I wasn't expecting that, but it made me grin nonetheless. She was feisty. I should have known by her words that she would be. I couldn't help but push her to see how far I could before she snapped.

"That is the least of my actions, *Aaron*," she growled in my ear, but when she pulled back, her face gave nothing away. She pulled herself up into the seat and gripped the handle to shut the door in my face.

I laughed under my breath and rounded the hood of the car. Silence greeted me as I started the engine and pulled off the curb. The dress shop they wanted to take Haven to was about a forty minute ride into the larger part of the city.

I didn't mind. With Bellamy in the seat beside me, I could steal little glances at her, burning her features into my brain. I had a feeling if I let her under my skin, she would dig her claws in and never come out.

Veronica and Haven conversed nearly the whole way there as Bellamy and I sat in silence. Pushing her nerves right now wouldn't do me any favors, and since I actually wanted to get to know her, I chose to keep my mouth shut. She always seemed to have nothing nice to say to me, but I didn't get the impression that was her go-to attitude. I needed to know more. I'd get her to warm up to me.

Eventually.

My sister loved her, even talked about her and Veronica all the time. So I knew she had to have a heart of gold. My sister knew good people. It was a true gift that neither of our parents had, but Holly-Jay was special.

The dress shop must have known we were coming. Once I pulled up to the doors, they swung open and men in sharp black suits stood at the entry. I unbuckled my seatbelt and told the girls to wait before exiting the vehicle. The last thing I needed was one of them getting run over in the middle of the street.

I opened the back door first, letting Veronica and Haven slip out onto the concrete before sliding up to Bellamy's door. She didn't wait for me to open it, instead pushing it open with her foot and nailing my hand in the process.

"Shit." I huffed. "You wound me Sunshine."

She eyed where I held my hand with the other to ease the sting, and a brief look of apology flashed across her face before she walled up again.

"I warned you I wasn't liable for my actions." She sauntered off after the other girls, but I noticed the way she swayed her ass a little more.

I was so fucked.

Bellamy

Dress shopping was arguably the worst part of wedding planning. How many dresses do you think the average bride had to try on before she found "the one"?

Too. Damn. Many. Approximately.

Upon entering the lavish store, attendants brought out champagne and orange juice. Of course they had known we were coming. I could only guess that Ronnie had told them it would be for a celebrity.

They had cleared out the entire space today just for us. A small mercy, because the place usually had about ten to twelve brides at a time, complete with all the feminine chatter about the way a bride looked in a dress, and each with one or two women from their wedding party to "hype" the bride up. Don't even get me started on the snide comments and hastily thrown in "no offense" after a truly appalling comment.

You would think it would be a happy time for a bride, but

more often than not, it was the worst experience.

Mothers, aunts, sisters, cousins, even best friends had their opinions, and by God they didn't hold back. I couldn't even remember the amount of times I had consoled a bride whose body had been torn apart for sport, all in the name of love.

We stopped at the carpeted area where Aaron reappeared after parking the SUV in the adjacent parking garage. He leaned against the lushly painted pink wall even though cream cushioned chairs lined the room.

We all took a seat as the champagne was poured. Since Ronnie and I normally drove, we didn't waste the opportunity to indulge in the sweet alcohol. Free booze was free booze after all, and I definitely needed it after that long drive with the veteran's eyes on me.

Aaron didn't take a glass, passing the attendant over and settling his sights on me.

I scowled at him and faced the head attendant. Gaby introduced herself to Haven, she was an older woman with blonde hair that was slowly turning gray and a tall, slim build.

She had the cutest little cat eye glasses perched on her nose. "We have a few designers on site at the moment that would love for you to try their latest creations."

I tuned her out as I went in search of what I thought would be the perfect gown for Haven. It might have been rude to walk out as the attendant was making introductions, but I loathed the choices that woman made. Ronnie and I didn't normally deal with her. Zoey was our main girl, but she was on maternity leave with the sweetest baby boy.

Since Haven was tall and willowy, anything would look stunning on her, but seeing her face back at the shop confirmed the dress pick in my mind. She wanted a quiet wedding, and her gown would reflect that. I could only imagine the extravagant dresses the attendant had secured for Haven to try on.

After heading to the back of the store, I slowly picked my way through the dresses there, looking for the perfect lace number to match the vision in my head.

"Isn't the bride the one who's supposed to be picking out her dress?" I heard Aaron's voice. Of course he didn't understand the extent of my job. Or his, apparently. Why would he? I guess I figured since his sister owned the company, he would at least have some sort of inkling. Oh well.

"It takes a village." I shooed him away from the rack with my hands, still combing through the lace numbers until I spotted *the one*. "Shouldn't you be watching Haven?"

I pulled the plastic wrapped dress from the rack and held it out. But since my arms weren't very long I couldn't get the full effect.

"You want me to watch her get undressed?" he replied in the same tone that had me squishing my thighs together.

"I don't particularly care who you see getting undressed."

I pushed past him with the dress slung over one arm, but the bottom was too long and I just ended up stepping on the plastic covering. Annoyed, I took a step back, right into his front.

He braced his hands on my upper arms, brushing the scrapes that still stung a little. But his touch is what sent me over the edge. I hissed and tore my arms out of his hands, which probably wasn't the smartest thing to do. My back hit the door jam and my breathing became labored as I struggled to gain my composure. The dress lay forgotten on the carpeted floor between us, the clear vinyl covering crunching against the lacy fabric.

"You seriously don't understand what *dont touch me* means, do you?" I screeched. "You just can't keep your hands to yourself. Why don't you get it?"

It was the third time he had touched me without permission, and I was about to come out of my skin over it.

But because I liked it, or because it was uninvited I didn't know.

To his credit, he didn't say anything, though it was probably due to shock.

I glared at him all while trying to calm my breaths. He couldn't really understand why human contact was such an issue for me. I should have been able to give him some grace. But he kept doing it, touching me as if he had all the right in the world.

"Why do you insist on touching me?"

He had his fist raised, teeth sinking into his first finger. With a huff, I picked up the garment bag and stomped off to the main pedestal. Haven should've had on a dress already, but Ronnie was on the phone and alone when I arrived.

"Yeah, we're here now," she said into the phone, glancing over at me. "Well…" She cupped the phone with her hand and mouthed "Xavier" with a roll of her eyes. "Just get here. Haven will be in her first look soon."

She cut the phone and looked between Aaron and I.

"This one is just stunning on you." Gaby praised Haven as she walked forward, stepping up on the pedestal, and saving me from the inevitable questions that were surely brewing in Ronnie's mind.

"You should go out in the waiting room," I threw over my shoulder, knowing Aaron probably wouldn't listen, but trying to put distance between us anyways.

His body almost brushed up against mine as he leaned down to whisper, "Not a chance."

Butterflies erupted in my stomach, and goosebumps covered my skin. But not the good kind.

"Please stop touching me," I whispered, hopefully quiet enough no one but him could hear. I was starting to form a slight headache.

He relented and backed away, giving me room to breathe without his scent invading my nose.

Instead of giving him any more of my time, I crossed around the pedestal, admiring the empire waist of the dress. A sash in bright blue had been tied around her slender waist, making her look entirely too small. The dress was plain—much plainer than I thought they would pull.

"It's too plain," I said with an edge in my voice. "The waistline makes you look too small."

Ronnie nodded and Haven looked relieved, and I would have bet my left tit this dress had been pushed on her. I handed Gaby's assistant the dress I pulled and asked to see it next. The look on Gaby's face told me she was not happy that I had picked a dress in her absence.

I get it, this was her job, but the moment I had seen Haven's eyes light up with the plan, I knew what the perfect dress for her looked like. I knew Ronnie would agree, but I wanted to surprise her.

The glass double doors of the dress shop flung open, revealing a frazzled, yet completely put together, Xavier-Micheal—a feat only he could pull off.

"I'm here! I'm here!" he cried dramatically as if he had to run the whole way here. I rolled my eyes as he leaned in to kiss Ronnie's cheek. He wasn't tall—a little taller than me—but not taller than Ronnie in heels. His frosted hair had been gelled back giving him a polished look. He was dressed in a bright, baby pink sweater, khaki slacks, and if he could have gotten away with wearing crocs he would probably be wearing them. Instead, he had brown Sperrys slipped on over his feet.

Aaron moved into action, his long legs ate up the distance toward where Xavier had hustled in.

"What are you–" I started.

Xavier turned at the exact moment Aaron reached out to grab him.

"Oh helllllo handsome." Xavier blushed and glanced to where Aaron's hand landed on his shoulder. "To what, or *whom*, do I owe the pleasure?"

"This is a closed event." Aaron clipped in a no nonsense voice.

Xavier gasped, literally, as if it was a crime that not all good looking men knew exactly who he was. "I'm Xavier-Michael, photographer extraordinaire, and you are?" He squinted up at Aaron but somehow still seemed to look down his nose at him. A talent I could never master.

Aaron looked to Ronnie and I for confirmation before letting Xavier go and stalking around me to lean against the wall, without answering his question.

Xavier hopped over the pedestal and pulled me into his arms, even though he knew I hated physical affection. He loved to push his luck with me, but I had to admit I liked the bastard. He was fun to be around, and he really did have the eye for this.

"Who are you?" Xavier asked again, his voice still edged on a flirty tone as he looked over my shoulder. I had to hide the snicker climbing up my throat.

"Aaron Lark." He held his hand out to shake Xavier's, and I swear the latter almost fainted from chivalry. His eyes damn near making hearts, he was still holding Aaron's hand, and it was starting piss me off.

"I don't know Mr. Lark very well, but I'd say your flirting is off-base," I snapped. Why I needed to claim him in front of Xavier was beyond me. It was a knee jerk reaction I would not be repeating.

Xavier and Ronnie shared a look, and I had to take a deep breath before Xavier opened his mouth again.

"Touchy." He smirked, and I swear I had never hated either of them more. My face had to show exactly what was on my mind. I was just glad Aaron was behind me.

Small blessings.

"What did I miss?" he asked as he made his way over to the champagne.

"Empire waist, plain satin, big sash," I stated the facts of the dress, knowing without seeing it he would hate it.

"She didn't!" he exclaimed, tossing his hands up in the air and turning to look at me. Thank God the glass he'd taken was still empty. He poured the champagne with the flair that only Xavier could pull off and took a long sip. "What's the theme? Details. What are we working with?" He snapped his fingers, but not in an annoying way. It was something he did while getting all the details.

I broke down the ideas, all while conscious of Aaron's presence behind me. He didn't utter a word as I spoke, giving Xavier the bones Ronnie and I would build on.

"That sounds lovely! You two came up with this last night?" Xavier beamed.

"You sound surprised, Xavier," Ronnie chided, knowing well we were always equipped when weddings were involved. He tapped his chin as Ronnie went on to discuss what she hoped the next dress would look like.

After three more dresses, I stopped Gaby. "Please put her in the dress I gave your assistant. This would go a lot faster." I didn't want to be rude, but the last three dresses were absolutely awful. Gaby gave me a tight nod and continued on.

The next was a mermaid gown with little pearls all over it. *Gaudy* was the first word that came to mind. I was positive Xavier thought the same thing judging by the look on his face.

Then she put her in a southern belle ball gown, and I thought Xavier was going to break down in tears before Haven even got to the pedestal. The last monstrosity was a simple strappy number that would do nothing to combat the cold.

"Where is the dress you picked, Ronnie?" Xavier asked, his fingers pinched between his eyes and his hand on his hip impatiently.

"Bell actually picked this time," she said proudly, and my heart swelled a little at the pride in her voice. Dresses were normally her and Xavier's thing.

He turned in my direction, and his eyes widened. I turned, but only found Aaron behind me, hands tucked in his pockets, standing stoically. His eyes met mine and I whipped my head back to Xavier.

Haven entered and my anger rose. Of course Gaby hadn't put her in my pick. I would be sick if we continued to stand here while they paraded poor Haven in dress after dress. I found the couch in front of the pedestal. The tri-fold mirrors directly in front of it gave me the best view I was going to get while sitting. Aaron stayed by the door, and I observed his eyes on me from across the room.

"For heaven's sake, Gaby. Put the girl in Bellamy's pick!" Xavier hollered after the last dress disaster. He and Gaby had a past. I don't even think Ronnie knew the whole story. Gaby straightened and led Haven back toward the dressing room. The tulle swirled in different directions as she walked away—it made her look like a cupcake. I couldn't tell how much time passed before Haven walked through the doors from the dressing room.

I stood, taking in my pick. It was beautiful on her. The base layer was a satin, floor length dress with wide vees down the front and back, exposing her small breasts, toned shoulders, and tapering at the waist. But what completed the gown was the delicate, long-sleeved, vintage lace overlay that fit like second skin along her arms, covering the vees with beautiful appliqué, and pooling over the satin skirt beneath. Both materials traveled all the way to the floor where the extra pooled at her feet, but we could have that hemmed right up.

Xavier held his almost empty glass to his chest. When he looked at Haven, his eyes lit up. "If you don't buy that dress, I will."

Her broad smile was telling. "I love it." She ran her hands along the lace covered bodice and slowly over the swell of the skirt. Her eyes were glassy when they met mine in the mirror. "It's perfect." A lone tear slipped from her eye as Aaron approached her with a box of tissues.

Where did he get a box of tissues?

Ronnie and Xavier fluffed the dress, talking about measurements and time lines for alterations. I couldn't take my eyes off Aaron.

"Keep staring at him like that and you'll end up pregnant," Xavier said not so quietly. Aaron's eyes met mine, and my stomach hit my throat. He winked before glancing away.

I swatted Xavier. "Why do you insist on annoying me?"

"I only speak the truth." He pursed his lips and shrugged, annoying me further.

Bellamy

R onnie secured the dress for Haven, locking in alterations for the next week. One of us would accompany her to make sure everything was on time; brides didn't need to take on that burden alone. Most weren't assertive like they sometimes needed to be. Being the voice for one of our brides was part of the territory, and I was damn good at it.

Xavier ended up riding back with us, once again making me sit in the front with Mr. Lark. The SUV was quiet for a while until Xavier spoke up, "So, Bellamy, how's that girlfriend of yours?"

I felt Aaron's eyes on my face. Good Lord, after everything that happened between me and Olivia, I still hadn't told anyone other than Ronnie we had broken up.

"We broke up," I mumbled, hoping he would drop the conversation. I didn't need him airing my dirty laundry out, especially not in front of Mr.

Too-Handsome-For-His-Own-Good.

Xavier laid a hand on my shoulder. "What happened?"

Kill. Me. Now.

I knew he was just being supportive, but I really didn't want to advertise my failure. Especially with Aaron hearing every word we said. Plus, Haven didn't need to hear about my sordid past.

"It's fine. We decided it was for the best. Besides, she's moved out already." My words were clipped, and I knew I was being rude. But I did not want Aaron to know the many reasons my last serious girlfriend left me.

Even though we both knew we weren't in love, I still felt like I failed her. I worked too much, I wasn't into all the physical affection she was, and at the end of the day we just wanted the other to be happy. At first we were, but after a while it just...fizzled out.

It happens—honestly it does. I really didn't want to consider it a failure because our relationship was doomed from the start, and that wasn't something I was just telling myself to try and minimize the hurt over her leaving or moving on with someone else. I also wasn't naive enough to think she didn't see the other people behind my back. That was the final straw. Olivia had cheated, and when I didn't freak out the way she thought I should, we realized neither of us cared enough to fight for the relationship any longer.

"I knew she was no good!" He leaned up in the seat so his face was close to mine. "If you need a night with the girls, let me know."

I cringed, remembering that Ronnie and I already did that. Which is how, unfortunately, I met Mr. Handsome. "Thanks."

"*Ooh*, maybe we could go to that club Ronnie likes. Get you a hot somebody to grind up on."

Well, if Aaron didn't know I was bisexual before, he did now. Thanks a lot, Xavier-Michael. I was so close to rolling my eyes, but kept it inside.

When men found out I liked both men and women, it would go one of two ways. They either assumed I would be down for a threesome—which, hey, to each their own, but I wanted someone that was mine, and mine alone—or they acted like they didn't care, but asked way too many questions.

Ronnie reeled him back, and drew her hand across her throat.

"What about your bachelorette, Haven?" Ronnie redirected, breaking up the tension of my thoughts.

Haven shrugged. "Adrian and I decided to kind of have a pre-honeymoon." Her cheeks pinked and her smile turned dreamy. "We're both so busy, it's hard to find alone time together."

No bachelorette? That couldn't be. She had to have friends coming in, right? Shouldn't they be throwing her a party?

Xavier clapped his hands and squealed. "We have to Bell! Obviously."

"I'll bet Mr. Lark here would agree. A night out is mandatory for a bride to be," Ronnie said, joining in on the revelry.

I had to remember that Xavier meant well, and that he was just trying to help. But I really, really wanted to strangle him. Like put my hands around his throat and squeeze. Honestly, I was well on my way to murdering the only two friends I had.

"Please, call me Aaron, and I could actually get you guys into a VIP room." Lark's deep timbre scattered those thoughts, surprising me. I didn't turn to meet the handsome man's gaze, but somehow I knew he was looking at me. "If you want."

Was he asking permission? From me? Haven just declined, and I had zero reasons to go out as it was.

Xavier and Ronnie jumped at the opportunity. I figured they probably didn't need Aaron getting us a VIP room with

Ronnie being a frequent flier and all. But I guess I'd let him have his moment.

"That's so nice of you, Aaron," Haven murmured, back to her demure self again but with a large smile on her face. "But really, Adrian and I hardly get any time together. We would rather spend as much time as we can alone."

The rest of the ride was filled with idle conversation about Haven's fiancé. How they met and when, and how he popped the question.

We pulled up outside the shop and I bolted. I couldn't sit in the car anymore. I needed air that didn't smell like Aaron.

"Bellamy, can you wait up a second?" he asked, his tone almost desperate.

Groaning inwardly at him, I stopped and let the rest go in ahead of me. Why me? What was it about me that he liked, or even remotely wanted? I was always falling over my own feet recently, so unless his savior complex hadn't met its quota for the century, I just didn't get it.

Not to mention my stellar personality. Nothing about me said "nice girl you take home to mom".

"Your scratches are bleeding." He brought a tissue up to my arm. Oh, well, maybe he wasn't hitting on me. "May I?"

I was surprised he even asked, but I nodded anyway. He swiped the tissue across my arm, and sure enough, a little trickle of blood stuck to the white paper. I guess I had picked the scabs without noticing in the car while everyone was talking.

"Thank you." I dropped my gaze to my feet, suddenly terrified to be alone with him.

"I feel like I may be pressing my luck here."Aaron rubbed the back of his neck. "But would you come to dinner with me tomorrow night?"

My eyes snapped up to his green gaze. Surely he didn't mean, like a date. Right? "I guess we could have dinner. It just depends on what our schedule looks like," I tested. Maybe he wasn't asking for me, but for our group. Yeah, that had to be it. Had to be.

"I didn't mean you and everyone else." His eyes searched mine. "Just you and me."

Well shit.

After Olivia I just figured I would be alone for a while. Honestly, work took up most of my time, so I wasn't that upset about being alone. Aaron didn't seem like the busy type, he also didn't seem like the type to want a woman who worked long hours and kept to herself.

I was a selfish person, I could admit that. I liked my down time, I really enjoyed my alone time, though I didn't get as much as I would like.

"You're my boss's brother. Don't you think that's a bad idea?" I was grasping for straws, and he knew it, too, if his smirk was any indication.

"Let's find out."

Before I could protest, he grabbed my hand and pulled me into the shop behind him, not stopping to chat with anyone. Holly-Jay's office door was shut, but not locked, so Aaron just waltzed right in. The door gave easily enough, but I had to cover my eyes the second I rounded Aaron's back.

Holly-Jay was on the desk, her skirt pushed up around her hips. Soft moans drifted from her mouth as a groan came from the other side of her desk.

"Whoa, sis!" Aaron shouted, causing Holly-Jay to jump clear off the desk and into her partner's arms. Kelly's laugh was throaty, and I couldn't help the little embarrassed laugh that escaped me as well. Oh God, I had just walked in on my boss, head thrown back in ecstasy. Could today get any worse?

Aaron pulled me back out into the hall. "Knock next time dumbass!" Holly-Jay shouted through the door, as Kelly laughed softly. I could only imagine their frustration. Hell, I was suffering from second hand embarrassment, and a little jealousy. It had been a long time since I had an orgasm that I hadn't delivered myself.

Not long after, Kelly opened the door to Holly-Jay's office. "You can go in, but don't say I didn't warn you. She's in a mood." Her rich umber complexion was flawless, as always. Dreadlocks flowed from her scalp to her waist in funky colors. Different jewels and hoops of gold looped throughout her hair. Her long bohemian dress fluttered after her as if the breeze was made just for her. Kelly had a way about her that just made everyone at ease. Even my anxiety melted away when we spoke.

I flushed, hoping Kelly didn't think less of me for laughing. She called over her shoulder telling Holly-Jay she would be waiting at home for her. I imagined she would be eager to get back to their *activities*.

"What could be so important, Aaron?" Holly-Jay snapped, and I ran my tongue across my top teeth, internally cringing at her tone. It was one I had only heard once before, and it did not end well for the other person.

Hearing Holly-Jay say his name had my thoughts tumbling. Aaron suited him, with his ginger hair and bright green eyes. I could imagine with his tall figure he would be jacked under his gear.

Nope, not now, especially now that I've seen my boss intimately with her partner.

"I asked Bellamy on a date. She seems to think you would

have an opinion on it," he stated nonchalantly, as if his sister wasn't glaring at us through narrowed eyes.

If only I could forget the way my boss looked on her desk. I would never be able to come into her office again for fear of my cheeks burning.

"I do." She harrumphed, and sat down in her chair before turning to me. "You don't want to date this turd."

I almost laughed because she was right, and wrong. I did kind of want to know more about Aaron, but I was also scared. While I was perfectly happy with my body, society was not. Not when all the layers came off and the extra skin from yo-yo dieting over the years weighed me down.

"Don't tell her what she wants," Aaron snapped back at his sister, and I felt like that was my cue—that I needed to head out.

I turned toward the door ready to do just that when Holly-Jay's voice stopped me. "I'm sorry Bellamy, it's been a rough day."

That was an understatement.

"If you want to go out with him you have my permission, but don't say I didn't try and warn you of his turdiness." She waved her hands around as if making her point. Her smile looked as genuine as it normally did, but her eyes looked almost hopeful? Confusion, anxiety, and embarrassment swirled in my gut, colliding and rallying against one another for control.

I did not need to have a panic attack in my boss's office.

Nope. No. No. No.

I tried the breathing techniques I learned as a kid, years of the most expensive therapy should have to work for something. You would think, right? My lungs were aching, my breathing heavy, but I held it together.

Looking around, I found three things I could see: Holly-Jay, Aaron, and the little vintage lamp she bought at a junkyard a few years ago.

Three things I could hear. My old psychiatrist's words rang through my head. The sound of Ronnie's laugh down the hall mixed with Xavier's. Aaron's breathing beside me and my own lungfuls of air sawing in and out of my chest. I hoped he couldn't hear, prayed he didn't notice.

Come on, Bellamy. Three things I can feel. I wiggled my fingers against my leg, wiggled my toes in my flats, and gently ran my hand over the textured wallpaper at my back.

I nodded and gave Holly-Jay a little smile. I knew the pause was a little dramatic, and if I told her what I had been doing she would understand, but for some reason I couldn't say the words. I didn't want Aaron to know what was going on.

Mainly I didn't want him to think it was his fault. But worst of all, I didn't want his green eyes to fill with pity, and I sure as hell didn't want a pity date from him.

"Bellamy, I hope you have a great night." She smiled, effectively dismissing me.

I let go of all the air in my lungs. Holly-Jay was giving me an out. Whether she knew it or not, she just saved me from myself.

"Aaron, stay for a second," I heard Holly-Jay say as I turned to leave. "I need to go over a few things with you for the benefit concert."

I could have kissed Holly-Jay right then and there. I could escape, face Aaron's question another day. I didn't have to answer him tonight. I could walk straight out of the office and go home. Smokie would be more than happy to see me, and I could use a good bubble bath. I could fill my little house with music and drown in my thoughts alone.

He turned, his large hand almost brushing my knuckles. "Wait for me?"

I felt myself nod without really thinking about it. Like a knee jerk reaction. I wasn't actually planning on waiting. No, I had a solid plan. Go home, bathtub, music. Plans. I had plans that didn't involve him.

Okay, that might have been a lie. I would do plenty of

thinking about Aaron Lark. But that was it, just thoughts.

He smiled, and I noticed for the first time he had dimples. They were so cute I couldn't help but smile back at him. Damn it, I needed to leave. No, I *had to* leave. I couldn't stay and face whatever this was.

I didn't have feelings for people I barely knew. Not me. Never me.

I drifted toward the front room. Ronnie, Xavier, and Haven were sitting around the white, distressed coffee table, whispering between themselves.

Xavier spotted me first. "Girl! Details, now," he demanded, exaggerating the words.

I couldn't help but hysterically laugh. It bubbled up my throat, completely unwelcome, but I couldn't stop it. I had just fought a panic attack in my boss's office in front of her super hot brother who, for reasons unknown, got under my skin, burrowing so deep I couldn't pluck him out.

I plopped down on the chair between him and Ronnie. "I have no fucking clue," I said honestly. How did I go from wanting to smother him with a pillow to agreeing to wait for him to get out of his sister's office?

I was giving myself whiplash.

"He is a fine specimen." Xavier pulled me out of my thoughts.

"I think you just have a uniform fetish," Ronnie added, winking at me and sending Xavier a scandalous smirk.

"You aren't wrong," he said, his voice full of sass. He pulled his leg up and placed his ankle on his knee. "But this isn't about me." His stare was focused on me, as if I had something to hide or confess.

I huffed a breath. "It isn't about me either." I could feel the headache from earlier coming back, and honestly all I wanted to do was go home and pretend the last few days never happened.

"Oh, honey. Even your denial is cute." Xavier leaned back in his seat. "But, you're right. It's not only about you. It's about the hottie Marine back there, too."

"How do you know he's a Marine?" I asked. The question popped out of my mouth before I could think about it.

"I looked him up in the car," Ronnie said with a shrug, like looking up strangers that you work with is totally normal. On second thought, we probably should have done that first. Shaking my head, I tried to expel that pathway.

I just figured Haven's people picked her security detail. So how did Holly-Jay's brother end up as the head of security for Haven? And why isn't he on active duty now? Isn't that a thing for the Marines? I had to reroute my train of thought before all these questions sent me into an anxiety spiral.

Aaron, it was a cute name. With his freckled face, and dimples. Oh, God, no. I could not go down that rabbit hole. Why was that the first place my brain wanted to take me?

"Talking about me already?" Aaron and Holly-Jay both approached our group, sharing a smile before he nodded at me and gestured toward the door. I didn't move, I was still debating on whether or not to flee.

I mean, what did I really know about this man?

Ronnie, Xavier, and Haven all stood, ready to drop Haven off. Another man approached the door. "Miss Macemore, my name is Greer. I'll be your escort back to Bedknobs & Broomsticks."

Aaron clasped hands with the man. Haven gave him a small smile and pulled Ronnie and Xavier after her through the door. Leaving me, Holly-Jay, and Aaron alone.

Great, now even Haven was #TeamAaron.

We watched them climb into another black SUV and drive away, all three of us quiet. I didn't know what to say, and I honestly didn't want to look at Holly-Jay, after the way Aaron and I found her in her office earlier.

"I'm gonna jet. See you two tomorrow?" she offered, erasing the silence. I nodded, unable to form a response. "Lock up when you leave."

With that, she was out the door, leaving me and Aaron in

the waiting room. It seemed impossibly small as we stood there awkwardly waiting for the other to speak. I was sure anything that would come out of my mouth would be stupid or embarrassing.

Lord, give me strength.

Aaron

I couldn't remember the last time I had felt this awkward around a woman. Usually I would just ask for what I wanted, and nine times out of ten I would get it. But I knew in my gut that Bellamy would rather chew nails than give me anything I asked of her.

The moment she chapped my hide at Dusk 'Til Dawn, I knew she would be a challenge if I ever saw her again. I didn't usually work in private security. Hell, I had seen my sister more in the past week than I had in the last couple of years.

Ever since I left the marines after my contract ended, I had been stuck. Stuck in a house that didn't feel like home. Stuck in denial that my dream job wasn't actually my dream job after all. I'd always wanted to become a Marine, only onceI finally became one, my family started dying. I realized I wanted to be closer to the ones I had left. I wanted a home, and a person to share it with.

I rubbed the back of my neck, trying to think of the right thing to say to get her to agree to dinner. I could tell she wasn't exactly comfortable, but after today, it felt like we had made a little progress.

"You stayed." The surprised comment left my mouth before I could help it.

"Call it a lapse in judgment." Her voice was full of disdain.

"We'll have to agree to disagree on that." I smiled at her, trying to seem teasing.

She turned, placing her fingers at her temple and rubbing in circles. Did she have a headache?

"Wait. Are you okay?" I asked, trying to sound genuine.

"I'm fine. Can I go now?" She didn't wait for my reply, just turned around and walked outside. I followed like a damn puppy.

"Can I at least take you home?" I had to get her to say yes. I wouldn't be able to think about anything other than her if she didn't agree to one damn date.

"No." She cut me down quickly and began walking down the sidewalk. It was late afternoon now. The sun was low on the horizon and the shops were just starting to pack up. It wasn't like me to pursue someone so hard, but hot fucking damn, I wanted time with her. I wanted to crack her hard exterior open and find out who Bellamy was, what made her tick. She was quick on her toes, and if the tongue lashing my sister just gave me was any indication, she was an amazing person. Someone you didn't fuck over. If you did, she would be out faster than lightning.

She stopped in front of Olde Elixir Parlor before pulling the handle and walking inside. She didn't hold the door for me, but I didn't think she would. I gripped the glass before it closed completely and walked in behind her.

The lady at the counter greeted us as we walked in. "Hey Bellamy, what can I get you two?" Her voice was soft, motherly. Her blouse looked like something straight out of the eighteen hundreds with a ruffle down the middle tucked into a dark green skirt that I imagine brushed the floor.

She stood on the other side of the low counter wiping down the linoleum top with an old rag. This place was quite the relic. Everything looked old, but functional. It was almost like a coffee shop with the old school soda fountain behind the low sitting bar, and the ancient looking glasses. It had been a long time since I had been over in this area of the quarter.

Bellamy glanced over her shoulder and scowled.

I chuckled. I wouldn't apologize for following her.

"Do you have anything for a headache?" she asked, totally ignoring me. I felt a pang of guilt in my chest. I should have gotten her something as soon as we got back, but I would have lost my nerve to ask her out if I didn't do it right then.

I'm an idiot. A selfish idiot.

"Of course, sweet thing!" The woman quickly grabbed a packet from behind the counter and handed it to Bellamy. "On the house." She wrapped her weathered hands around Bellamy's and gave her a smile.

"Georgie, you know I can't do that," Bellamy said like they've had this conversation before. She sighed, gearing up for a fight.

I pulled my wallet from my back pocket and laid down a twenty. Georgie lifted her eyes to mine and smiled brightly. "And who is this fine fellow?"

"No one," Bellamy grumbled. "I can buy my own damn medicine."

She wouldn't look at me, but Georgie smiled and made change at the vintage cash register. I was shocked it actually worked. It was so old and tarnished, but I had to admit it was charming.

She handed me the change and grabbed a glass from under the counter, filling it at the old soda machine closer to the door. Orange soda sputtered from the funnel attached to the old thing into the cup. I focused on Bellamy as the woman came back to where we stood.

Bellamy waited until the fizz settled down, then downed the powder Georgie had given her before taking a healthy swallow of the orange soda. Her eyes watered, from the carbonation if I had to guess. She dabbed her mouth with the back of her hand. I watched every movement, completely ensnared by her.

"Oh!" Georgie exclaimed, breaking my trance on the way Bellamy's lips looked. I had already fantasized about that mouth, but now it was ten times worse. "Before I forget..."

Her eyes bounced to where I stood, looking between me and Bellamy before she hurried toward the pharmacy cabinets that ran along the back wall to our right, motioning for Bellamy to follow. Whatever it was, she didn't think I needed to hear it.

Unable to help my curiosity, I slowly made my way to where the two disappeared. I couldn't see them, but I could hear Georgie's low whisper. "Henry filled your prescription, but your mother called again."

Bellamy made a noise, it sounded like an annoyed huff, and by God, it made me smile. At least I wasn't the only one who she was annoyed with. If she was annoyed with her own mother then there had to be a chance for me too, right?

"I'm sorry, Georgie," she said, and it was low, so low I almost didn't catch the hint of sadness in her tone. My smile immediately faded. Why would that make my sunshine upset?

"Henry doesn't mind telling that woman that he won't be giving out your information." Georgie began digging through bins of medicine ready for patrons. "I just worry for you, sweet girl."

I was beginning to miss the closeness of the community here. Bellamy seemed to be an active part, which meant these people knew things about her.

"Everything okay here?" I asked, stepping around one of the isles and raising an eyebrow. Georgie and Bellamy both lifted their heads in unison. It was a little eerie, but also endearing.

"Everything is fine, young man," Georgie said, plucking a brown paper bag out of the bin I heard them rustling in earlier. "Here you are."

"Prescription?" I asked, even knowing damn well it wasn't my business, but I wanted it to be. I wanted to know everything she put into her body. Well, maybe not everything. Jealousy wasn't a good look, and I had only known her for two days. No where near long enough to have any right to know anything too intimate.

But I would be a lying son of a bitch if I said I didn't want to know all of those things, too.

She flushed and passed by me, heading toward the counter. She sipped more of her orange soda. Not meeting my gaze, she said, "Anxiety."

It was the only thing she said, and I had the distinct feeling she was ashamed. I wanted to tell her she had no reason to be but before I could respond, Georgie placed another paper bag on the counter in front of Bellamy.

"This one too." She huffed. "Golly me, sweet thing, Henry would lose his marbles if I told him I forgot to give you the other one."

Bellamy's cheeks heated, coloring her olive skin a flushed red. It was cute, and I wondered what the other prescription was for.

Which I knew was insane. I knew next to nothing about her.

"Thank you, Georgie," she whispered, her voice a little hoarse.

"Don't you mention it. I'll tell Henry you said hello." She waved as we made our way out the door. I guess the pharmacy didn't close until later, all the other shops looked dark and locked as I swept the area. It was a habit; always have your head on a swivel. You never know when it could save your life.

Bellamy clutched the bags to her chest and continued

walking past the closed shops and around another corner to a brick path with minimal light.

"You walk this every day? Alone?" I couldn't help but imagine the worst, especially with the things I'd seen. This would be the perfect place for a predator to snatch her up off the street.

"I've worked for your sister for nearly two years," she said, interrupting the lashing I was giving her in my head. "I'm fine."

"You don't know what happens in dark alleys like these," I stated, annoyed that she would be so nonchalant about the situation.

She didn't even falter, just continued on like I wasn't losing my mind thinking about her walking alone everyday.

"What about your girlfriend?" I responded. "She never walked you home from work?"

She stopped, and I had to halt my stride not to run into her back. "Ex." I could tell by the slight moon light seeping through the canopy of trees overhead that her jaw was tight. She turned, and since I was so close, she had to tilt her head back to look me in the eyes. "And no, because I am a grown woman. I can handle myself."

This five-foot nothing sass mouth thought she could handle herself? Against a predator. No. I had watched too much investigation discovery to not be paranoid.

"Just, humor me." I wouldn't be able to sleep tonight if I let her walk home alone.

"Please?"

Bellamy

*P*lease.

A look between panic and pleading crossed his face as he said it. He got closer somehow, without touching me. My back hit the hard brick wall, my head tilting up to stare into his eyes almost involuntarily. I couldn't process whether he wanted to kiss me, or if I wanted to kiss him.

The path was small, barely big enough for two people to walk side by side.

"Please, Sunshine." It was all he said, whispered on the softest of breezes of his breath against my mouth. I could almost taste the sugar from the tea he kept in his SUV. I was too stunned to move, captivated by his closeness.

"Can you give me some space?" Weakness slithered through my veins. I could hear it in the way my voice broke, and my body shook. My brain couldn't settle on a feeling, butterflies erupted in my stomach, confusion broke the fog of my mind, and longing for a connection pulsed in my heart.

"Let me walk you home. Please?" he asked again, lifting his hand tentatively to brush the outer shell of my ear where I had a barbell shoved through the inner and outer cartilage.

"Okay," I said quietly. He was smiling, and it was smug. I didn't want to acknowledge that it was also cute as hell. We stood there for what felt like an eternity and not nearly long enough when he finally stepped back. His hand fell away from the side of my face.

Once the heat from his body disappeared, I set a fast pace to where the end of the brick path emptied out into my street. Since his legs were damn near twice as long as mine, he kept up with no problem.

We didn't speak as we walked. Occasionally his hand would brush mine, sending shivers up my arm. I stopped in front of my house and unlatched the gate to my walkway. My "little white picket fence" wasn't as picturesque as I'd imagined it. With its slightly chipped white paint that covered the wooden panels, it was more of a fixer upper than anything. The shrubbery really needed a good cut. I would have to get someone out here to fix it before the ferns and bushes took over my path.

Anxiety flooded my system wondering what he thought of my yard. Was I going to let him in my house? No, I wouldn't.

I didn't keep the gate open for Aaron. Instead, letting it

slip from my fingers and slap into his legs. I had to admit, it was a little satisfying hearing the small bite of pain in his voice when he made it to my porch.

"I'm sorry I didn't answer you earlier," he began. "I don't really have an answer for wanting to touch you."

"Oh." I didn't really know what to say.

"It's just..." He looked around as if the shrubs would give him answers. "I like you." He stepped closer to me so I had to incline my neck to look into his eyes. He shook his head, as if dispelling more thoughts. "Go to dinner with me tomorrow night." he said instead.

"No." I crossed my arms over my chest and waited for him to leave, that moment in the alley forgotten as my walls reformed at lighting speed.

I stole a glance up at him. He was smiling down at me. "I'll pick you up at seven, wear something nice." He ran the back of his hand down my cheek and disappeared off my porch and across the street before I could respond.

Didn't I say no? I distinctly remembered saying no.

What the fuck? I wouldn't go. I couldn't. It was a terrible idea. Horrific, really.

The house key was warm from holding onto it tightly in my hand. I slid it into the lock and twisted. Once through, the door closed with a heavy thump, and I flipped the lock, earning the satisfying click of the tumble settling into place.

I turned, sagging against the wood. "What just happened?" I whispered to no one in particular. Before I knew it, my butt hit the floor, and I found myself praying against my better judgment that this wouldn't end with my heart broken for real.

The next morning, I had to relieve myself of the ache between my thighs. Self love was my favorite form of stress relief. Just remembering the way Aaron's body hovered against mine had me clenching down low.

Smokie had curled up at the bottom of my bed. She blinked open one of her yellow eyes and yawned.

"Rough night?" I teased her. Too often I found myself talking to Smokie. She stretched and repositioned herself before laying back down. Spoiled cat.

I stripped out of my sleep shirt and made my way to the bathroom. Flipping the shower on, I waited for the water to heat up, scrolling through my phone. I had a few missed texts from Ronnie and Xavier, but for the most part all was quiet on the home front. I checked our business page, replying to comments and sharing tags. Overall, it was a sea of thank yous and congratulations.

I turned on my morning playlist and blasted the volume as I got ready for the day. The bluetooth connected and *Moves Like Jagger* by Maroon 5 pulsed through the speaker and I couldn't help but sing along.

I pulled on a long-sleeved black dress that cinched at my waist, accentuating my breasts and the flare of my hips. It fell to the floor, covering the shoes I decided to wear. It was warm and comfortable—two of the most important things in my world.

In the kitchen, I put together a small breakfast as little nervous butterflies fluttered in my belly. Pulling all the fruit containers from the fridge, I threw grapes, strawberries, blueberries, and pineapple into a bowl.

However, I couldn't eat much in anticipation of seeing Aaron. I wondered if he would be wearing his baseball cap like the second time we met, or leave his hair perfectly tousled on top of his head, showcasing the shaved sections above his ears.

Giving up on the fruit, I pulled some Saran wrap out of a drawer and placed it over the bowl as best I could. The stupid stuff clinged to everything except what you wanted it to.

Throwing the bowl in the fridge, I gathered up my keys and wallet, shoving them in the pockets of my dress. Thank God for pockets. Whatever person invented pockets in dresses better be a rich bitch. I absolutely loathed carrying a bag.

I made sure the lock engaged before making my way down the path of my drive, surprised to find Ronnie at the gate.

"You look mighty chipper this morning," she said in greeting, handing me a cup of what I assumed was hot cocoa. I was rewarded by the sweetness of the warm chocolate coating my insides. The slight zing of peppermint awakened my body, something coffee could never do.

"Peppermint, my fave." I gripped the cup with my opposite hand to loop my arm through hers.

"I know." She rolled her eyes dramatically which made me snort.

We walked in silence, gearing up for the day as we covered the same path Aaron and I traveled last night. I couldn't help the blush that peaked through my face, sneaking a glance at the spot where Aaron practically begged to walk me home. The butterflies from earlier erupted in my belly again, but a lot stronger. Oh fuck, this was going to end badly. I needed to turn him down...again. But this time, make it stick.

"What are you hiding?" Ronnie asked, pulling my

attention from the wall. I didn't realize I had almost slowed to a stop as we passed.

"Nothing." I ducked my head, hoping she didn't catch the blush I knew was staining my face. But she knew me better than anyone, and she definitely didn't believe me. I could tell by the way she unhooked her arm from mine.

"Liar, liar," she taunted, all but jumping around me in a circle. "What happened with the hottie last night?"

She poked at my ribs, trying to get a reaction out of me.

"He walked me home." I tried to sound impassive.

"And did you hate fuck the shit out of him?" she prodded.

I smacked her arm, sending her hot drink to the sidewalk in front of Misty's flower shop. I covered my mouth with my hand before laughing.

I couldn't help it, she deserved it for that question.

"My mocha!" she dramatically cried as I took a sip of my warm peppermint cocoa and made sure to dig it in a little further by moaning in delight. "You owe me a mocha and the dirty details of your sexy time!"

I laughed again, trying and failing to settle down to explain to her we didn't get past the front door. She picked up the paper cup from the street and placed it in the waste bin at the corner of our shop's street.

"There was no sexy time," I said, barely containing

another fit of laughter at the way her brows furrowed. I shrugged, still holding my now almost empty cup."I promise, he walked me to my door, then went wherever he went."

Xavier was walking from the opposite direction, coming toward us with a frown on his face. It was nine in the morning, what did he have to be cranky about already?

Ronnie didn't ask any further questions as we made our way into the shop, flipping the lights on and setting up the portrait space. Xavier didn't utter a word as he set up his equipment. But I could tell something was off with him. He grunted and sighed, glancing at his phone every now and again.

"What gives?" Ronnie finally voiced my thoughts.

Xavier spun around to face us, his face flushed. "I had an employee interview this morning."

He didn't offer more than that, so I asked, "And?"

"And he was great, but I don't know if I could trust him with my clients." He looked away and started to fiddle with the camera directly in front of where Ronnie was settling the background.

"What do you mean?" I couldn't help but feel a little remorse for him. He had never needed another photographer, but now that he was double booked for the first time I could tell he was struggling with the control.

I gripped onto his problems, hoping mine wouldn't walk through the door with Haven today.

"He's got a reputation." He dropped his arms and placed his hands on his hips, letting out a long breath. "He's also a blast from the past I never thought I would encounter again."

That got our attention. We both crossed the space to where he was standing. "What do you mean? From *your* past?" I asked.

"I mean he's my ex from high school." His voice was barely audible over the buzzing camera equipment.

I couldn't recall a time when Xavier wasn't boisterous, so whatever this man had done to him in high school must have been heartbreaking.

"Oh, Xavier! Is he the one that got away?" Ronnie asked.

He nodded as silent tears fell down his cheeks. I hated seeing him so upset, but couldn't bring myself to wrap my arms around him like Ronnie did. She followed him to the floor and stroked his back where he silently cried.

"What did I miss?" Haven entered then, looking beautiful in her makeup. Ronnie had texted me last night saying she had asked Haven to have her makeup team do a Christmas look for her portraits. Her lids had been painted perfectly in nude with burgundy eyeshadow blended from the outer corners of her eyes into the crease of her lids. Long black lashes had been added to her already bold ones, making her dark brown eyes even darker. They applied a deep matte purple-red to her lips, looking fuller with the contrast of her skin. Her skin appeared like porcelain, with a little shimmer to make her cheekbones pop.

Xavier wiped the tears from his face and gave her a big smile that did appear genuine, but I knew he was struggling. Seeing the love of your life after so long had to be taking a toll on his thoughts, especially if said man was also a photographer.

"You look stunning! And you aren't even in the dress!" He gave her an air kiss, making sure to keep a distance so he didn't mess up her makeup. She blushed, which made her look absolutely adorable. He pointed at her face. "Keep that, right there."

The air swirled in the room, and I swore it was hotter than it had been a second ago. My eyes connected with Aaron's as he made his way into the large area. It felt immensely smaller now, like all at once the air was sucked out of the place and the walls closed in.

He had on a pair of light wash denim jeans that clung to his thighs and covered the top portion of his boots. The T-shirt he wore molded perfectly to his shoulders and bulging arms under the black fabric.

I wondered if he had a plethora of black shirts just waiting to be used in his closet. Then I thought about what he would look like out of it, and his lips tipped up in a smile like he could read my thoughts.

Ronnie whisked Haven into the dressing room, leaving Xavier, Aaron, and me in the room alone.

Double fuck.

Xavier lifted his eyes, blinking them between the two of us. Reading our *energy* if I had to guess. Xavier could be blunt and a bit uncouth when he got excited, and what better fodder than the supposed chemistry Aaron and I had?

"So stud," Xavier started. "You wanna date our Bellamy here?"

I groaned. "Can we not?"

"Oh, we shall." Xavier snickered. "How else will I ever get to know what this fine specimen wants with our little ol' Bell, hm?"

"Nothing. That fine specimen wants nothing." I turned in Aaron's direction, willing him to agree.

"I didn't think this fine specimen was going to get to speak." Aaron's lips tilted up in a smirk.

"He really shouldn't," I warned, not at all vaguely.

Xavier clapped his hands together in excitement. "See! There it is. The *spark*."

"We have a spark!" Aaron gloated.

I shook my head. "I'm not going on a date with you."

"Why not!" Xavier shouted at the same time Aaron grumbled, "Why not?"

Piercing Xavier with the best side eye I could manage, I answered, "Because..." I struggled to find something other than the equivalent of stomping my foot like a child. "Just—because!" *Goddammit.*

I sped off in a rushed excuse about needing to use the bathroom. I walked down the hall and shut the bathroom door—just in case anyone actually came to look—and crossed the hall into my cramped office.

Bellamy

A few minutes passed when I heard Aaron's booted feet clomp over the carpeted space heading for the bathroom. He knocked—timidly, but still. I had a clear view of his back behind my desk as he remained near the door. I didn't know if I wanted to speak. It didn't matter though. He turned around, glancing past me at first, then snapped his head back in my direction. We stared at each other for a few minutes before he broke the silence.

"What do you like to eat?" I wasn't expecting the question, so the look on my face must have spoken for me. "I want to take you somewhere you'll actually enjoy, Sunshine."

When he had called me Sunshine before, it was unnerving. But now? It was kind of cute. Even I had to admit it because I was anything but a ray of sunshine. I was the rain cloud you had to think about before leaving the house.

"Doesn't matter because I told you no." I tried to be casual, but the heat in my words felt like knives. I should have felt bad, but I was running out of resolve.

"We'll see about that." His long legs ate up the distance, and when he was just a step away from me, he asked again, "What do you like to eat?"

I looked up at him and raised my eyebrows, not willing to give him an answer.

"I'll tell you one thing right now, Sunshine." He took another step forward and I had to tilt my head up to keep eye contact. His tone had changed, taking on a hard edge that made my blood rush through my ears and heat up my body. "I enjoy the chase. It will make it that much sweeter when you surrender to me."

I laughed. He was awfully sure I would eventually give in to him.

Not. A. Chance.

"I told you, my answer is no."

His smile was all wolf, predatory, and I had to fight my body's instinct to rub my thighs together. No way would I give him anything more than my words.

But looking at him made everything else in the room melt away. Like there was nothing else in the world. It was scary, and I was relieved when Ronnie and Haven came back. I crossed the room, but not before walking around Aaron. His fingers grazed mine as I passed, leaving goose bumps in their wake. I couldn't tell if it was the usual icky feeling of being touched that did it or the little flare of need that traveled through my body. I couldn't focus on that right now, I had a job to do.

Since Haven's dress wouldn't be ready until the wedding, we improvised, putting her in an elegant, white, off-the-shoulder gown that made her otherwise boxy frame curve. With Xavier directing her body's movements, he would be able to capture the best angles to make her look like the blushing bride she was.

Misty had put together a bouquet of deep red roses, separated with sprigs of eucalyptus and sprinkled with a few delphinium stems. It was beautiful, and I found myself cataloging the combination for future brides.

Ronnie and I stayed while Xavier snapped a few test pictures, giving Haven direction and only intervening when she didn't quite understand a move. She didn't move with the grace I would picture for a young celebrity like her. She was stiff, and a little scared.

I eyed Aaron by the door and caught Haven's quick look his way. "I'll be right back," I whispered to Ronnie.

Crossing the room, I gripped Aaron's arm and pulled him out the door into the hallway.

"If you wanted to get me alone all you had to do was ask,

Sunshine."

I scoffed. Of course he would think I was trying to get him alone twenty minutes after I turned him down again. "You're going to stay out here while we finish these frames." I held up my hand to stall his argument. "She's stiff, and it will show in her pictures."

"What does that have to do with me?" he asked, genuinely confused. I guess he didn't realize the presence he had, this big man with eyes like a hawk.

"You're intimidating as hell," I snapped a little too harshly.

"Intimidating?"

I wanted to smack the smirk off his face. "Careful," I warned. "Wouldn't want me to be violent now would you?"

He leaned forward slowly, showing his straight white teeth. His parents probably had him in braces for his smile to be so damn perfect. "Spoiler alert. It's my favorite version of you."

I couldn't hide the surprise from my face. He couldn't like a woman constantly wanting to punch his throat and reject him. That only happens in the fantasy romance novels that I was secretly trash for.

Placing my hand on his chest, I leaned in close, almost rubbing my breasts across his stomach. When he leaned down, I pushed him out of the doorway, and shut the door sealing him outside. He laughed, the reverberations traveling through the wooden door.

I took a minute to compose myself. I had touched him and didn't feel absolutely disgusting afterward. Progress.

When I turned, all of them were staring at me wide eyed. "Can you guys not mind your own business?" I grumbled, only a little perturbed, knowing good and damn well I would have totally been eavesdropping too.

"I may be gay, but even I can admit that was hot," Xavier said, effectively making us all laugh.

After that, the photoshoot went perfectly. Ronnie and I even jumped in for a few at Haven's request.

"We should schedule the cake samples while you're here," I said, speaking through the tri fold partition where Ronnie was helping Haven out of her dress. "When will your fiancé be arriving?"

"He should be here Friday." I could tell by the lift in her voice that she was excited to see him.

"I'll call the baker and let him know to have samples ready by Saturday. How does that sound?" I asked while I typed out the message to the baker. He was the confectionary genius Ronnie and I had found a few months back. His treats were always the stunner of the show.

"We could show you around town afterward," Ronnie

offered. We didn't have any other plans so I was down with doing whatever.

"That would be lovely," Haven said.

Dressed once more in her street clothes, she joined me and Ronnie. We headed to the screening room for a few minor details, but the biggest parts of the job had been done. We had her dress in alterations, floral arrangements had been ordered and Misty would have those ready when they came in. The groom's tux had been decided and measured, chairs had been rented, and music acquired. We had a wine tasting later in the week, so we had the rest of the day to catch up on errands for the shop.

"Let's grab lunch before we head out," Ronnie said. She knew I was a sucker for food and didn't even ask anymore. "Xavier is all packed up. Haven, would you like to join us?"

She nodded and we followed Ronnie out to the main entrance. Xavier's car was idling at the front door. It was one of those little boxy cars, and it always made me giggle. It was bright red and totally him. We had lovingly dubbed it Red Rocket.

Aaron stood up from the couch, placing his phone back in his pocket. Damn, I forgot he was even here. "Where are we heading?"

"We're going to lunch. Haven is joining," I told him, feeling a little guilty for kicking him out of the portrait room like I did.

"Let's not keep the ladies waiting." He swept his arm in relation to the door. Xavier jumped up to open the door and Haven crossed the street toward the SUV.

I hesitated before climbing into the back of Xavier's little car. I didn't look at Aaron before closing the door, and I definitely didn't watch him walk to the SUV.

He had a job to do just as much as we did.

Aaron

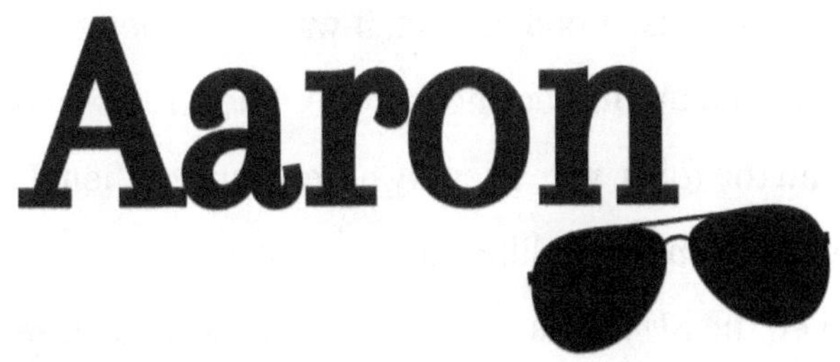

She chose not to get in the car with me. That shouldn't have upset me. Not in the slightest; we barely knew each other. So why was I so grouchy over her riding in the car with her friends? Maybe because I was a jealous asshole. It had always been one of my worst qualities.

What was even worse was the fact that I craved her attention; an alarming sign of a forming addiction. I couldn't give her that control. If I did, this job would slip through my fingers before I really had a chance to decide if I liked it.

I followed Xavier's car through town, recognizing the flower shop close to Bellamy's house. We drove for a few more blocks before Xavier turned the car into the gravel parking lot at Billy's Chicken Pit.

I remembered eating here as a kid. Holly-Jay and I would order our sodas in a glass bottle and pretend to be in a different era. The thought made me smile and really think about the time I had lost while I served my country.

Living here wasn't bad. In fact, it was much better than where I ended up purchasing a house. The streets were clean, and the folks were friendly here. Some of them I even recognized from my childhood.

I parked the SUV in the gravel lot under a shade tree to help prevent Haven from too much exposure. She had fair skin like I did, but her hair was a deep brown, almost black. We exited the vehicle, and I walked a few steps behind her as she led the way to the trio. I tried not to seem obvious in my jealousy. Bellamy peeked at me through her lashes, presumably thinking I wasn't looking at her.

I was determined to get her to go out with me tonight, come hell or high water. If I had to corner her friends and ask what she liked, so be it.

She led us into the little hole in the wall restaurant. The smell of grease and barbecue hit my nose right off the bat, and I noticed a table full of college boys near the register.

A large man carrying a tray of cornbread and yeast rolls swung by, giving Bellamy a quick peck on her temple before flinging his hand in the direction of the kitchen. She made her way around the tables, guiding us to where a large table waited in the back.

We took our seats, and waited for a waitress to come around. "Are we even going to get any service today, Bell?"

Xavier groaned, and I had to admit I was starting to question it myself.

"Billy's had a hard time with this new waitress. I'll go get drinks. I know what you two want." She smirked, not giving Ronnie or Xavier time to change their mind before turning to Haven and I. "What would y'all like?"

"Tea is fine. It was delicious last time," Haven answered.

"Whatever is fine with me." I gave her a smile that I knew would grate her nerves.

"Be careful what you wish for," she said sweetly, but couldn't quite get her face to cooperate. She would probably spit in whatever it was she was bringing. I didn't care. I had her full attention for just a second and that was enough for me.

I watched her saunter off through the tables, headed toward the big man from earlier. They talked for a few minutes and Bellamy disappeared into the kitchen, emerging a few minutes later with a tray full of drinks and pitchers of refills.

She sat them all down in front of each of us, pulling straws from the pocket of her dress.

"Billy's new girl didn't come in today, so, I know it's probably bad etiquette, but would y'all mind if I helped Billy out for a few?" Bellamy shrugged like it wasn't a big deal to be waitressing while entertaining a client.

"Do you need us to do anything?" Ronnie asked, while Haven said, "No honey, you go help your family."

"What will we have?" She beamed.

She didn't pull out a notepad to write anything down, just listened as we all named off what we wanted. Ronnie and Xavier ordered chicken tenders and fries. Since she didn't offer us menus, I followed their lead even though I really wanted the country fried steak and rice. If it was half as good as it used to be, I would be in hog heaven.

Haven piped up, asking for the macaroni and cheese from the last time she was here. Her cheeks turned pink at her sudden outburst. Everyone around the table gave her an encouraging smile.

Even Bellamy. Fuck me, she was pretty when she scowled, but her smile? Goddamn gorgeous. Like a beacon to my soul.

She walked back to the kitchen as the rest of the table fell into idle chit chat. Why was I sitting there when I should have been helping Bellamy? Because I was supposed to be watching over Haven, that's why. But after watching Bellamy bounce around the place, I couldn't sit any longer.

Fuck it. "Y'all don't leave this table." I looked at each of them before feeling satisfied they wouldn't leave.

Following the path Bellamy took, I hesitated at the kitchen doors. I couldn't very well just step right in like I owned the place. Lucky for me, Bellamy pushed open the swinging metal door and walked right into my chest.

"Do you need something?" Her nose scrunched up as if she smelt something sour. Did I stink? No, couldn't be me.

"I came to help."

Her eyes went wide before narrowing at me. "Why?"

"You look like you could use it," I offered, knowing good and well she didn't need the help.

She nodded and hollered into the kitchen, "You need someone to run food?"

A loud voice answered, "Go sit with your friend's, Kitten."

Kitten? I raised my brows, glad she wasn't looking at me.

"You need the help, old man. It's either a runner, or a server." She turned back to me and looked me over from head to toe. "Better choose a runner. This one might scare off your customers before they even sit."

The old man, as she called him, was the same gray haired man from earlier with a graying mustache, wrinkle lines from a life well lived, and a smile toward Bellamy. Why did he get to call her Kitten when I couldn't call her Sunshine?

Billy came through the swinging doors of the kitchen, "You alright, son?" he asked, wiping his hands on the apron tied around his waist. Bellamy turned to look and I tried to school my expression back to normal. Or at least what I thought was normal. "A veteran shouldn't have to wait on tables in this place."

How did he– did Bellamy tell Billy about me?? I'm not sure if I should feel flattered or embarrassed.

"Billy, let us help you with the rush." Bellamy fisted her hands and rested them by her sides. She wasn't about to take no for an answer. Even I could see his defeat clear as day.

"I really don't mind sir," I added, hoping to help.

Bellamy gave me an appreciative smirk and my pride preened like a damn peacock. Billy nodded into the direction of the kitchen and began to give me the quick rundown of how orders were processed and the layout of the place. There weren't many tables so it wasn't too hard to catch on. I watched Bellamy float from table to table, making sure no one's drink emptied, and their food was satisfactory. She smiled at almost everyone and looked radiant, even with the light sheen of sweat covering her brow.

The college boys must have been getting on her nerves though. I could tell from where I stood waiting on another order that she was close to punching one of the pricks. Violence looked so sexy on her, but I did not want to start a brawl here if one of them laid a hand on her.

They were giving her a hard time about waiting for their food. Hungry men weren't the friendliest. "Billy, you got table seven's food yet?" I urged.

"Yeah, coming up," he hollered back. "Why?"

He came to the door just in time to see one of the boys swat Bellamy's ass. It was like red mist coated my vision. She'd told me more than once that she didn't like to be touched. Hell, she didn't even hug her loved ones much. So I wasn't about to let this fly.

I gripped the tray Billy handed me and turned in that direction before I could think better of it.

But Billy gently laid his hand on my arm. "Let her handle it."

The room had descended into hushed murmurs. Her face was flushed from embarrassment and all the running around. She stared at one of the college pricks, leaning low, whispering something to the table. Before they could respond, she hauled the tea pitcher up and emptied it over the dick's head.

The other boys laughed and the one now soaked in tea grabbed her wrist.

I'd had enough. No one disrespects a woman like that in front of me.

"It's time for you to leave," I rumbled, carefully brushing

my hand along her lower back, letting her know it was me.

She whirled. "I don't need your fucking help." She poked my chest, and all it did was give me a semi. Fuck me, I loved her viciousness.

"Too bad, Sunshine." I gripped her hand, watching for her reaction. Waiting for her to pull away. When she didn't, I addressed the boys still sitting at the table. So much for good behavior. "Billy, theirs will be to-go," I said in my most lethal tone.

Our table was staring at Bellamy with their mouths wide open. If I didn't have her hand solidly in mine, and these assholes to deal with, I would probably be gaping at her too. As it stood, I was still waiting for them to move.

When none of them did, I pulled Bellamy behind me and told her to go help Billy box up their orders. She wanted to argue, but one look into my eyes she saw there was no point. These fuckers were leaving, and if I had to haul them out one by one, so be it.

I watched her disappear into the kitchen before swinging my attention back to the boys. I growled. "You are some kind of stupid to put your hands on a woman who clearly didn't want anything to do with you."

"Hey man, we're leaving," one of the younger ones said. He wore glasses that he had to push up the bridge of his nose to see me. I stood back to let them rise. They all laid down a few bills to cover whatever they ordered. Billy handed them their to go containers and on the way out I heard one of them mumble, "I wouldn't fuck that fat bitch if she paid me."

Bellamy had just opened the door to the kitchen, carrying a full tray of food that she almost dropped, clearly indicating she'd heard what he said. Her face gave nothing away, and that's why it hurt. She was one of the most expressive people I knew. So for her to lock it down at his words made my heart ache knowing this wasn't the first time she'd heard them.

"Who the fuck said that?" I was barely holding on to my sanity. None of them turned around, ignoring my question. But I wasn't about to let them get away with that shit. I followed them out, of course these assholes drove high end cars.

"I asked you a question." I was seething, and if I didn't get an answer soon, I would do something stupid. Very, very stupid.

Bellamy

Aaron stormed after the group of boys, following them outside. I didn't usually have a problem with patrons, but then again, I wasn't the one usually serving them.

When the dickwad frat boy not-so-subtly made comments about how he could fuck the bratty attitude out of me, then proceeded to smack my ass, I had reached my limit.

But I'd had it covered. I didn't need a big, strong man to come save me. I could stand up for myself, and Aaron would be sorely mistaken if he thought otherwise.

I passed the tray of food off to Billy, hooking my thumb over my shoulder. "I need to handle that."

He nodded and it was all the confirmation I needed. Aaron looked pissed, his body poised to fight. His biceps looked like they had grown twice in size as he held one of the boys by his collared shirt against the side of the silver sports car.

"Aaron, stop!" I yelled over the car, not willing to get close to the four men. Who knew what they were capable of. His face flicked up to mine, trying to communicate with me. I shook my head. "They aren't worth it."

He slowly lowered the man to his feet, brushing off his shoulders. I heard him say, "If I find out you or any of your little friends here touch another woman without their permission again, I will personally see to it that you become acquainted with four concrete walls."

They all mumbled a quick apology and Aaron rounded the car stopping just a foot away from me. His eyes were fierce, face contorted in wrath. What I didn't understand was why he was so pissed.

I had to admit, I was a little scared of the way he looked at the moment.

"I took care of it," I told him. "You didn't have to intervene."

"I really did." His eyes were closed, breathing deeper. I recognized the calming technique from when I had learned it in therapy. Maybe he had anxiety too, alongside anger management issues.

I could understand why he would be upset with them putting hands on me, what I didn't understand was his extreme reaction to what one of them said.

It wasn't like he had any reason to protect my feelings.

"No. You didn't," I retorted. His eyes snapped open, but I laid my hands on his chest to stop whatever response he was thinking. "But I appreciate it."

I was just as surprised as he was. Accepting his help and touching him all in the same day. Who was I? I felt a little dizzy pulling away from him, leaving him out in the parking lotI made my way back inside where conversation had started once more.

Billy had caught up with everything and was sitting at the table with my friends, our food on the table, untouched.

"You okay, Kitten?" Billy spotted me first. I nodded, letting him know I didn't really want to talk about it. But I knew he would dig deeper the next time I was in here.

"I don't know about y'all, but that..." Xavier drifted off, attempting to find the right word to describe what just happened. He waved his hands, gesturing to the table the boys had vacated."...was hot."

I couldn't help the laugh that erupted from my chest. Maybe it was a little hot. Xavier had a way of making heavy things less...heavy.

"If you don't like him, I will definitely give him a try," Ronnie agreed in her own way, shooting me a wink.

I desperately wanted to stop talking about the events of

the past ten minutes. Haven was quiet, eating her macaroni and cheese. I knew it would be out of left field, but I asked, "How did you get the mayor to agree to your venue at the fountain?"

"Oh!" She wiped her mouth, holding the napkin up until she was done chewing. "That's why I'm doing the benefit. For the historians, I believe."

"So the mayor agreed to your venue choice to raise money for the historical preservation?" I asked, just to clarify.

"Yes. That's what it was." She snapped her fingers. "You know, my fiancé picked the location?"

"That's sweet. Is there any reason why?" Ronnie asked.

Haven nodded. "He's way better at telling the story. You'll have to ask him when he gets here." Her face lit up talking about her man, and it made her look so cute.

"Can you sing *Black Roses* at the benefit concert?" Ronnie practically vibrated in her seat. I knew she had been waiting to ask her since we found out about the benefit. It was her favorite song and I had to suppress a giggle at her fangirl ways. I was surprised she hadn't secretly asked Haven to autograph something.

"Of course! It's one of my favorites too!" Haven's cheeks glowed when talking about her music. It was adorable.

We ate, and as we did, I waited for Aaron to rejoin our

table. When he didn't, I grabbed a box from under the counter.

"Is he still outside?" I asked Billy. He was standing at the register cleaning up the mess from the lunch rush.

"I haven't seen him. But, Kitten, that was a mighty strong reaction." He eyed me hard over the bills he was counting. "There something you need to tell me?" He lifted his eyebrows, as if I were hiding a secret from him—as if I *could*.

I shook my head. How could I even describe Aaron to Billy? I was still circling around my own emotions on whether or not I actually wanted to go on a date with him. Almost every time I argued with myself, I came back to wanting to try, but couldn't bring myself to allow it to happen.

"Nothing to tell. We haven't even kissed, old man!" I hollered.

Embarrassment wrapped around my insides and squeezed. Why would I shout that out loud? I didn't even know if I liked the guy.

Of fucking course the door had to open just as I was shouting my personal business like I was advertising it on a freaking billboard. I buried my face in my hands. I was a train wreck.

"Does this mean you want to kiss me?" Aaron just had to

tease me as if it wasn't already bad enough. I retreated to the kitchen, where he followed, pressing for an answer. "Do you?"

Truthfully, I wanted to feel his pale pink lips on mine. I wanted to know how he would hold me as he did. I wanted him to ravage my mouth. Maybe Ronnie was right, we should just hate fuck and get it out of the way.

Carnal attraction. That's all it was, right?

"What took you so long?" I asked, finally uncovering my face, but keeping my back turned on him. I found a stack of unwashed silverware and began loading them into the industrial dishwasher

His steps were slow, measured. He stopped, not close enough that I could feel the heat coming from his body, but close enough he could touch me if he lifted his hands.

"I had to calm down." He spun me around slowly, barely brushing his hand on my arm. "I didn't like the way you looked at me out there."

His eyes were trained to the ground, as if he was ashamed.

"I don't know you well enough to know if I'm safe with you." I gave him the truth. By the look on his face, it wasn't what he wanted to hear.

"You will always be safe with me, Sunshine." His gaze captured mine. Sincerity lined every word, and I believed him. "I'm sorry I made you think differently."

His hand cupped my face and I leaned a fraction into his warm palm. It was calloused, as I suspected it would be. But it wasn't uncomfortable. "I'm sorry you had to deal with that," I said honestly. He didn't need to deal with the drama that seemed to follow me these days.

"Never apologize for those types of assholes." His eyes took on the hard edge from earlier, before softening again. "No one should ever put their hands on a woman without their permission."

I raised my eyebrow at him, his cheeks tinged pink at my silent call out. He coughed, his hand leaving my cheek, taking its warmth with it. "I'm learning," he admitted.

"Do you still want to take me on a date?" I asked, trying to sound nonchalant, but failing miserably if the hiccup in my voice was any indication.

"Are you kidding me? I've saved you three different times, arguably four, let you scold me and talk about my underequipped manhood, and now I've defended your honor." He smiled, a wicked slash of his mouth, dimples shining. "We're practically engaged, baby."

I giggled—actually fucking giggled at him. He was teasing and I liked the way he purred the word *baby*. It had me biting my bottom lip and my stomach doing somersaults.

Save the Date

Aaron and I made our way back to the table. It looked like everyone was as good as finished. Ronnie was sitting back in her chair and had her jeans unbuttoned. I knew it from the little outline showing through her shirt, barely noticeable unless you knew what to look for.

"Sorry about all that." I shouldn't have been apologizing, but Haven was pretty cool and I really didn't want her thinking my life was a complete disaster. Although, it most definitely was. "Things aren't normally this chaotic."

Haven smiled and nodded, the only acknowledgement I guess she was going to offer.

"Don't let her fool you. Things are always chaotic with Bell." Ronnie laughed.

I scowled at her. "Thanks."

She rounded the table and pulled me into a quick hug. "You know I love you."

"I love you too." I couldn't help but smile at her. Ronnie

made everyone feel like she had known them her whole life.

The rest stood, Xavier stretching like a cat who just ate a feast. "Well, come on, love birds. I've got places to be," he snapped, making Ronnie and I stick our tongues out at him. Jealous hussy.

"I'm going to hang around and help Billy with the restaurant. Y'all go on," I said, releasing Ronnie's arm.

Ronnie and Xavier both shrugged and blew air kisses as they passed by, saying goodbye to Haven and Aaron.

Aaron, who had stood by quietly throughout the exchange, spoke up, "I'll be at your place by seven."

I flashed him a quick smile and turned to Haven. "I'll see you Friday. I can't wait to meet your fiancé."

She smiled and offered a small wave before she walked to the front door, leaving Aaron behind.

"You better go since, technically, following her is your job," I teased. Some people had stopped her on her way out, pulling out pens and napkins to capture her autograph.

I didn't envy that. Poor Haven.

"Don't forget, wear something pretty" he whispered before stomping off toward her. Instead of watching him, I started picking up the dirty plates from our table, emptying the little food that was left and realizing Aaron didn't get to eat.

"Aaron." I waved him down, motioning for him to wait as I boxed up his food, and handed it to him. "Wouldn't want you to starve."

He smiled down at me and took the box from my hands.

The few people who had asked for Haven's autograph lingered, so I shooed them back toward their tables so Aaron could make his way out the door.

I turned after watching them all drive off, ready to face Billy and his million questions.

I couldn't find him in the kitchen or the dining area, so I continued to clean up the few abandoned tables, throwing uneaten food in the trash and stacking plates on the bar. Once the tables had been wiped down and readied for new customers, I took the stack of plates to the dishwasher, leaving the few patrons in the dining area with full drinks and satisfied bellies. Loading the dishes in with the silverware from earlier, I let them go through the wash cycle.

I wondered where Aaron would take me tonight. I had to leave here in a little while or I wouldn't be able to shower. Then I would smell like grease, and that wasn't a cute look for anyone. It was the least I could do, especially if we could just figure out what we wanted out of each other.

The washer stopped, so I pulled the crate out that held the

plates and found a clean towel under the industrial sink to dry them off before placing them near the runners area. The silverware stood up in cylindrical drying racks, separated by spoons, forks, and knives.

Once done, I checked Billy's office where he normally retreated for a little peace. I couldn't blame him. He probably had to fire the new girl and that was always hard on him since he liked picking up strays off the side of the road. I was convinced that's why he called me Kitten.

He was sitting behind his desk, hunched over the keyboard to his ancient computer. He wouldn't let me or any of his grandkids buy him a new one though. So until this one crashed, it was stuck.

Every time I saw him and didn't mention the possibility of Tennessee and the new shop, I felt a little guilty. I knew he would be so happy for me. I would be lying if I said I wouldn't miss the heck out of him. Plus, it wasn't a done deal yet. I couldn't get him worked up if nothing came of it.

"You really need to get some reliable help," I tried teasing, but I could tell the weight was settling heavy on him.

"My best waitress went off and became a sought after wedding planner," he chirped back. It made me smile.

"She was already a wedding planner when she started working here part time," I countered. I knew he was happy for my success. He had always made sure to celebrate each one with me.

"That vet sure does have a presence, huh?"

"Yeah, he does," I agreed. "He asked me to dinner."

Talking about Aaron with Billy kind of felt like what I would imagine talking to a father should feel like. My own father wasn't a good man.

Billy's face turned down. Anytime a veteran came through his doors, it made him sad because it made him think about his son, and his grandson who was in the Navy...wherever he was. I hurt for him, and I could never understand that pain, not really.

He looked up at me again and nodded his head, waiting for me to continue.

"If I tell you how we met, you promise not to laugh?" I was suddenly feeling anxious about telling Billy what I said to a perfect stranger in a night club.

"I can't make that promise, especially knowing how your mouth runs away from you sometimes." He grinned.

The half smile that pulled at my lips told him everything he needed to know. "I may have told him that he didn't have what it takes to satisfy a woman."

"You did what?" He couldn't hold it in any longer. His belly shook with his laugh, making me think about Santa and

Christmas being not so far away.

"Ronnie and I were at that club, you know, Dusk 'Til Dawn, and we had been fending off mens' comments and paws all night. I was irritated and ready to be home." As if that was enough of an excuse. "I thought he was the same guy that had bothered Ronnie and I earlier, but all he was trying to do was return my clutch that had fallen on the ground."

"Kitten..." He sighed, still chuckling. "Well, I hope he knows exactly what he's getting himself into."

I smiled at him, knowing he was right. And tonight I would make sure to wear something that showcased all my curves so there would be no doubt if Aaron made the move to fuck me, he would know everything he signed up for. I was a *whole lotta woman.*

Billy and I cleaned up the kitchen. Marcy, his regular waitress, had slipped in while we were talking, taking care of the few late lunch stragglers.

He offered to drive me home, and since I was already sweaty, I accepted. His dinner rush wouldn't be for another few hours anyway, and it would be good for the man to get away from his restaurant.

He dropped me off at my house with the promise that I would come see him after my date and tell him all about it.

"Be good, Kitten," he hollered as I unlocked my door.

Not tonight. Tonight, I wanted to try my hand at *bad*.

Bellamy

I rushed through a shower, making sure to shave my legs and under arms. Everything else had been waxed not too long ago so I wasn't too concerned with that. Just the thought of Aaron seeing me naked sent a thrill through my body and my anxiety skyrocketing. Although, I would definitely be a liar if I said I hadn't thought about what he had going on underneath his jeans.

Of course I was getting ahead of myself, especially if it didn't work out. Talk about awkward. We still had a few weeks until Haven's wedding. What if he asked to be taken off the assignment?

Smokie walked figure eights between my legs as I brushed my teeth and applied a thin layer of moisturizer. "I just put lotion on," I whined, knowing I would have to wipe stray cat hairs off my legs since they were still a little sticky. She didn't care, wanting pets. I bent down to pick her up and placed her on the counter, stroking her chin for a minute as I let the moisturizer do its thing.

I was still wrapped in a towel, my hair bound tightly in a T-shirt. It was the secret to perfect curls, or at least my curls.

Looking at all the makeup in my drawers, I couldn't decide on a look. I had barely worn any makeup the last few days, so would he expect something a little more? Or did he even care?

He hadn't even said where we were going, so I had no clue how to dress. I suddenly wanted to cancel, but I didn't have his phone number. Something I totally didn't even think about.

I picked my phone up off the counter and sent a quick text to Ronnie.

Me: I should cancel, right?

Seeing that she had already read it, I waited for the little three dots to pop up.

Ronnie ♥: What's going on? Cancel what?

I was going to be sick, especially because in my hasty acceptance, I somehow forgot to tell my best fucking friend the hot Veteran asked me out. I was such a mess, my emotions were all over the place. "First things first" I said to myself as I typed out my reply.

Me: Aaron asked me out. I said no, like, ten

> times. But he kept coming back. I have no idea where he's taking me. What if it turns out disastrous? My track record recently hasn't been too stellar.

Her picture flashed on my screen with an incoming FaceTime call. I answered, propping my phone up on the bottom shelf of my mirror.

"I need you to take a deep breath, Bell." She smiled at me. I could see her little dining set behind her over the couch.

"Okay." I took a few deep breaths with her leading, then admitted, "I'm freaking out."

"He's already seen the messy you, playa! Let him see the masterpiece you are." Her tone was light, playful. Exactly what I needed, and as I processed her words, I knew she was right. I had basically already had an anxiety attack in front of him, but hopefully he hadn't picked up on it.

"You know I'm bound to say something stupid."

"Since when do you care?" Her response was immediate.

"He's different..." I didn't know exactly how to put it in words. I knew he liked when I fought him—he admitted as much. But what if I stopped being so combative? Would he lose interest like Olivia?

"It's going to be okay." Ronnie sighed, looking from the TV to me. "Look, take me to your closet. Let's find your outfit!"

This was definitely a good idea. Ronnie knew fashion, and

I knew whatever she picked out would be fantastic. I pulled my phone from the little shelf and walked the short distance to my bedroom. Flicking on the light to my closet, I turned the camera around so she could see.

"Let's see, move to the right. No, my right."

I rolled my eyes, even though she couldn't see.

"We really need to go shopping." Ronnie sighed. "Why is everything black?"

"It's simple and professional," I murmured, knowing she would have me shopping for new clothes soon by the look on her face.

"Wait!" she cried. I stopped moving the phone, trying to see exactly which article of clothing she would be looking at. "That one. The deep green. Pull that out."

I did as she asked and pulled out the emerald dress. It hugged my curves, fell just a little over my knee, and hung off the shoulders, exposing just a little bit of cleavage. It was a little chilly today so I would have to wear a cardigan over it.

Ronnie must have put that together too. "Uhhh no, too cold for that. Toss it." She looked determined to find the perfect outfit. "Pull out all of the items that aren't black, Bell."

"Bossy," I muttered, but did as she wanted. I placed the

phone down on the edge of my bed to pull out everything I had that wasn't black. I laid the few pieces out in a neat row across my bed before picking up the phone and showing her the options. I had a navy wrap dress that was more of a casual dress than first date material, a gray sweater dress that was probably the coziest piece of clothing I owned, and a red number that still had the tags on it.

"That one."

I pretended like the red dress wasn't an option and pointed to the gray sweater dress. "Yeah, I like that one too."

She rolled her eyes. "No, Bell, the red one. It's perfect."

I picked it up a bit begrudgingly, holding it up to my body to get a better idea of what it would look like.

"Yes!" she squealed. "Pair it with those black point-toe heels and even I would want to undress you."

"I don't know if I want him to undress me yet," I lied. I did want him to undress me. I wanted him to think about it all night.

"Liar!" she shouted. She was up and dancing around her kitchen, making what I assumed was her dinner. I looked at the time.

"Shit! He'll be here in an hour and I still have to diffuse my hair." Panic tried to grip its claws in.

"Damn, Bell. Cutting it close, huh? Tame that gorgeous

mane and stop panicking!" She stopped dancing to look into the phone all serious. "You have amazing hair, and with that dress, trust me. He'll be eating out of the palm of your hand."

"Okay, love you! Bye."

"Deets later, playa. Love you!"

I hit the red button to end the call, scrambled to the bathroom, and began to diffuse my curls. As I let my hair rest—plopped on top of my head—I applied primer and foundation, then swiped a nude color over my eyes, smoking out the shadow with a deeper brown to add dimension. I finished off the look with eyeliner, a thousand pounds of mascara, and setting spray, forgoing the towel. I was melting, hot from the dryer, and even more from nerves.

Back in my room, I pulled out my best bra. Grabbing a lacy number to cover my plump booty, I pulled it on and over my hips, then shimmied into the dress. It was soft—much softer than I anticipated. The sleeves touched my wrists, the top dipped into a low cut V, and it had ruching across the stomach. The dress hit just a tad below the knee, and with every twist and turn, the extra skin around my stomach moved with it.

No hiding here. I loved that the color made me feel powerful, and the fact that I refused to put on shapewear was freeing. I wasn't about to be uncomfortable. If he wanted me, he would have to want all of me.

I slipped my feet into the heels Ronnie told me to wear before taking a deep breath and looking into the floor length mirror in my hall. I was surprised by my reflection. Getting dressed up wasn't new to me; I attended weddings for a living, but this felt different. Seductive almost.

I loved it. I loved the high I felt looking at myself, thinking about what Aaron would think when he saw me.

My lips still hadn't been painted so I rushed to the bathroom to fix it before Aaron showed. It was about five minutes till seven, and my nerves rushed back in. I pulled my anxiety pills out of the cabinet and placed one on my tongue, drinking a little water to get it down.

I rifled through all my lipstick, trying to find the one I wanted. It was a dark nude that made my lips look full and my teeth whiter. I was applying the matte color to my lips when I heard a knock at the door.

Instantly, I felt like a rock had been lodged in my throat, and my legs started to shake. Oh, God. I took a few deep breaths, gripping the edges of the porcelain sink, lecturing myself for not having the foresight to take my meds sooner. I knew I needed to stop leaning on them so heavily, but knowing my mother called Henry and Georgie the other day didn't help.

Filling my lungs as much as I could, I let out that breath in a slow, steady stream, balancing myself on the sink. I finished my lips, meshing them together to properly coat both, then stood up straight. With one more calming exhale, I walked across the living room to open the door.

Aaron

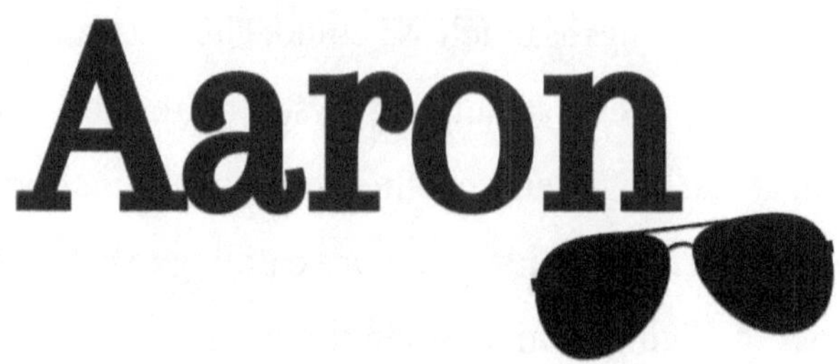

She answered the door, and once my eyes found her standing there in a sexy-as-fuck red dress, I knew I was done for. I wasn't going to be able to focus on driving to the damn restaurant with her beside me looking like that.

The red material sculpted to her body, and I couldn't help but be jealous of the damn thing. I couldn't form words for a moment. Her hazel eyes were bright under the low lighting in the house, accentuating the little upward tilt of them.

I probably looked like an idiot ogling her, but *fuck* she looked like sin in those tall, thin heels.

I cleared away the lump in my throat. "Screw the reservations. Let's stay in."

She laughed, throwing her head back, her cheeks darkening under her smooth complexion. "Absolutely not. You think I'm wasting all this after you badgered me for a date?" Tilting her head back down, I noticed the wink of a silver hoop in her nose. It was the first time I had seen her wear any type of jewelry on her face other than the various earrings she wore.

Running my hand over my mouth so I didn't say anything stupid, I nodded and waited for her to shut and lock her door.

Following her down the little stone pathway toward my truck, I watched as she swayed her hips, her ass bouncing perfectly. I had to adjust my dick before opening the door for her. I was already halfway hard, and goddamn that dress gave me all kinds of fantasies.

Once she was settled, I closed the door and rounded the vehicle. I had kept it running to keep the heat on. I didn't want her to be cold, but I also didn't want to waste a second of our date. For however long she would let my ass stick around.

"You look absolutely beautiful." It wasn't enough, she looked better than beautiful. Unearthly. Her lips were full, and if I didn't put the truck in gear right fucking now, I would ruin the date before it even started.

"You don't look half bad yourself," she quipped back. Her smile pulled at my heart, and I made a note to make sure I told her everyday how pretty she was if it meant she'd smile at me like that every time.

I had dressed in black slacks and a gray button down, and

had dusted off my nice shoes in hopes of impressing her since all she ever saw me in was jeans and a black henley. Not that I thought she minded. I had caught her looking at me almost as much as I looked at her.

"I clean up nice, huh?" I teased, wanting to touch her, but respecting that she wouldn't want that. Yet. Eventually, I'd have her begging for it.

"So where are we going?" she asked. The lights from the other cars lit up her face, making her look like a damn angel.

"*That* is a surprise." I didn't think she'd had many before. She seemed like the type to always be the one doing the surprising. I wanted to do this for her, to make sure she didn't have to lift a finger tonight.

"Give me a hint?" she pleaded.

I just smiled. Bellamy sat back in her seat with a huff and I had to chuckle at her impatience. I hoped she didn't mind a little drive further into the city of Charleston. It was a little authentic Italian place that had the best handmade pasta I had ever eaten. I had bribed Veronica to tell me Bellamy's favorite food since the stubborn woman wouldn't tell me herself. I just hoped she loved it. I laid my arm on the armrest between us, palm up in hopes she would lay hers in it.

Focusing on the drive, I navigated the way toward downtown. I pulled into a spot not too far from the restaurant.

"It's been a while since I've been into the city for anything other than a wedding," she said. I raised my brows at her, knowing she was just here a few days prior. She amended, "Well, and a drink the other weekend."

"Well tonight is about you. No work talk." I laid down the most important rule. I selfishly wanted her to think about me.

She nodded and I clicked open my door, rounding the back to let her out. I had engaged the child locks earlier to make sure she couldn't get out without me opening the door. Which I could tell aggravated her.

"Child locks, really?"

I did a silly bow as if she were royalty before offering her my hand to help her down. She let out a little giggle and it was the sweetest sound my ears had ever heard. When her feet hit the ground, it was all I could do to hold myself back from smothering her in my arms.

"Can I hold you?" I didn't want to freak her out, but I really wanted to pull her into my body. I couldn't explain it, but I needed to feel her against me more than I needed anything else in this moment. Her eyes widened, surprise evident on her face.

Torture. That's what it felt like as she just stared at me.

I could see the gears working in her brain. I just hoped it wasn't fear of *me* holding her back.

Did I ask too much, too soon?

She tilted her chin down so I could no longer see her face, and slowly, so agonizingly slowly, stepped into my chest. I immediately wrapped my arms around her.

She fit perfectly in my arms, and I wanted to keep her there.

Her shoulders were stiff but only for a moment before she relaxed. I blew out a breath, looking down at her as she looked up at me.

"Thank you," I murmured. She didn't have to trust me, but she did. Enough to agree to come out with me, and to let me hold her. If only for a moment.

She ducked her head and stepped away, interlocking our fingers and pulling me toward the sidewalk. I took the lead, trying to keep my steps short so she didn't have to struggle to keep up.

We made it to the maître d', and since I ate here way too often, he directed us straight to our table even though there were patrons waiting in the lobby.

He pulled the chair out for Bellamy, and gently pushed her seat in once she got comfortable. I gave him a nod in thanks.

"Well, this is nice," she said, her eyes trained on me. If I hadn't known any better, I would have said it sounded like a purr. The low lighting in the room and the candle burning in the middle of the table cast her in a beautiful golden glow, making her eyes look darker than her normal hazel, completely obliterating the green.

"Everything is delicious, so get whatever you want." I had to stop staring at her. If I didn't I wouldn't be able to eat. I was so nervous, but hopeful she would love it as much as I did.

"Pasta," she murmured as she looked over the menu. "Someone's been talking to you."

Her eyes met mine, and I detected a smile over the menu. Points for me.

"You like pasta?" I tried playing innocent.

"Cut the shit. Which one of those idiots talked to you?"

"Let's just say I have informants everywhere." I couldn't take my eyes off her.

She hummed, and I swore I started sweating. She was easy to read most of the time, but tonight it was like she had put up a different wall, schooling her features perfectly so I couldn't guess what she was thinking.

We ordered and the server brought out a red wine that he said would pair well with our meals. I hadn't had anything I didn't like here, so I allowed him to pour us both a glass. She didn't touch hers, seeming uninterested.

I took a sip. It was smooth, earthy almost. Not terrible, but not my favorite. I was starting to wonder if she didn't drink when she lifted the glass to her perfect lips and took a sip.

"That's," she paused, "not terrible." She looked between my glass and hers, clearly trying to swallow those words back.

I chuckled, knowing that was exactly my thoughts. We didn't bother with the rest of the bottle as our food was delivered. We ate and took turns asking questions in between bites. I learned she was an only child, her parents didn't communicate with her often, and she loved the color green.

"So, retired Marine, huh?" she started, and I felt a pang of sadness resonate through my body.

"Veteran is the correct term," I answered, "I left after my contract was up for renewal. I didn't want to re-enlist since my parents died while I was deployed. Especially since Holly-Jay and her wife, Kelly, are all the family I have left now." I shrugged. "I miss it and my brothers like hell every damn day, but I know I made the right choice."

Sitting here with this gorgeous woman, everything seemed like it might work out. Like fate or some cosmic shit my sister-in-law talked about.

"So, how did you end up with the private security gig?" Her face flushed in the candle light. "I mean, obviously your sister. But was that always your backup plan?"

I chuckled. Her attempt at talking had made her face turn sour, as if she were biting on a lemon.

"Actually no, I didn't have a backup plan. I never thought I'd be anything but a Marine. But to answer your question, I was in a rough space. I felt lost, and without a purpose. Holly-Jay saw it and she begged me to talk to someone." Bellamy was so easy to talk to, so I kept going. "I reached out to Benny, one of my best friends, who works in private security. He's a bouncer at Dusk 'Til Dawn. I talked to him about it and he gave me the encouragement to at least apply."

She sipped her wine again, eyes never leaving mine as I spoke. Like she couldn't get enough of my words. A thrill shot straight to my brain and I couldn't stop talking once I started. "It's been a few months now and when Holly-Jay found out about Haven Macemore wanting you and Veronica for her wedding, she let me know."

"It hasn't been easy, especially since I never saw myself doing anything other than serving. But I have to admit, from where I'm sitting, the view is much better."

At the first mention of the place we met, she had set her

glass down, fingers turning white from holding the glass so tight. Her face showed a mix of embarrassment and...was that a smirk?

"About Dusk 'Til Dawn, Aaron. I'm so sorry."

I couldn't help the laugh that came out. She was sorry for the best first impression I'd ever had?

"Why are you laughing?" she asked, her lips turned down and her eyes stared daggers at me.

"I don't think you understand how much I wanted to get to know you after that introduction."

Her face morphed through several different emotions, landing on embarrassment. Her skin paled, cheeks rosy. It was adorable as fuck.

"I'm not sure you know what you're getting yourself into," she started. "I haven't spoken to the people that procreated and gave me life in years, I generally stay away from people as much as I can outside of my job, and I really suck at relationships. Like forgetting my partner exists sometimes."

I sat back for a moment, watching as the word vomit spilled from her lips. The same lips I had been fantasizing about wrapped around my cock for a week. I admired the fact that she was a straight shooter. Most women I'd met tried to hide their faults.

The comment about her parents was shocking. If I could

have had one more day with my parents, I knew I would have taken it no matter the cost. But I didn't want to push her for more than she wanted to give me. I had a feeling if I did, she would clam up, and considering this was the best date I'd ever been on, I wanted it to continue. We continued on well after we had finished eating and the table had been cleared. I loved hearing her tell stories so vividly.

A shadow fell over our table and I expected the waiter. Instead, I found the one person I never wanted to run into again.

Molly, a woman I went on one date with over two years ago, stood beside our table, her body turned to face me. "I thought I saw you over here, darlin'."

Bellamy's eyes widened and her brows shot up her forehead. I knew I was in for one of two things by that look, and I sent up a silent prayer that she would listen to what I had to say before making assumptions.

Bellamy

What. A. Bitch.

She really just sauntered up to our table, completely ignored I was sitting here, called him *darlin'*, and ran her finger up his arm.

"Molly, this is my date, Bellamy." He had the good sense to introduce me, at least, or else this date would not have ended well for him.

She flicked her gaze to mine, looked me up and down, and completely dismissed me refocusing on Aaron.

"Nice to meet you too," I snapped. She turned back to me, piercing me with her stare. But I was not easily swayed and she was about to learn it.

"Wait..." Her eyes narrowed. "You're that wedding planner, right? The one in that magazine." She placed her expertly manicured finger on his shoulder. "Yes! With the company your sister owns!" She turned back to Aaron like he was going to give her a damn cookie for putting two and two together.

She just had to bring up that fucking article.

"She's the best in the business." Aaron beamed at me, taking me by surprise.

"But you're a team. I'll bet your partner wouldn't be too happy to hear that." She giggled, and I swore the sound was just like the scratching of a fork on good china. "She's so pretty and thin. Have you thought about asking her for dieting tips?"

"Fuck off." I was getting irritated fast. "You don't get to act like you know anything about me or Ronnie because you read a damn article. And for the record, I don't need a diet to look better than you in that gaudy dress."

Her jaw dropped open as if the fat girl really just said what she did. Let the record show: fat girl 1, jealous barbie 0.

She looked back at Aaron with incredulous eyes. "You know my number." Again she ran her finger over his arm, and squeezed his shoulder before flouncing away back to her own date.

Aaron closed his eyes and ran a hand down his face. "That went well."

I pushed up from my seat, ready to get the hell out of here. I was actually having a good time. I couldn't remember the last time I actually wanted to answer personal questions, but the genuine look in his eyes as we spoke had me spilling little details about my life.

I wanted to tell him things about me, just like I wanted him to grab my hand again and pull me into his arms. But whatever the hell that was back there? I didn't want any fucking part of it.

Throwing the cloth napkin over my dessert plate and turning on my stiletto, I made my way to the door.

"Sunshine," I heard Aaron behind me. "Sunshine, hold on."

I didn't wait. I stepped out into the cool night air trying to remember which way we parked.

"Bellamy," he said more forcefully.

I turned on my heel to face him, nearly losing my balance.

"What are you doing?" he asked, as if it wasn't completely fucking obvious I wanted to go home. I'd been stupid to think opening myself up to someone was a good idea. God, why did I do this to myself?

"Was this a pity date?" I asked, my thoughts working up into a frenzy of emotion. "Let me guess. You take me out on a date, it goes great, and what, you've checked that box off on your do-gooder list?"

Thoughts swirled in my head. The way he allowed her to continue touching him, as if she had any right... Maybe she did, and I was the odd one out.

"Hate to break it to you, but I'm not a woman who plays mind games."

He stood there, jaw so tight I could almost see him working his molars over. "Are you done?"

"With you? Hell yes!" I shouted. I didn't care that people were walking by. I just wanted to go home. I pulled my phone from my little clutch to call an Uber. It wasn't that far, and I was sure I could find somewhere to wait that wasn't in the cold November air.

"What are you doing?" His voice was closer.

"Getting a ride."

"Bellamy, would you hold on a minute?" Exasperated, he ran his hands through his hair. "She's..." I could tell he was trying to choose his words carefully. "Well, she's a friend I've known for a few years now."

"Some *friend*." At this point I didn't know if I was angry with myself or him. "A little fatphobic friend? Let's see, Aaron. How many friends do you have that wonder if you've asked for dieting tips?"

"Okay, so *friend* is not quite the right word. Acquaintance? Someone I knew from a while ago?" He gripped the hand that held my phone and lowered it, hitting the cancel button on my Uber app so smoothly, I just gaped.

"Last I checked, I don't let my friends touch me and fawn all over me," I snapped. "Or talk to strangers like they owe them any amount of answers about their bodies. But shit, maybe my version of *friend* is different from yours."

His chuckle sounded panicked. "She's not..." He ran his hands over his face, leaving mine eerily cold, before his knuckles grazed my fingers. "What she said. It wasn't okay, and I'm sorry I let Molly get that far.. I should have said something. And I know you can stick up for yourself. But you shouldn't have had to, I don't know how to do this. I like you, Bellamy. A lot."

I didn't want to trust the sincerity in his eyes. I didn't want to feel this sick feeling in the pit of my stomach either.

"Do you want me to go back in there and tell her off? Because I fucking will."

"No." I chewed the inside of my lip, waiting for him to decide I wasn't worth the effort. Instead he pulled me into his arms and took a deep breath.

"Just so you know, I found that extremely attractive." He pulled back and I swatted his chest. Of course he found it attractive, I just confessed to *feeling something* for this big idiot.

"Can we just walk for a bit?" I asked. I wanted to cool down and Charleston was so pretty this time of year. He didn't say anything. Instead, he grinned and held out his hand like a footman waiting for Cinderella to dismount her carriage.

Horses hooked to buggies pulled couples around the block, garland hung from every lamppost, red bows dotted the windows, and I loved the twinkling lights they put in the bare trees lining the sidewalk.

We walked side by side down the street. People passed by carrying hot drinks and murmuring amongst themselves. It was a clear night, the stars above us painting the sky with bright freckles.

I could feel Aaron's stare on my face as I gazed up. Maybe I'd see a falling star and make a wish. It was close enough to Christmas, right?

His hand came up around my face, thumb swiping a little back and forth movement over my cheekbone.

"I don't think you know how beautiful you are," he whispered, so quietly I couldn't tell if he was talking to himself, or if I was meant to hear it. Our eyes connected, and we stood there locked in sight, his hand warm against my throat, his other arm banded around my waist.

I shivered under his touch. The hand that held my face so delicately ran featherlight down my shoulder to my hand. We slowly made our way back to the truck, and he helped me into the passenger seat before getting in himself and starting the engine. It was loud. I smirked as he pulled away, slightly disrupting the peaceful night.

Bellamy

onight hadn't been as disastrous as I thought it would have been. Other than his *friend* making an appearance, it was a great first date. I had been on some terrible dates, and this was probably the best one I had ever been on.

He drove back to my little town, a complete change from the city where I imagined people still milled about. All the little shops were closed, lights turned off besides the ones lining the street.

It was cozy; a sleepy town where so much of my life started. Where I had learned to rework my future into something I wanted. Not what my parents thought I should have wanted. I had learned how to truly be me.

To take no shit, protect my heart, and learn to love myself.

Although, looking over at the man sitting in the driver's seat with his hand on my thigh, I was starting to think I could let him love me. Maybe I could trust him with my heart. Not a piece like I gave Ronnie and Xavier, but the whole damn thing.

The thought scared me. Obviously, I wasn't ready for that yet. We'd had one date. A good date, but only one nonetheless.

"Tell me what's running through that pretty head of yours." Aaron smiled my way before looking back at the road. I liked that he took time to glance at me. It was sweet.

"Just thinking about how different my life is now."

"Are you talking about your parents?"

I nodded, and he didn't pry. But I knew when I was ready to talk about it, he would be willing to listen.

Not long after, we pulled up outside of my house and he turned the truck off, the cloth seat stretching and dipping under him as he turned to give me his full attention. "Can I take you out again?"

I giggled as he blurted his question. I couldn't blame him for wanting a redo even though it was one of the best nights of my life. I nodded again slowly, hiding my mouth behind my hands.

I hadn't smiled like this in a long time; freely and without thought. It felt liberating, and I didn't want it to stop. He smiled so wide his dimples showed and I had to stop myself from launching across his console to kiss him. I wanted him to want to make that first move.

He was still smiling when he slipped out of the truck and made his way to my side. Which was still locked. It was silly, but oh-so-cute that he engaged the child locks so I couldn't open my own door just because he wanted to be the one to do it. It made my heart skip a beat.

And they say chivalry is dead.

He offered me his hand and I took it, not letting myself think twice about it. I liked his touch; it was soothing and strong. Everything I wanted in a partner.

He unlatched the gate and stepped through, twisting his arm so I could walk in behind him without parting our hands. "Do you have your keys?"

"Of course." I laughed. Why wouldn't I have my keys? As I pulled them from my clutch, I slipped on a rogue pebble on my walkway. Aaron caught me, with one arm around my back, and the other cradling my head.

If I had to guess, we looked like that sailor and his wife in all those old-timey pictures. It was cheesy, but it felt perfect. His gaze held mine, and I held my breath, scared to make a move, fearful that he would drop me.

He leaned down closer to my face, eyes searching mine for permission. Ever so slowly, he closed the space and I let my eyes drift shut. My eyes popped open just as I heard a growl erupt from the bushes behind me. I screeched and flailed in his arms.

He was so close, I ended up head butting him in the mouth. Stunned, he reached up to cup his mouth and I fell to the walkway. I yelped, "Ow, fuck!" as my ass took the brunt of the fall, and I swore if I had broken my tailbone, I would never see the light of day again.

Aaron groaned in pain as he kneeled down beside me. There was a little cut on his lip, and I wanted to cry or fall into a black hole.

"Sunshine, are you okay?"

Our first kiss was always meant to be a disaster. Tears fell as I laughed hysterically. I couldn't help it, but the concern in his voice registered in my brain and I felt bad for my reaction.

"I'm fine," I wheezed, trying to hold the laughter in.

"I didn't mean to drop you." He laid both hands on the sides of my face, using his thumbs to wipe away the tears that had surely messed up my mascara. But I didn't care, this was perfect and I wouldn't want it any other way.

Smokie trotted out from the bush, tail puffed, and a new fit of laughter hit me.

"Oh my God," I howled. My own cat scared the shit out of me. Why was she even out here?

"Why are you laughing?" Poor Aaron was so confused, and I couldn't blame him.

"This is Smokie." I held my hand out for the Maine Coon to come to me, warning through my laughs, "Smokie, this is Aaron, be nice."

When all the pieces seemed to catch up to him, he laughed along with me, throwing back his head in a full belly laugh.

Once Smokie had enough pets, Aaron stood and helped me back up. We reached the porch without any more pebble mishaps, and he gripped my hips and pulled me flush against him.

He didn't waste any time as his lips came down on mine hard. He crushed his lips to mine like a man starved, like he wanted to devour my soul through my lips, and I melted into it. When his tongue flicked my lips, I opened for him. He teased my tongue with his own. It was a toe curling kiss, lasting forever and not nearly long enough in the same breath.

When he finally raised his lips from mine, he whispered, "I've been thinking about doing that since I saw you in Dusk 'Til Dawn."

My heart was racing in my chest, and I was sure he could feel it being as close as we were, but I didn't have a care in the world. I wanted all of his kisses. He tasted of wine and chocolate, with a little tinge of copper from the cut on his lip. A deadly mix that had me craving more.

Smokie meowed loudly, ending our trance. He took a slight step back and helped me unlock my door. Probably a good thing because my whole body was shaking like an addict ready for their next fix.

Smokie darted in and I turned back to Aaron, desperate for one more kiss before he left. I wasn't working tomorrow, so I knew I wouldn't see him. And even if I did, would I kiss him in front of my friends? At this point, I would do anything to have him look at me like I was the last good thing on earth again.

He leaned down, lightly pressing his lips against mine before pulling back and heading to his truck. I had a feeling if I let him come in, there would be no more talking and way more than I was ready to give him.

"Thank you," I called once he got to the gate. "For tonight, it was...." I tried to search for the right words to tell him how fucking wonderful tonight was.

He spoke instead, "I know."

His lips twisted up, and if I didn't get my ass inside, I would launch myself down the stairs and pull him inside with me. I quickly turned and locked myself in the house, placing my hand against my lips that still tingled with his kiss.

I couldn't wait to see him again. It shocked me. That was the first time I had ever let myself have something that I never wanted before.

Bellamy

I slept hard that night. So hard, I didn't wake up until almost lunch time. My nose was stuffy, and I hoped I wasn't getting sick. Good thing I had the day off. Ronnie and Xavier had texted to our group chat, wanting to know how the night went.

> **Ronnie: Bellllll! Give us the dirty deets!**

> **Xavier: Yes, girl. Spill the tea!**

> **Ronnie: She's probably still asleep. That dick must have been good!**

> **Xavier: Good? Honey, he looks exactly like big dick energy. I want pics!**

I laughed at their antics, but ultimately put my phone down. Picking up a pint of Ben & Jerry's new *PB Over the Top* and a spoon, I got comfy on the couch with a big fuzzy blanket. I had pulled on some sweatpants under my shirt since the heat in this house didn't work the best.

My phone had dinged a few times while I was up, but I ignored it.

My head was starting to hurt and my nose ring was really starting to bother me. I figured if I took a nap, I would feel better. I hadn't been sleeping much since we had been so busy at the shop.

Burrowing under the blankets and snuggling down into the widest part of the couch, I thought about Aaron and wondered what he was doing. But without his phone number, it would be hard to connect.

With my thoughts focused on him, I drifted off to sleep.

I woke up sometime in the middle of the night, my stomach rolling as bile pushed its way up my throat. I threw off the covers and made it to the toilet just in time to empty my guts.

Sweat rolled down my temples and I knew I needed to start hydrating. The stomach bug was no joke, and I was supposed to meet Ronnie today to finalize little details for Haven's wedding.

Once I was sure I didn't have anything more to purge, I

went in search of my phone. The TV had long since turned off so there was minimal light. The end of the couch came out of nowhere and I bashed my toes into one of the wooden legs.

"Mother fucker!" I hollered to no one. Smokie didn't even lift her head from where she was laid out at the end of the couch. "I think I lost the toe," I told her, to which she cracked an eye and promptly closed it, signaling she couldn't care less.

I rolled my eyes. *Maybe I should get a dog.* I laughed to myself. I barely had time for myself, I would never have time to take care of a dog.

Swiping my phone open, I let my eyes adjust to the bright light. The group chat had way too many messages for me to deal with at the moment. I found Ronnie's text thread. She had sent me a few things since yesterday. I ignored those to tell her I wouldn't be in today, that I was sick, and left it at that. Misery loves company, but seeing as it was close to three in the morning on a Friday, I didn't want to bother Ronnie with a phone call.

I didn't want to miss Haven's fiancé's arrival, but I didn't want to get anyone sick. Adrian Scott owned a ton of hotels, and I secretly hoped he would be open to a business proposal while here.

It wouldn't look good if I wasn't there, but if I didn't listen to my body and give it the rest it needed I wouldn't have a choice.

Sliding through the house on my fuzzy socks, I flicked the light on in the laundry closet, looking for the bin I usually kept medicine in. Shuffling through the bottles, I found a few tablets for cold and flu symptoms and popped two in my mouth. Hopefully I'd wake up refreshed and ready for Adrian's arrival.

Swallowing the large pills with a swing of water, I made my way back to my bedroom. I didn't want to be any further from the bathroom than I had to be. Soon enough, I was feeling the drowsy effects of the pills and let them take me into dreamland.

I was still miserable by late morning. I had eaten a breakfast of plain toast and had kept that down. I prayed it would pass today and I could be there tomorrow for the cake tasting.

Billy called to tell me about his grandkids. Turns out they are coming into town for Christmas this year and he wants to have dinner one night. I told him I would be there as long as he made me a Peter Paul Mounds cake, to which he chuckled and agreed. He even asked if I would bring my friends, which warmed my heart.

Ronnie called confirming everything we had on task was complete. She offered to bring me soup, but I declined. I was disgusting and I really didn't want company. She mentioned Aaron briefly, but I shut that down.

I really didn't want to talk about him. He took up too much of my brain space as it was. Plus, I was still trying to work through whatever it was that I was feeling for him. I needed to do that on my own.

I was suddenly glad he didn't have my number, or he would be offering the same thing. I had already embarrassed myself enough this past week. I didn't need to add this.

> **Unknown: Missed you today. You ok, Sunshine?**

Well shit, speak of the devil and he shall appear. I didn't recognize the number so it had to be him. Ignoring the message, I forced myself to drink some water. I did not want to get dehydrated.

I stripped my clothes, then my bed and picked up the clothes I had lived in for the last two days, throwing it all in the washer. I poured in Clorox and laundry detergent, shutting the lid and starting the clean cycle.

Sometimes I hated being an adult. I just wanted someone to take care of me. Was that too much to ask? Glancing into my drawers, I debated putting underwear on and ultimately decided against it, pulling another large shirt over my body and sweatpants over my hips, then went in search of more fuzzy socks.

It was freezing in my house and as I walked by, I checked the thermostat. I had it set to seventy, but the screen said it was sixty-four in the house. I hoped my heater wasn't going bad. It was no secret this wasn't my forever home, but I didn't want to move quite yet. The location was perfect, but the repairs were not.

All I had on the walls were a few pictures of me and Ronnie. Some with Xavier, and some that Xavier snapped from weddings. I didn't have any pictures of my parents or anything linking me to them. I didn't want anything to do with them.

I picked up my phone from the bathroom on my way back to the living room, flopped down on the couch, and turned on Netflix hoping to find a feel-good movie to raise my spirits. My phone buzzed in my pocket. I had four new texts from the unknown number and clicked on it right when someone knocked on my door. I told Ronnie not to come, but that didn't mean she wouldn't send Xavier instead. They were sneaky like that, but it made me love them even more for it.

Since I didn't have a peep hole, I pulled the chain into the slot and cracked the door. Aaron stood there with brown paper bags in his arms, looking like a man on a mission. I wasn't sure what to do, so I slammed the door shut.

"Open the door, Sunshine," I heard him rumble from the other side.

"I'm sick." It wasn't a lie, not completely. But I didn't know if I could handle being in close proximity with him after Tuesday night. I figured I would've had a few times in between with at least one other person in the room.

"Why do you think I'm here?" I could tell he was confused by my reaction, but my house was a wreck. I had a stack of used tissues overflowing in the trash can by the couch, cartons of empty ice cream laying on the end tables with the spoons still in them, and I didn't even want to think of the state of my bathroom.

"You can put that stuff on the porch. I'll grab it." I felt silly talking through the door, but what else could I do?

My phone rang, the noise jarring me. I raced toward the couch to answer it, without looking at the screen I swiped the answer call button. "Hello?"

"Are you really going to make me stand out here all day?"

I checked my phone, noticing the odd number that had texted me earlier.

"Bellamy?"

"Aaron?! How did you get my number?" It wasn't remotely what I wanted to talk about, but I was curious.

"How about you open the door and I'll tell you while I cook you some soup."

I smiled. He wanted to *cook* me soup?

"I don't want to get you sick." I tried a weak attempt at getting him to leave. He seemed to notice, chuckling through the line. Which was weird since I could hear him outside too.

"I wouldn't be here if I didn't want to be." I could hear the sigh in his voice. "I will stand out here all day. Try me."

A little part of me wanted to, but the other part really wanted him to take care of me. It had been a long time since anyone had.

"You can't."

"Why not, woman?"

"Because I'm sick." What if I had to throw up again? I did not sound cute upchucking into a toilet. Or even worse, what if I got the shits? No, fuck no. I was not letting him into my house.

"I have a strong immune system, now let me in."

"Fine, but if you get sick I won't take care of you." The big idiot would haunt my doorstep all damn day.

He chuckled again. "Deal."

Disconnecting the call, I padded over to the door, releasing the chain and opening it just wide enough he had to squeeze through. His big booted foot almost stepped on mine.

He walked right into the kitchen. Not like he couldn't find it. He deposited his bags on the floor and went back to the door. Good Lord, what had he brought me?

He stopped at the door and bent over, giving me a perfect view of his ass. He unlaced his boots and slid them off one after the other, then hung his keys on my key hook like he owned the damn place.

"What are you doing?" I asked, completely stumped. I thought he was just going to heat up a can of chicken noodle soup and leave, but he looked like he was planning on staying a while.

"Making you soup." He didn't elaborate. Instead, I watched the muscles in his back shift under the dark henley and I had to stop myself from drooling.

"You're...making me soup."

He gave me a wink over his shoulder. "You didn't think I was just going to heat up a can of soup and leave you, did you?"

I was too stunned to form a response, because that is exactly what I thought. He stalked close to me slowly, his eyes never leaving mine. Placing a hand on my cheek, he kissed my forehead before waltzing into the kitchen.

"I'm confused," I said, tilting my head. "Aren't you supposed to be on Haven and Adrian duty?"

"I traded shifts with Greer." He pinned me with a look like I had two heads. "I'm making you soup. You're going to eat while I clean your house, and hopefully take a nice long bath afterward."

"You are not cleaning my house." I folded my arms over my chest, remembering I didn't have underwear on. He could probably see my nipples from here. Because it was cold, not because he kissed my head, not because he looked absolutely delicious in just his shirt and pants.

"I am and that's final." He pulled so many groceries out of the bags that I wondered if he was making soup for an entire army. Celery, carrots, chicken stock, and a whole ass chicken. It was like Mary Poppins loaned him her bag of fun.

"Are you feeding an army?" My mouth must have been hanging open. He crossed the space between us and with a finger under my chin, shut it.

"Don't argue with me. Go sit down and watch your movie."

He tilted his head as if telling me to try him. I was so shocked, I did as he asked, settling into the couch and picking my movie. It was a Christmas one Ronnie would have liked. She was a Christmas freak.

About halfway through, he brought me a steaming bowl of soup. He managed to find my checkered pot holders. The red gingham covered the bottom of the bowl, but I still felt the heat through the fabric. It smelled wonderful and I immediately wanted to know who had taught him to cook.

But he didn't stick around. Instead, he walked straight to my bedroom, and I had to keep myself on the couch. My room was a wreck. I still hadn't cleaned up from when I FaceTimed with Ronnie.

He didn't say a word, instead went about like it was his own, throwing things into the hamper, putting new sheets on the bed. I guess I kept things in a semi-normal place since he seemed to be finding everything okay. Or maybe it was because there weren't many places to store things.

"I don't hear your movie," he shouted, and I jerked forward, spilling the hot soup down my body.

"Fuck!" I shouted, shooting up from the couch. Aaron came running into the room like a bat out of hell, immediately taking the bowl out of my hands and putting it on the end table. He gripped the hem of my T-shirt and went to lift it over my head. "Wait!" I swatted his hands.

"You have to get out of that shirt. You don't want to scald your skin." He reached for me again, and I took another step back.

"I c-can't," I stuttered out. It burned, holy shit did it burn.

"Sunshine, it's fine. I won't even look." He held up his hands in surrender and took a step closer. I stepped back again, stepping on Smokie's tail to which she hissed and my heart hit the floor.

"Smokie! I'm so sorry." I twisted to pick her up and the heat seared at my skin. I ripped the shirt over my head, completely forgetting why I didn't want Aaron to take it off in the first place.

When cool air hit my skin, I yelped and covered my breasts. Not well, I might add. My breasts were bigger than my hands, so Aaron got an eye full. He offered me the blanket and I knew if I could see myself, I would be flushed from head to toe.

Aaron

S he wasn't wearing a goddamn bra.

I don't know how I didn't notice before. Maybe because I was actually trying to be a decent guy? When she tore the material off her body and I got an eyeful of those perfect fucking tits, I could have come in my pants.

Jesus, forgive me. All I could think about were her breasts as I quickly grabbed her a blanket and held it out for her.

That glimpse was all it took to have my cock standing at attention, aching for release. I would have to rub one out in the bathroom while she watched her movie at this rate. I had it bad, and I hoped it never went away. Her face flamed, emotion flicking over her features. I tried not to stare.

I groaned.

"I'm sorry," she said while taking off toward her bedroom.

"Hey, no." I crossed the distance to where she had slammed the door. "You didn't do anything wrong."

I had the distinct feeling that she would shut herself in and worry over her thoughts, let her mind wander and create scenarios in her head. I stood at the door, trying and failing to hear her on the other side.

"Can I come in?" I didn't want to barge in, especially in her own space. She needed to be comfortable, to feel safe.

The door creaked open and I took my opportunity. Entering the room, I spotted her going back to sit on the edge of her bed, wrapped up in the blanket, eyes red and puffy. She found new sweatpants somewhere; I spotted the gray material around her ankles.

"Why are you crying?" I knelt in front of her, lifting her face to mine. "Sunshine, talk to me."

I felt the overwhelming urge to pick her up and wrap her in my arms, to just make her understand I wasn't going anywhere. She was not in the right headspace for that though and I didn't want to push her too far.

"I didn't mean to flash you." Her voice was small, barely above a whisper.

"You won't hear any complaints from me."

Finally her eyes met mine, searching my face as if she'd find a lie. She wouldn't. I was rock fucking hard under my jeans.

"Why are you being so nice to me?" Her eyes glazed over with unshed tears. I hated seeing her cry, not because it made her vulnerable, but because I didn't know if I had caused it or not.

"Because, Sunshine, if I haven't made it clear, I like you." I brushed the pad of my thumb across her bare face, adding, "I like you a lot."

She laughed then. It was small, but I counted it as a win. "I like you a lot, too." Her face was completely open, letting me see just how much she meant those words. She sniffled, clearly still stuffy from being sick. "And that scares the shit out of me."

I needed to kiss her. Maybe it was stupid, and maybe I would end up with the virus next, but I needed to feel her lips move against mine. Ever since that first kiss, I couldn't get the weight and feel of them out of my head.

I had to know it was real.

She met me in the middle, her arms coming around my neck. The blanket fell away, leaving her bare breasts pressed against my chest. When I groaned in approval, she swiped her tongue into my mouth. That was all the acceptance I needed to deepen the kiss.

I pushed her back against the mattress so she laid flat against it, trailing my mouth along her neck and back up, electing soft moans of encouragement from her throat. My lips found hers again as I made a path with my hand, gently taking one of her soft breasts into my palm.

Her back arched off the bed, pushing herself into my hand harder. I continued kneading and rolling her nipples between my thumb and forefinger as we kissed, our tongues twisting and tangling. Slowly, I braced myself with one arm beside her head, making sure I didn't have her hair pinned, and placed my knee between her legs.

She rolled her hips up to meet mine and I chuckled into her mouth.

"Needy," I murmured in her ear, placing a kiss below it,while I teased the waistband of her sweats with my fingers. "I need you to tell me when you want to stop, okay?"

I pulled back to look into her eyes, sneaking a peak at her breasts and the way they fell to the sides of her body. She nodded, and I took her hardened nipple into my mouth.

"Words, baby." I wouldn't go any further if I didn't hear her sweet voice beg for me.

"*Please*," she panted, and I let go, watching as her breast fell back against her body.

"Please what?"

Her eyes popped open, and the fire I saw in them had to match my own lust shining through.

"Touch me." Her pants were breathless as I slowly pushed my hand further into her pants. I sucked in a harsh breath when I found her completely bare.

"No panties?" God, I wanted to live between her fleshy thighs. I was still staring down at her as I teased my fingers over her clit. "You're wet as fuck for me."

She wiggled beneath me as I coated my fingers with her arousal. "Tell me, baby. Were you this wet the other night?"

She groaned as I made her clit harder with another pass over. "Yes—"

Her voice caught as I pushed one finger inside of her, hips pushing against my hand, seeking the friction she wanted. I wasn't ready for her to come just yet. With her splayed out below me and panting, I pushed another finger inside her and curled my fingers, looking for the sweet spot that would send her over the edge.

She gasped as my fingers moved inside her, and when I brushed my thumb over her clit, her back bowed off the bed and I knew I found the spot. I memorized the way she gripped my hand as I brought her to the precipice of her orgasm.

As I moved my fingers in and out of her, I crushed my mouth to hers, rubbing hard circles over her clit with the heel of my hand. She detonated under me, moaning into my mouth, her walls squeezing around my fingers. I absorbed every fucking sound she made, moving inside of her throughout her orgasm until she gripped my arm hard enough to draw blood.

I peppered her face with kisses as I pulled my hand from her pants. Her cum coated my hand, wet and slick between my fingers. It was a beautiful sight that made my mouth water. I brought it to my lips and licked them clean while she watched through hooded eyes. "Fucking divine, baby."

When I was done, she gripped the back of my head and pulled my mouth to hers. We kissed for minutes or hours, I didn't fucking care. But my cock did—he was straining against my pants with a vengeance.

I planted a kiss on her nose and went into the bathroom to clean up. I didn't want to push her, and I definitely didn't want our first time together to be like this. She was sick, and God help me, I should have waited until she got better to do anything like that with her. But I couldn't help myself.

Her taste on my tongue was enough to turn me into a mindless asshole. I was not about to unleash on her like that.

Not yet.

Bellamy

Aaron actually made me orgasm. A man who didn't fumble with his fingers or apologize for missing my clit for the twentieth time since we started. I didn't even care that I was still half naked laying on my bed.

I was blissed out fucking happy.

It didn't escape my notice, however, that Aaron had not finished. A pang of guilt washed over me for not thinking about him. I would have to rectify that as soon as possible. Especially if my reward was more orgasmic bliss.

I found a clean shirt in one of my drawers and pulled it over my head as Aaron came out of the bathroom. He didn't appear out of sorts as he leaned against the door. Which made me a little suspicious. I sat on the bed anyway, legs still a little limp post-orgasm.

"You're fucking perfect when you come." His smile was firmly in place, and I felt a blush creep across my face.

"Can't say I've ever heard that before." Honestly I couldn't remember the last time I had orgasmed at another person's touch.

"In that case." He towered over me while I was standing, but sitting? He looked like an angel of death. "You are fucking perfect when you come *for me*."

Sweet babies everywhere. He was going to work me up again, and I still wasn't quite ready to make that final plunge with him. So I needed him to stop being so...*amazing* didn't feel like the right word. Fantastic? Perfect?

"I'm glad you think so," I muttered, not able to look him in the eyes.

His hand gripped my chin, not roughly, just enough that I had to follow whatever movement he wanted. "Don't ever be ashamed of taking pleasure from me. Do you understand?"

I don't know where this alpha male came from, but I'd be damned if it didn't turn me on. "I just—"

He cut me off with another kiss. The position couldn't have been comfortable for him, but I wasn't going to turn him down. I wasn't ashamed of what we did, I was more worried about his needs. He had been so good to me ever since he walked into my house that I wanted to return the favor.

"Don't worry about me, Sunshine," he said as if he had

read my mind. When he pulled back, he gripped my hands and hauled me to my feet. "Soup is probably good and cold by now." The smirk on his face told me exactly what he thought about that. He didn't give one single care in the world. "Let me heat up another bowl for you, and this time please try not to drown yourself in it."

I swatted his arm.

He heated another bowl as I got comfortable on the couch. When he placed it in my hands, he planted a soft kiss on my brow before going back to what he originally had planned for today. He cleaned until my whole house sparkled and I finished two movies on my watch list.

When the last movie went off, he picked me up from my place on the couch. I squealed in protest, but that only made him hold me tighter. He walked me into the bathroom. It was a tight fit so he had no choice but to sit me down on the sink to start the hot water.

As the tub filled, he kissed my cheeks, my eyelids, everywhere but my lips. Going as far as brushing his lips against the sides of my mouth.

I almost mewled in frustration, but he was already lifting my shirt and tossing it aside. I sat there, breasts sitting heavy between us, but he made no move to touch me. Instead, he plucked one of the bath bombs from my basket and chucked it into the water. It fizzled immediately and the smell of coconut quickly took over the room.

He went to duck out as soon as I stood to remove my sweatpants, but not before locking his lips with mine and squeezing my hip.

Tease.

I was glad for it because this was definitely not how I wanted our first time to be. But I don't remember ever being this strung out and horny before.

I lowered myself into the tub. The hot water felt wonderful against my clammy skin. The water turned a milky white, and I tilted my head back against the makeshift pillow Aaron had made out of a towel.

I soaked for a while, until the water went cold and my skin turned to prunes.

Aaron knocked on the door. "Your phone keeps ringing. Want me to bring it to you?"

"Who is it?" If it was anyone from work, I'd answer before rinsing. If not, it could wait.

"It says *Alice*."

My heart immediately went into overdrive. Why would my mother be calling me? I've managed to evade my parents' radar since they cut me off all those years ago. Other than the occasional phone call to the pharmacist to demand they refill my weight loss drugs.

I pulled the plug and waited for the water to drain before standing to turn the shower on. I needed to rinse and wash my hair. Then I could make a plan.

"Sunshine?" Aaron asked. I heard the creak of the door opening.

"Leave it. I'll call her back," I lied, but Aaron wouldn't know that. I hadn't told him my parents' names. Even if he did know who she was, it wasn't his place to run interference with my mother.

What should have been a relaxing soak and shower turned into my mind going a mile a minute with all the possibilities of why my estranged mother would be calling. Of course the first thing my mind went to was either her or my father was dying. But that couldn't be it. I was fairly certain when they cut me off, they changed their will too. Not that I cared. I had enough of everything I needed here.

I finished rinsing and washing my hair, then quickly toweled down my lush curves, walking from the bathroom wrapped in a towel that didn't quite wrap all the way around my body, leaving one of my hips exposed. In a way, it made me feel sexy, like a tease just waiting to be seen. Even after days of feeling sick. I took a deep breath, trying to block out thoughts of my mother.

I was a bit nervous to parade in front of Aaron in only a towel, despite what we did just mere hours before. The door squeaked as I made my way straight to my bedroom, trying to seem unaware of his presence. But my body knew where his was. He had made himself comfortable on my couch, and I could hear a sportscaster in the background.

After drying off fully, I put on a pair of leggings and pulled a sweater over my wet hair. Locating an old T-shirt, I made my way back into the bathroom. Flipping my hair over, I lathered it in curl crème, making sure to get all the individual strands, scrunching the excess water out with the shirt. It would have to do. I didn't want to waste another minute with Aaron in my house.

In the living room, he turned my way before I took the cushion beside him and snuggled up under his arm, surprising myself, and by the look on his face, him as well. After a beat, his arm tightened against my shoulders, and he turned my head to face him.

His lips ghosted against mine. "Feeling better?"

I nodded into his hand, unable to find words. I had already given him more than I would anyone else, and I think he understood. We watched one of those comedy action movies and laughed at the same jokes until I eventually passed out on his shoulder.

I woke up sometime that night to my phone ringing. I had to blink a few times to register where I was. The last thing I remembered was being warm and tucked under Aaron's arm. The wood paneled walls of my room came into focus, but the chirp of my phone told me it wasn't in here.

Slowly, I padded out of my room on bare feet in search of the stupid device. The light from the phone lit up on the table beside my couch. I swiped the phone off the table and almost tripped seeing my mother's name on it again.

I couldn't remember the last time I had even heard her voice. The abuse my parents put me through was not something I like to spend time thinking about. Especially when they withheld my trust fund from me once I turned twenty-one. When I left, they tried reeling me back with promises to release that same trust fund. The trust fund my grandmother set up for me because she knew she raised an awful woman and felt like the money she left me might help.

But they had pushed me too far. I wouldn't even entertain the idea.

Both of them were toxic. Neither appreciated the creative

daughter they had, and they each had their own way of torturing my thoughts. I had been working on myself far longer than I cared to admit to erase all of the negativity I grew up in.

A voicemail popped up on my screen not long after the last ring I ignored. I should have deleted it. *Just delete it and move on.* But I was stronger than them, right? I could handle whatever vitriol they wanted to spout at me.

"Bellamy, I hope your childish games will end soon," I heard my father's deep voice boom through the tiny phone speakers. *"All this nonsense after that article was published. You should be ashamed of the way they made you look."*

"And your outfit! Bellamy, honestly, could you have chosen anything less flattering?" my mother shrieked in the background. I felt my eyes prick with tears, and I hated it. How did they still make me feel so small? *"I think you do this just to embarrass us."*

"Did you gain even more weight after you left?" she continued. *"Bellamy, some good news."* My father's voice turned business-like. *"We will call you every hour until you pick up. This is no longer a child's game to be played. This is your life."*

I couldn't imagine the news would be good if they would threaten to call me every hour and berate me all in one voicemail.

I had finally found happiness within myself, with my friends whom I had chosen as my family. I didn't need my parents any longer. So I finally did what I should have the second they figured out my number. I blocked their number, much like how I blocked them from my work number, email, and any other type of communication they could use to get to me.

I crawled back into bed and fell asleep to thoughts of my chosen family

Bellamy

R onnie and I were waiting at the shop the next morning. Standing in the bright sunshine of the windows, my pale blue top stood out in the glow, especially since I usually never wore color. Aaron was bringing Haven and Adrian to us so we could view her bridal portraits together.

They pulled into the lot across the street and Adrian stepped out, extending his hand for Haven to take, Aaron following behind them. Our gazes snapped to one another through the window and I smiled. My heart was beating a mile a minute.

As if we were connected, his feet ate up the distance to where Ronnie and I stood. He ripped open the door, making the glass rebound in its frame. Immediately, his hands cupped my cheeks as he bent down and kissed me. It didn't feel real. This man who was damn near perfect wanted me, and God did I want him too.

"Good morning," he finally said as he pulled away from me.

My cheeks tinted pink and I pulled my bottom lip into my mouth. Letting it go, I whispered, "Good morning."

"If you two are done, Xavier sent over Haven's proofs," Ronnie said and clapped her hands.

Haven's pictures were gorgeous. Xavier had done a phenomenal job as always. The contrast of the black studio background and her white dress made the pictures stand out. It was as if we were looking at her in real life, and not a picture at all.

I pulled out my computer and dialed Xavier's FaceTime. He answered on the first few rings. "I assume you're ready to spill all the deets from your date?"

Embarrassed, I glanced around the room. Ronnie was trying to stifle a laugh, Haven's smile was soft, and poor Adrian looked a little lost. I assumed Haven hadn't caught him up—it wasn't her business—and my respect for her skyrocketed.

I cleared my throat, unwilling to look at Aaron. "Uh, no." It wasn't like I wanted to hide it. I just wanted to keep it.

"Well, boo. I'm busy." He hung up and I rolled my eyes, hitting the button to call again. Seeming exasperated this time, he said, "I told you I'm busy."

"Haven and Adrian wanted to ask you a question," I blurted, getting slightly annoyed that he would think this was a personal call when he knew we would be looking at his proofs.

"Oh!" I could tell he was scrambling to look presentable. When he had first answered, his hair was a little askew. He must have been editing another session. "How can I help our happy couple?"

I turned the computer around to face them.

"Hello, Xavier." Adrian took charge, his voice even and commanding. "My fiance loves your work."

I just knew, without looking, that Xavier was swooning. Adrian was a very attractive man, and it didn't take much for Xavier to swoon.

"Well, thank you," he replied, his southern accent coming through stronger. I had to bite my lip to keep from laughing. One quick glance to Ronnie and I knew she was doing the same.

"Would you be available to capture us touring your city?" Adrian asked, as if it wouldn't blow Xavier's mind.

"Of course!" he almost screamed through the computer. I could hear him flipping pages and throwing pens in the background. "Unfortunately, today is the only time I have available."

Adrian looked to Haven, who looked at Ronnie and me. The baker would be here in a few hours with their cake samples. Something Xavier could document as well; it would make great pictures for a slideshow at the rehearsal dinner.

Ronnie clapped. "We'll be ready in no time. What time can you get here?"

"Give me twenty."

"Ronnie, the cakes will be here around lunch." I didn't want them to miss out on arguably the best part of the wedding process.

Haven, who seemed more at ease with her fiance here, spoke up, "I'm sure you and Mr. Lark could pick our flavors, right?"

My eyes snapped up to Aaron, who stood silently by at the exchange. He smiled when our eyes connected, sending the dormant butterflies erupting in my belly.

"That's a great idea, song bird." Adrian wrapped an arm around Haven and kissed her temple. The act almost made me melt, and I was not a lovey dovey type. Her little nickname had me thinking about how Aaron called me Sunshine. Maybe I didn't hate it as much as I originally thought.

"I can have Greer here in ten minutes to escort you

around the city." Aaron's eyes didn't leave my face. As always, I knew he would be on board, but this was something a couple should do together, especially for their wedding.

"But, you two really should be the ones to pick your flavors," I pleaded. "It's one of the best parts of planning."

"We already know what we want it to look like, and you and Ronnie have done such an amazing job already. I trust you," Haven said, leaving no room for argument.

"That's settled!" Ronnie sang, ushering the couple to the front of the shop to wait on Aaron's replacement.

Aaron didn't waste a minute once we were alone. He crossed the room, and his lips captured mine like a man starved. He took his time, pressing soft kisses to my neck. "It drives me crazy when you bite your lip."

I laughed. Of course that's all he could think about. I was a little sad that Adrian and Haven didn't want to do the cake tasting, but I knew Aaron would make this a fun experience.

"Thank you for yesterday." I had to arch my neck to look him in the eyes.

He smiled again, showcasing his pearly white teeth. "It will forever be one of my favorite memories."

It would be for me too, remembering the way he took care of me so carefully and made me soup from scratch.

Also, the orgasm. Definitely the orgasm.

Greer had long since picked Adrian and Haven up from the shop by the time the baker arrived.

"Where is the happy couple?" Jeremy, the baker, asked as he loaded up the table in the tasting room with all sorts of yummy looking cakes.

"They're out touring the city," I answered. He was our very best pastry chef, and I knew he would be a little disappointed to know they wouldn't be tasting any of his delectable creations.

He furrowed his eyebrows, but didn't comment further. When everything was set up, I walked him out the door. I promised we would reach out as soon as we had a decision on flavors, and mentioned him creating some desserts for the benefit this coming Friday, which he seemed all too happy to make. With an air kiss to both my cheeks, he was on his way.

Aaron sat at the table smothered with pretty little cakes, each labeled with different flavor combinations. This felt intimate in a way I couldn't describe, as if we were picking flavors for our own wedding.

Whoa girl, slow down. I barely knew the man. But everything about what I already knew had me fantasizing like a love sick teenager.

I shook my head at my thoughts. Too soon, Bell. Too soon.

"Where do we even start?" Aaron asked, running his hand through his perfectly styled hair, giving it a little messy look.

There had to be at least twenty different options, and I knew for a fact if it wasn't a celebrity client there would be maybe five tops. Lucky for me, I loved cake.

"Which one catches your eye?" I asked, observing him as he searched over the flavor cards.

He skipped over all of the options with lemon, which surprised me. Lemon was a popular flavor, though I personally detested the taste. He picked a chocolate cake with dark chocolate ganache topped with an orange glaze.

Pulling the little plate forward, he lifted his fork and took a bite. I watched, waiting for his reaction. Since this was his first option, I wanted a gauge of how this was going to go. He closed his eyes, jaw moving before declaring, "This is the one."

"You've tried one option." I chuckled at him. "You can't possibly know that's *the one.*"

He stuck his fork back into the cake and held it near my lips. The heat in his eyes caused my veins to light on fire.

Feeding someone shouldn't have felt this erotic. I opened my lips, letting the cocoa and orange burst over my taste buds.

He was right, this one was delicious. The hint of orange balanced out the heavy chocolate flavor so well. The cake itself was moist and fluffy. I had to hold back a groan.

Believe it or not, I barely ate anything at the weddings we organized. Mainly because Ronnie and I would be running around trying to make sure nothing went wrong and everything was exactly as it should be.

"See," he said. I popped my eyes open to see him smirk. I didn't even realize I had closed them.

"It's good, but let's try more." Taking my eyes off his handsome face, I searched over the options. Vanilla, strawberry, chocolate, red velvet, even lemon were the sponge options. I promptly put the lemon to the side since Aaron had an aversion. The real flavor was the filling and icing. Some were just lightly glazed, while others had a thick coat of frosting. I chose a red velvet base with cream cheese icing. It was a little too sweet for me, but the color was beautiful. Aaron tried it and determined the same thing.

We had sampled a few more when my eyes snagged on a four layer chocolate base with peanut butter filling and peanut butter glaze. I knew that one would be my favorite.

Pushing all the other plates out of the way, I pulled it in as close to my body as possible. Taking a huge chunk, I placed it in my mouth and hummed as the combination hit my tongue.

It was heaven in my mouth. The finely chopped roasted peanuts in the filling gave texture to the otherwise fluffy cake, and I noticed Aaron's fork invading my plate from the corner of my eye. I hit his fork with mine, knocking it away. His eyes snapped up and I gave him a cheeky smile.

"It's like that?" he said playfully.

I nodded. Even though we had sampled at least half of the options, I was determined to finish this little slice. It was perfect, and I would definitely be recommending it for Adrian and Haven, adding a mental note to offer a second option in case any allergies need to be addressed.

He tried again, slowly pushing his fork closer to my cake.

"Mine." I fake growled at him. He threw his head back and laughed as I shoved another chunk into my mouth.

His eyes flared with challenge and I tightened my thighs together under the table. He went to grab for the plate, which I snatched at the last minute, pulling it dangerously close to the edge of my side of the table.

I shoved the orange and chocolate cake he loved in his direction with a little too much force. It slid right off the table and into his lap. Icing and ganache coated his pants and I giggled.

"Whoops?"

He looked down in his lap in disbelief before looking back up at me. "Oh, you're in for it now, Sunshine." His smile turned feral and I squealed when he picked up the closest cake and slung it in my direction, hitting me in the chest.

"Aaron!" I shouted.

He shrugged his shoulders. "Whoops."

Oh, it was on. I picked up the closest piece of cake and squashed it in his perfect, smug face. Licking the stray icing off my fingers, I sat back in my chair to admire my handy work.

"Sunshine," he growled while wiping the cake from his eyes. Anticipation was lighting up my insides and sending pulsing waves straight to my lady bits.

He stood above me in one quick movement, wrapping his arms around my legs and threw me over his shoulder. I took the opportunity to swat his perfect ass, which earned me a satisfied yelp.

He sat me down carefully on the table, taking my mouth in a hot kiss. The cake and icing on his face smeared onto mine. As long as he kept kissing me like this, I didn't care. He tilted my head, wrapping his hand in my hair to give himself better access to invade my mouth with his tongue.

He tasted like all the flavors of cake we had tried and something uniquely Aaron. It was dirty and messy, but oh-so fun. Adrenaline pumped through my veins as he dominated my mouth. His tongue licked off icing and cake from my lips and I opened my legs wider, circling his hips.

"Ahem," Ronnie's chuckle pulled us out of our vigor. "This looks like it went well." I felt my blush from the tips of my toes to the roots of my hair.

Embarrassment flooded my system and I pushed Aaron away, making him laugh. He was still licking his lips, his eyes trained on my face.

"Don't stop on my account," Ronnie voiced, making her way to the back room. "I'll be gone soon. And Bell, unless you're suddenly an exhibitionist, I wouldn't suggest fucking on that table."

I knew my face was turning a furious shade of red, completely forgetting that Holly-Jay had a surveillance camera in this room. "Oh, my God," I groaned, not meaning to say it out loud.

"Exhibitionist, huh?" Aaron's eyes glittered.

"No," I said, putting that to a stop before he convinced me to forget about the cameras.

Aaron disappeared for a few seconds, returning with a

bunch of napkins. He wiped up my face, getting the icing and cake from where it had smeared. I shifted, feeling what suspiciously felt like cake under my butt squish around.

"Come to dinner at my place tonight?" he spoke softly, continuing to wipe the stray pieces of cake off my face. I was suddenly glad I decided to forgo makeup this morning.

"I can't." I was already regretting my acceptance to girls night with Ronnie, Xavier, and Haven tonight. But I needed a little time with my friends, especially to work through the feelings I had bubbling up about him.

"That's right, buddy. She's mine for tonight." Ronnie appeared from around the corner, bouncing happily on her feet.

"I'm free tomorrow." I laced my fingers through his, hoping he would understand. New relationships were always hard to navigate, but I didn't want to blow my friends off.

He leaned down to place a quick kiss on my lips. "Promise to call me when you get home?"

I nodded, giving him my sincerest smile.

"I'll see you tomorrow." He let go of my hand and walked out the door. I still had cake on my clothes, but luckily I had shoved a few outfits in my office not long ago, just in case.

"Let me get another change of clothes real fast. I'll lock up and meet you outside," I told Ronnie who had a shit eating grin on her face, and I knew tonight would be a game of twenty questions.

Bellamy

Xavier had the foresight to pick us up some food before we made our way to my house. Greasy fries and juicy burgers. We sat around my little dining table and scarfed it all down. It was perfect, and I couldn't remember the last time we got together like this.

"Have you found an assistant yet, Xavier?" I asked.

Ronnie looked over at the man in question. Her smirk had my senses on alert. I had missed something since Tuesday.

"No," he said begrudgingly, side eyeing Ronnie.

"But he did call the first interviewee back." She rested her chin on her hand, elbow on the table. "You remember, Bell? The one that broke poor Xavier's heart?"

I remembered him being upset about it. Why call him in for a second interview if he didn't want to see him again?

"A second interview?" I raised my brow. How had I missed that? I was sick, and Aaron, well... he had distracted me. In more ways than one. And then my parents. I hadn't heard anything since blocking their number.

Thank goodness.

"Come back to us, love puppy," Xavier clipped.

I rolled my eyes. Someone sounded jealous—a little more than normal if you asked me.

"It was just a second interview."

"That can't be true." I scoffed. No one who'd had their heart broken would call said heartbreaker if there wasn't a chance they could get back together.

"It's not," Ronnie piped up, diffusing the little tension. "Tell her what you told me." She nudged him with her elbow, giving him her no-nonsense expression.

He sighed dramatically. "I wanted to hear him out, okay?"

"And?" I pressed.

"And... he apologized." Xavier was being difficult, but I could give him time. It was hard seeing an ex, especially if you were still in love. I wanted Xavier to be happy. I felt a little wave of hope that maybe this guy would be it for him.

Maybe he would take this opportunity to lean on the assistant he chose so he could carve out that time for himself.

"Well that sounds nice," I goaded, knowing he would crack.

"He told me he still had feelings for me. We're going on

a trial date." He tried not to smile. His little shrug wasn't so nonchalant; his joy was transparent in his expression. I knew him better than that.

"I'm happy for you Xavier." And I really was. He deserved a little love in his life. "But be careful. I'd hate to have to sick my Marine boyfriend on him."

Oh God, I just called Aaron my boyfriend. As in *exclusive!* It made me giddy with excitement. I had been so out of practice I didn't know if I should wait for Aaron to ask me, or if I should ask him.

As my feelings grappled with themselves, Ronnie and Xavier both squealed.

"Boyfriend, huh?" Ronnie demanded while Xavier said, "Tell us everything!"

We all laughed and I glanced at my phone, smiling because Aaron had saved his name in my phone as *Mr. Handsome* with the little heart emoji beside it. He had texted a few times, but I hadn't checked it yet, and my fingers were itching to look.

Ronnie stole my phone, screaming at the time and telling us we needed to start getting ready, but that our conversation wasn't over.

I let Ronnie style my hair and makeup like she always did in college. I wouldn't let her dress me though. I wanted to be comfortable, plus I didn't want roaming hands on my body if I could help it. The only two people who would be allowed to touch me tonight would be Ronnie and Xavier.

We would Uber to Dusk 'Til Dawn and retire here. Xavier in his normal spot on the couch in the living room, while Ronnie and I went to my bedroom. We couldn't very well pile into my queen bed as three grown adults. I would normally be the designated driver, but I felt like letting loose. Even though I wouldn't get too out of hand. I couldn't let myself. After spending a lifetime of trying to gain some semblance of control, I just couldn't relinquish it, even if I knew I would be okay with my best friends.

Ronnie's shimmery, short number made her long legs look slim and toned. Xavier was dressed in black snug pants and a sheer black top that refracted different colors depending on the light.

The Uber dropped us off at the doors of Dusk 'Til Dawn. Benny, the bouncer, nodded at Ronnie. "We're a little full tonight, party girl."

Xavier slid up to Benny and grinned. "Don't worry, stud.

We're on the list."

Benny didn't even check it as he lifted the velvet rope and we slipped right in..

Thank you, Xavier.

"Let's find our spot," I heard Xavier call over to Ronnie. We snaked our way through tables, dodged waitresses, and found the low booth that would be our home base for the night. Xavier had a client get us in so all our drinks would be free.

"I wanna dance!" Ronnie exclaimed over the pounding of music, already pulling Xavier and I toward the dance floor. We followed willingly—I did say I wanted to let loose. Ronnie's hips swayed to the music as she sashayed to the middle of the dance floor. We stopped in an area that wasn't too far from the table. Xavier started gyrating to the music, making me laugh and sway with them.

We danced for a few songs before Xavier went for shots, leaving Ronnie to close the distance between us. Her hands hit my shoulders, her fingers tangling in my hair. "You look so happy."

"I am." I chuckled.

She looked at me like I was unhinged, but didn't get the chance to respond when Xavier popped up with enough alcohol for our whole table and the grabby hands around us to delight in.

"Drink up, bitches!" he yelled before we clinked the glasses together and tipped them back. We continued dancing until I couldn't feel my feet, my low heels squeezing the offending appendages. I knew I would regret it tomorrow.

"I'm gonna go sit for a minute!" I got Xavier's attention. He nodded and grabbed Ronnie. We made our way past bodies writhing and grinding on one another, finding our way toward our table. A waitress came our way immediately. She was dressed in a skimpy black tube dress, sky high heels, and dark makeup.

Ronnie ordered for us, "Rum and coke, lemon drop martini, and I'll have a Jameson." Her eyes sparkled as she batted her long lashes. The waitress made her way to the bar, waiting on our drinks. Ronnie turned and zeroed in on me, "Now dish, playa!"

I smiled. I knew no matter what, they would get details tonight. Might as well spill while I was still sober-ish. Who knew what would come out if I were drunk.

"Our date went well." I chuckled. "He even turned on his child locks so I couldn't open my own car door."

Ronnie's eyes widened and Xavier looked deep in thought. "I guess that's one way of getting your way," he said. I could see the wheels turning—he was thinking about stealing that move.

"We had dinner at this fancy Italian place." I gave Ronnie a glare, knowing she was probably the one to spill those secrets. "It was nice until this woman showed up and started running her hands all over him."

"Noooooo!" Ronnie gasped at the same time Xavier squealed, "She didn't!"

I nodded. "Then had the audacity to pretend I wasn't even there."

"That bitch!" Xavier declared and I smiled. Naturally my peeps would have my back. "I hope you gave her a piece of that Bellamy magic!"

I couldn't help the laughter that spilled up my throat. He called my bitchiness *magic* ever since we first met, and had unfortunately been on the receiving end of one of my rants during one of my not-so-great moments.

It just kind of stuck.

"I stormed out of the place. Looking back it was probably childish, but that bitch mentioned the article..." I kept my eyes on my hands in my lap.

"Oh, Bell." Ronnie threw her arms around my shoulders. Xavier laid a hand on mine, covering my shaking limbs. "I don't know why they keep trying to tear you down."

Guilt ate at me with the subtle mention of my parents. I still hadn't told anyone about the ominous voicemail they'd left me.

"Because she's successful and thriving," Xavier said, squeezing my hand. My heart was heavy and filled to the brim with the outpouring of love. It made me itch, but also made me thankful that I had found these two souls.

I didn't need to be the pretty one, nor the fun one. I just needed them. They made me feel accepted, weird quirks and all. They never made me question who I was, and it was why we were friends.

I wanted to change the subject. It was getting too heavy, and tonight was supposed to be fun. "I really like Aaron. He showed up at my house while I was sick and took care of me like I was the most precious thing in this world." I was aware of how gone I was for this man, and I was done denying the spark between us. Especially after today, when he'd kissed me with cake all over his face and didn't care who saw.

"That is the cutest thing I've ever heard." Ronnie placed her hand on her heart.

The waitress sat our drinks on the table and sauntered off to tend to other customers. The club was getting busier the longer we stayed.

"Have you...?" His eyebrows jumped around on his brow.

Leave it to Xavier to tease. If our booth wasn't shrouded in dim light, my face would be on fire.

"There may have been an orgasm involved," I said loudly.

"Spill, you little slut!" Ronnie encouraged.

Just thinking about what Aaron did to me made my body flush with heat. Now all I could think about was calling Aaron to come get me. Maybe we could finish what we started earlier.

"I swear we haven't fucked!" I cried, trying to hide the lustfulness in my voice. I should have known better. They knew all my tells.

"Okay, you may not have had sex, but an orgasm? Bell, tell me it was yours and not his." She took a swing of her drink and I downed mine, letting the alcohol burn and the soda bubble down my throat. Lord, give me strength.

"Oh, definitely mine." I bit my lip and screwed my nose up, hoping that would be enough.

Xavier and Ronnie squealed and leaned into my sides, effectively caging me in.

"Did he go down on you? How was it?" Ronnie asked, one of her arms still slung over my shoulders.

"I'll bet that man is skilled with his tongue." Xavier sipped his martini like he was dishing out the tea.

I tried laughing it off, but they both looked at me

expectantly. "He fingered me, and it was so hot. Unlike anything I've ever done before." It wasn't that I was embarrassed that was all we did, but compared to these two, I was practically a saint in the bedroom.

"If the heat coming off your body is any indication, I'd say so." Ronnie winked, and I felt the tension in my spine melt away.

Xavier's mouth was still hanging open. "You let him touch you?" Xavier was a touchy man. He craved physical affection, and lacked that in our friendship. I didn't think he would be jealous though. "And you were sick?!"

"It's a long story," I told him. Truly, I felt bad for my non-touchy ways. But I had to keep my boundaries if I wanted to avoid any unnecessary panic attacks.

A dark haired man came up to our table, looking only at Ronnie. "Care to dance gorgeous?"

She laughed and flipped her hair off her shoulder. "You wish, stud." She stood. "I'm here with my friends. Now, if you would excuse us."

Pulling us again onto the dance floor, we left the guy gaping at our table.

Aaron

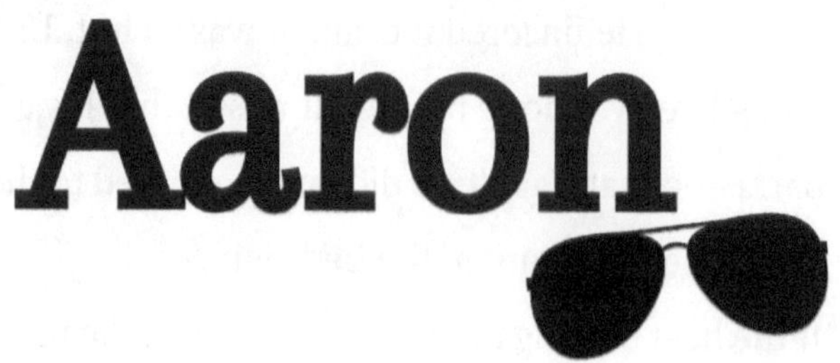

I decided to go to Dusk 'Til Dawn just to make sure they were alright. I could sit up on the balcony and none of them had to know. Veronica seemed like the party hard type, and I didn't want Bellamy to struggle if she needed help with her.

Plus, Finn had been badgering me to come see him since he wasn't in town the last time I stopped by. The night I met Bellamy.

I arrived just as Benny was closing the door, the club at capacity. Girls in dresses that barely covered their asses pouted at Benny, but he ignored them. They sauntered off, dejected and probably already a little tipsy. He saw me and waved me through. "Hey man. Didn't think I'd see you tonight."

"I wasn't planning on it, but my girl's inside." I shrugged, liking the way that felt. Bellamy was my girl, and by the end of the night she would know it.

He nodded, catching my meaning. If shit hit the fan, she would be my number one priority. Benny and I met at basic training, but didn't resign when his girl opened Dusk 'Til Dawn. He was a solid dude, and fit in with Finn and our group well.

I missed my Marine brothers, but my friend group was solid, and even though I hadn't seen a few of them in years, we stayed close. Benny, Finn, Landon, and I kept in touch regularly though, and I dropped in to see them when I could.

I made my way to the VIP section quickly, noticing Finn at his usual spot against the railing, scouting the dance floor. His sister owned the club, and it just so happened we'd been best friends since elementary school.

He even brought me to the recruitment center.

His strong square jaw was dusted with dark fuzz. He obviously hadn't bothered shaving today. His long hair was styled messily on his head, half pulled up in a bun leaving rest to flow down to his shoulders.

"Should have known you'd be here." I said by way of greeting.

"Lark, my man. I didn't know you were coming out tonight."

"Me either, but I figured why not." I leaned against the railing, matching his stance.

"I would have had some women waiting!" He clapped my back with one hand, the other had a whisky. I nodded toward that hand and all he had to do was twitch his fingers and a drink magically appeared, delivered by a glitter drenched woman.

"Nah, man. No need." I chuckled.

"No?" Finn asked, his voice gruff and demanding. Needless to say, he was thinking about getting his own dick wet.

"Nope." I smirked, knowing he was interested now. I searched the floor for Bellamy, spotting Veronica first, her blonde hair so bright in the twirling lights of red, green, yellow, and blue. Xavier of course had a shirt—if you could call it that—on his frame that resembled sparkly fishnets.

Then my eyes zeroed in on Bellamy. I loved the way her dark hair bounced against her skin as she swayed. She looked stunning tonight in a long sleeve, low cut top, and jeans covering every inch of touchable skin. She had to be sweltering in the heat. Even I could feel it radiating from here.

My eyes clocked her every move as she let Xavier and Veronica dance and grind on her. Her cheeks were flushed, and if I didn't know any better, I'd say she was tipsy.

"You got a girl?" Finn asked, trying to track my eyes. But

there were so many bodies, if you didn't know what you were looking for, it would be damn near impossible to find her.

"Yeah." I didn't think I would ever get tired of saying it.

"What are you doing then? Bring her up." His blue eyes twinkled with mischief. "I want to know what she sees in you, yeah?"

"No can do, bud." I laid my hand on his shoulder, pointing in the direction of the trio. Xavier pushed his way through the crowd with shots in his hands, bumping to the music. They each did a little *cheers* and tilted them back. Bellamy noticed a guy closing in on Veronica and gripped her closer. *That's my girl.* Even tipsy, she kept aware of her surroundings.

"The blonde, or the brunette?" he questioned, but it seemed a little more territorial.

"Brunette," I answered.

"Who's the blonde then?" he asked, and the earlier hint of possessiveness dissolved.

"Why? You interested?" I asked, genuinely curious.

"I may have seen her around a few times." His eyes slid to mine, and his lips tipped up in a smirk, "In a dark hallway where no names are required."

I pursed my lips and nodded. We didn't speak again as we

watched the trio dance. Bellamy was beautiful. Her hazel eyes looked dark as night from here. Her perfect pouty lips were painted dark, making her olive skin shine. A few more songs and she was pulling the group toward the side where tables sat. I could just see the end of their table. It wasn't ideal, but I didn't want her to know I was here.

Unless she needed me. That was the deal I made with myself before coming here. I would only intervene if necessary. I didn't want her to think I didn't trust her. I didn't believe for one second that Bellamy would let anyone close enough to touch her, even tipsy.

She was perfect, and when she let me taste her, I knew she was mine. I would make sure she knew who she belonged to as soon as I could.

It was closing in on one in the morning by the time Xavier stood from the booth, a little sway in his step. He was drunk, but was taking care of himself so far. I didn't mind when he placed his arm around Bellamy's shoulders, but I noticed another man walking up to their booth. Since Bellamy was standing, I could see her face, and she looked irritated.

I motioned to where Finn was sitting with the waitress from earlier straddling his lap. He swiftly picked her up and placed her on the couch. Her dress pulled up around her hips and I quickly looked away.

"You know that guy?" I asked, nodding in the direction of the trio's booth.

"Fuck, man." Finn ran his tattooed hand over his face. "I kicked him out a couple weeks ago for groping the servers. Dude doesn't take no for an answer."

Bellamy was yelling at him, her face red and brows furrowed. Xavier looked just as furious, but I still couldn't see Veronica.

"Where's the blonde?" Finn asked, watching just as I was.

"I can't see her from here. She's got to be in the booth still." My instincts were screaming at me to go down there. Bellamy was yelling, waving her arms and when the man reached into the darkened booth, my control snapped.

"Fuck!"

Finn was already at the stairs by the time I decided to move. The crowd parted for him. He was a big dude, outweighing me by pounds and muscles twice the size of mine, but we were matched in height. Something that definitely came in handy in a time like now.

The man held Veronica by her arm, and she was clearly not enjoying herself like she had been a few moments ago. As if our eyes were magnets, Bellamy's found mine as Finn approached the table. They went wide in surprise.

"Unhand the lady." Finn's deep rasp sounded like the

reaper himself. "She was just leaving with her friends," he continued. "Weren't you, love?"

Veronica's scared eyes locked with Finn's and I swear I saw a flicker of heat in his eyes before he slid them to the man whose hand was still clasped around her arm.

"No, she and I were about to have some fun." The man said as he yanked her up and out of the booth, and I watched as her hip hit the table painfully. She didn't make a sound, letting me know she was way more intoxicated than Bellamy or Xavier.

Finn's knuckles collided with the man's nose. Blood poured out of it, down and over his lips, but his hand remained on Veronica. He pulled her into his body, as if she was a shield. She sobered as much as one could in the face of danger, her eyes seeking out her friends, or Finn—anyone to help her. And by the look of terror on my sunshine's face, I couldn't just stand by.

Rounding behind him, I waited for Finn to separate them. Grabbing the man's other hand and pulling it behind his back.

"The fu–" He tried to swing on me, but missed, and Finn threw his fist into the guy's throat. His hand dropped away from Veronica to protect himself. He sputtered, trying and failing to catch his breath. It was the opening I needed to grip his other arm, and twist both up into an uncomfortable position he had no way of getting out of.

Finn held Veronica's shoulders, checking her over. Xavier said something to Finn and he nodded.

Benny appeared, took the man from me and started to lead him toward the back office to where I assumed they would wait for the local PD.

"Benny?" Finn snarled. Benny stopped, looking over his shoulder at his friend.

"Never let that asshole in again." It was the most commanding tone I'd ever heard come from him.

Bellamy

Aaron was here. Currently staring at me, with a look on his face that I couldn't place. I was grateful he was here, but I wanted to strangle him at the same time. I wanted to believe he was only here coincidentally with his friend, but it was hard to put aside the nagging thought that he was keeping tabs on me. Which I hated, mostly because it meant he didn't trust me.

Aaron nodded his head in the direction of the emergency exit nearest our table. The big, tattooed man led Ronnie and Xavier through the door and into the cold night air.

I'd never seen him before but the tattooed man dripped money and violence. He had come to Ronnie's rescue, looking over her for possible injuries like he was concerned and yet it didn't escape my notice that he happened to have glitter on his face. The waitresses were also covered in body glitter.

Aaron tried to approach once the bouncer led the jerk out

through a back entrance that read *employees only*.

I held up my hands in a gesture showing I did not want to have this conversation here, instead going to where his friend still had Ronnie by the shoulders. Xavier was just as stunned as I was by the look on his face.

"I'm sorry." Xavier lifted his hand like he was waiting on the teacher to call on him to ask his question. "What the hell just happened here?"

I crossed my arms over my chest. It was blessedly cool, a wonderful contrast to the heat rolling off the bodies inside, but I would soon start to shiver if I didn't get into a coat.

Something warm slid over my shoulders and I immediately smelled Aaron. I still wasn't ready to talk to him to find out why he was here, but it didn't mean I didn't appreciate the act.

His jacket was soft and fleece lined. It was still warm which made me wonder how long he had been here. I didn't see his jacket on him when he arrived with his tattooed friend.

"I threw that asshole out a few weeks ago. Same issue," the man grunted.

"So then, why did he come back?" I asked, trying to work through the issue at hand. I was a problem solver. I could figure this out. "What about security? How did he get back in?"

"I'll find out." His words were clipped, sharp like knives. "Until then, I want to know if your friend here is okay."

Ronnie just shook her head, still swaying from the alcohol in her system. She teetered on her heels and the man swept his hand under her knees and cradled her against his chest. "We'll take my truck."

Aaron nodded, placing a quick kiss on my temple before running around me to help get the door open for his friend.

Xavier and I exchanged questioning looks. What the fuck was happening?

I must have said the last part out loud because Xavier muttered, "I would also like to know."

Aaron looked up and motioned us over to the blacked-out truck. It was large, much larger than Aaron's truck. But then again, the muscles on the other guy were twice the size of his, too.

"I drove, so you can either ride with me, or your friends." He placed his hand on my cheek, then swiped his fingers over the back of my neck. "But I trust Finn with my life. He wont do anything but drive them home."

I nodded, looking at Xavier as he waited in the back seat, then back to Aaron. Ronnie was slumped over in the front passenger seat, already passed out. Her blonde hair was a mess, all in her face. Slobber already starting to pool in it.

I really wanted answers, and if Xavier was riding with her, I felt better about riding with Aaron.

Seeming to see my internal battle, Aaron whispered, "He's going to follow me to your place. Whether or not you ride with me, I'll see you at your house."

I nodded, looking up to where Xavier was slowly starting to lose his battle to sleep, too. Finn looked scary, in that big biker kind of way. If Ronnie wasn't passed out, would she have trusted him? My stomach clenched as I tried to make the right decision.

Maybe I'd had too much to drink, because I should have gotten in the truck with my friends. I should have directed Finn on how to get back to my house and told Aaron to get lost. But I couldn't, not with the way he was looking at me like he might lose me if the wind blew too strongly.

"I'm going to ride with Aaron," I told Xavier as I risked a glance back to catch his reaction. He looked relieved and a bit surprised. "I'll see you at home."

Xavier nodded, and Finn exchanged a look with Aaron that communicated something to him.

Getting into the truck, I buckled myself into my seat, loving that Aaron had turned on the seat warmer for me. I didn't speak, mainly because I couldn't think of which question I wanted to ask first.

"I didn't mean to surprise you tonight." He broke the silence. "I just remembered how we met, and knew I would regret it if anything happened to you."

I stole a glance in his direction. His face was open, and I wanted to believe that was all it was. But a small part of me still felt like he didn't trust me.

"You weren't there with anyone?" I asked, not knowing exactly how to approach the topic of monogamy. If I was going to share my body with someone, I sure as shit didn't want him to share his with anyone else.

"I was with Finn." His eyes slid to mine questioningly.

I threw my hands up, word vomit spilling out of my mouth. "Look, I'm not sure where we stand, and honestly I don't even know how to ask, or what I'm even asking." I was frustrated and a little intoxicated. Now was *so* not the best opportunity to talk about a heavy subject like this, but my mind wouldn't stop churning out questions and possible scenarios.

I covered my face with my hands and leaned my head back against the seat.

He chuckled from the driver's seat, and I had to peek between my fingers to see him. Why was he laughing?

"You're cute when you're drunk," he said, gently pulling

one of my hands down to hold as he maneuvered the streets of the quarter.

"I'm serious, Aaron!" I practically whined, feeling the headache from the booze coming on. "I can't take not knowing."

"I think we're pretty exclusive, Sunshine." I knew if he could look me in the eyes, he would. His tone was deep conversation, serious. "Don't you?"

"I can't help but think of *Molly*." I exaggerated her name, hating that I sounded exactly like a jealous girlfriend, but I couldn't help it. I needed to know now, before going any further with him, if he was still into her. I had a feeling if I slept with him and he wasn't fully in this, my heart would never recover.

"Jealousy looks even cuter on you, baby," he cooed before laughing, his whole body shaking with it. "I have no ties with Molly." He paused. "But if I did, I would have ended it before starting this with you."

He sounded sincere, and that was enough for me. He had never lied to me before, why would he start now?

We pulled up outside of my house and I yanked the handle to get out. The door didn't budge and if Aaron's grin told me anything, I would say the child locks were still engaged. I groaned, letting him have his little chivalrous moment yet again.

He took my shoes off the second my door opened. I lifted my eyes curiously, and I could see the behemoth's truck pull up to the curb behind us. Aaron reached into the truck and pulled me over his shoulder in one jerk.

I screamed, scared that he would drop me. "Put me down!" His hand landed on my ass, the smack echoing loudly on the empty sidewalk. "Did you just spank me?" My voice was breathy, and if I would have been in my right mind, I probably would have face-palmed myself for it.

"I did, Sunshine." His hand rubbed the sore spot he had made. "And I'd bet if I were to slide my hand into these tight little jeans, I'd find you wet for me."

He wasn't quiet about it either, if his friend's chuckle was any indication. I felt my face heat, and I was suddenly glad I was staring straight into Aaron's back. He was so tall that my fingers barely brushed his waistband. We walked through the gate, and even though Aaron tried not to jostle me, his shoulder dug painfully into my belly.

He didn't put me down until we were inside my house. Finn still had Ronnie cradled in his arms like she weighed nothing. "Where do you want me to put her?"

I pointed in the direction of the air mattress. It was comfortable, way more so than the couch Xavier would take.

He gingerly laid her down, and I pulled a blanket from the back of the couch to drape over her. "Where's Xavier?" I asked, waiting for him to stagger through the door.

Finn placed his hand on his neck. "He's passed out in the truck. He's staying here, too?"

I nodded, noting the uncomfortable look on Finn's face. Aaron seemed to notice, too, and offered to help carry him inside. He had an odd attraction to Ronnie, but if he worked at the club, they would have probably run into each other a time or two. Hell, she could have already slept with him.

Aaron nudged my side and ducked behind me to hide his obvious smile. Finn scowled, his thick brows drawn in toward his eyes. It almost made me laugh. "Hey, Behemoth, chill. He's going to be on the couch, plus he's gay."

They returned quickly with Xavier. Aaron had him under his armpits and Finn had his legs. They carefully laid him on the couch and I watched Finn steal a quick glance at Ronnie before nodding and clapping Aaron on the back. He left without so much as a goodbye, and I felt bad about not saying thank you.

It had been a long night, and all I wanted to do was clean up and climb in bed, but I didn't know if Aaron planned to stay, so we stood there awkwardly in the lamp light between my two passed out best friends.

I started, "Do you..." at the same time he said, "So..."

Aaron chuckled and held his hand out. I took it and he pulled me into his body.

"Do you want to stay?" I asked sheepishly—a little drunk and very horny, feeling like I shouldn't be inviting him to stay but doing it anyway.

His chest rumbled as he laughed.

"I'd love to." He nuzzled and placed chaste kisses into my neck. I loved the feel of his lips on my skin, heating it and cooling it at the same time. He pulled away before he got to my collarbone and I almost whimpered.

"I need to shower," I whispered. Even though we hadn't been out until the late hours of the morning, I still felt like I needed to. With all the people at the club, inadvertently hitting or brushing me, I felt dirty.

Aaron nodded and walked with me hand in hand to the bathroom where he turned on the shower for me, placed a light kiss on my nose, and then closed the door quietly behind him.

I was glad he was giving me my space, but also a little disappointed because I wanted him to see me. Maybe it was the alcohol still humming through my veins, but I felt more confident in my body tonight than I ever had.

I stripped down and stepped into the shower. The hot blast felt amazing against my skin. I scrubbed my body, washed my hair, and stood there for a few minutes letting the water crash over my face.

By the time I finished, the little haze of booze was gone, but the confidence never left. Was I ready for this? Yes. It had been so long since I had wanted something like this for myself, and I wasn't even slightly embarrassed.

I toweled off my body and wrapped my hair in the T-shirt I left in here the other day. Leaving the bathroom in only a towel, I walked the two steps it took toward my bedroom.

Opening the door to my room, it was dark save for the bluish light coming from the TV in the corner. Aaron was already in my bed, wearing only tight black boxer briefs which did nothing to hide the heat he was packing.

His eyes held mine and his arms flexed as I lazily drank him in from the top of his light ginger hair to his socks. His thighs were muscular, the defined quad muscles right down to his large calves. But he wasn't as ripped as I had imagined. I mean, he was physically fit, but he had the most adorable pudge above his waist band I wanted to trail my tongue over. Just to hear the sound he'd make.

He was a sight I didn't think I would ever get tired of.

"Come here, Sunshine." He patted the bed beside him,

and I blurted the first thing that came to mind.

"You aren't as bulky as I thought you'd be." Oh, God! Sometimes I hated my nonfiltered brain. Especially when the remnants of alcohol remained.

He laughed, his stomach muscles contracting into his sides. "That's what retirement will do to a man." He slapped the little pudge, and I could have jumped on him then. He was perfection personified.

Feeling brave, I dropped the towel, giving Aaron a view of me— all of me. Pulling the T-shirt from my head, I shook out my wet curls, very aware of the way my body moved. By the hungry look in his eyes, I would have said he found my body just as attractive as I did. He looked like a man starved, and I was his choice for his last meal. It made me feel powerful, like I could conquer anything.

Standing from the bed, he prowled over to where I stood. His hands found my hips, the callouses rough against my soft skin. His eyes roamed my form, and I felt it like a physical caress, igniting my body, buzzing with the energy between us.

His hands traced the skin that lay over my hips, up the hills and valleys of my stomach, to the outsides of my breasts. I arched into his chest, feeling my hardening nipples brush his bare skin.

A whimper slipped out of my mouth, sounding way too breathy. If he kept looking at me like he was, I was going to combust on the spot.

"Sunshine." His voice took on a growl, and I felt the slickness between my thighs increase. "The first time we fuck, I want you to scream my name when I make you come." His lips found mine before I could protest.

Wait? What?

He pulled away, just enough that he could speak against my lips. "I want to be inside of you. I want to mark you with bites, and fill you with my cum so you won't ever question whether you're mine."

His breath smelt of whiskey and mint, an intoxicating and heady mix. I had to clench my thighs together at his words, trying to get any type of friction I could to ease the ache there.

"But I'm not going to do that with your friends in the next room. I selfishly want all of your noises, and I don't fucking share."

He kissed me again, his hands still roaming my body, but not touching me anywhere that I wanted. I was aroused and frustrated as hell. I bit down on his bottom lip, not hard but enough it earned me a growl from low in his chest.

He reached behind me to grab a shirt, and slid it over my

body, shielding my skin from his. This time I didn't hold the whimper back. He peppered my face with kisses and chuckled in between.

"Needy thing."

The shirt wasn't as big as my normal sleep wear. It didn't even cover my ass. The material clinging to my body was most definitely not mine. The soft cotton grasped every dip and curve on my body, making my breasts sit tighter against my ribs, but it smelled just like Aaron.

Forgoing my underwear, he led me to the bed and pulled back the covers. Once settled, I lifted the shirt and inhaled a deep breath. When I opened my eyes, his were staring straight back at me. They were like a molten sky.

"Is this your shirt?" I asked like an idiot. Something in my brain needed verbal confirmation.

"It is, and I want you to wear it every night. So when you close your eyes, I'll be here. Even in your dreams."

I could have melted into a damn puddle right there. His words and actions held me in the palm of his hands, and I knew deep in my soul that we were made for each other, and I would do anything to keep it that way.

Bellamy

Monday morning came around too fast. Aaron was busy yesterday, so I didn't get to see him.

I stopped by Olde Elixir Parlor to see Georgie and Henry, and to get out of the house. Georgie mentioned that my parents' calls had become close to five times a day since I blocked their number from my phone. I apologized and told them to block the number they were calling from.

I needed to clear my head and get my thoughts refocused on Haven. With her benefit concert this Friday, Ronnie and I would need to get the details finalized and the event space coordinated. The rest of Haven's band would be here on Wednesday to set up, so we had to have the stage ready by Thursday morning. They would need somewhere for a sound check to fine tune their instruments and set list.

I chose to wear dark wash jeans and a black off-the-shoulder sweater today. It was getting colder here everyday the closer we got to Christmas. Which reminded me—I needed to get in touch with Billy before Haven's wedding. Since he mentioned the dinner we usually have every year already, I knew he would want a final head count to make sure he had the produce and ingredients he needed.

I made a mental list as I scrambled through breakfast. I loaded my toast down with peanut butter and headed for the door. I hadn't seen Smokie since last night, but I had a feeling she would be prowling around outside.

Gripping the toast between my teeth, I locked my door. Tearing the rest of the bread from my mouth, I set off toward the shop. I wasn't late, but I also wasn't early. It was one of my...well, irrational qualities. I had to be early, or else it was a bad sign. Logically, I knew that wasn't the case. But I couldn't help that my brain just wouldn't listen to reason.

As I rounded the corner and the shop came into view, Ronnie fell into step with me. "Alterations are done. Want to take Haven with me for her fitting?"

I really needed to stay at the shop. We had a lot of things to confirm today, and I really didn't have time to drive forty minutes both ways to see if the dress fit. But I couldn't get my nerves to settle. I could make phone calls from the car, but Haven may think it was unprofessional.

"We have the vendors and historians to confirm for this weekend," I reminded her. Maybe if I gave her a valid reason to stay behind, she would let me.

"We can make those calls tomorrow!" She wasn't going to give me an out. I saw it in the way she turned her pleading blue eyes in my direction.

"Okay, I'll go," I relented. It wasn't like they wouldn't be there tomorrow. Everything had already been confirmed once, so maybe I was just being overly thorough.

We walked arm in arm to our offices, unlinking to sit and take care of the things we each had on our desks from Friday. Haven and Adrian chose to have a traditional vanilla cake base with buttercream icing cake for their alternate, so I made sure to update the order ticket with Jeremy's assistant Chloe. We didn't need anyone going into anaphylactic shock at their reception. She was a nice older lady who pretty much took care of Jeremy's business so he could focus on what he does best—flavor combinations and culinary art.

The front door opened and Haven called out, "Good morning!"

"Back here!" Ronnie shouted, so loud I felt a ringing in my ears. I gave her a look over my computer, pointing to my ears. All she did was laugh.

Haven walked into the small space with Aaron on her heels. He smiled at me, but we only had so much room with me and Ronnie's desk.

"Are you ready to try on your dress?" Ronnie asked.

Haven's face lit up. "Yes!" Her eyes glossed over, as if she was seeing the dress in her head. It had been almost a week since we took her to try on dresses. "No offense, but the bridal portrait dress just doesn't compare."

Ronnie and I laughed. No, it didn't. But having the bridal portraits done was a great way to tease her future husband. There was something magical about him seeing her in the real thing when she would walk down the aisle toward him.

"Let's let Bellamy tie up a few loose ends and then we'll get going!" Ronnie gently guided Haven out to the kitchen, most likely to get her something to drink. I didn't have any more loose ends than she did.

She probably did it so Aaron and I could reconnect in private.

He slid in behind my chair, but he didn't exactly fit, causing my chair to squeeze my body against the desk tightly. "Can't breathe," I teased, although it *was* becoming difficult.

He shifted so I could push my chair back a little further, then bent and placed a gentle kiss on my cheek, trailing down to cradle my jaw. "Good morning." His hand slid over my thigh, down to my knee.

"Good morning," I said, almost as breathless as I would have been had he not moved. But the way his hand moved down my leg, combined with the way his voice dropped when he spoke, sent my brain haywire.

His hand trailed up from my knee, skimming over my bra, and over my collarbone to my chin. He tilted my head with a finger, planting his lips on mine. It was quick, much quicker than I anticipated.

"Come on." He offered his hand to help me stand. I took it like a princess would take a prince's. He hauled me out of my chair into his chest, wrapping his arms around me in a tight embrace. "Let's go get this wedding dress."

He sounded thrilled, and I laughed at his exuberance. The smile that plastered his face made my knees weak and I was suddenly glad he had his arms around me.

We made it to the dress shop just as the doors opened. It wasn't a complete lost cause like last time, thank God. I didn't think I could handle another "Gaby knows best" incident.

I watched Aaron work, admiring the way he took his

job seriously while also making an effort to make Haven comfortable. Ever since I told him he was intimidating, he had lightened up. Or maybe that was because of us.

Once inside, it was just us three and a few seamstresses. Aaron stood firmly outside the door.

The head seamstress led Haven into a dressing room. Ronnie's legs bounced with what I could only assume was anticipation as we sat on the tufted bench seat across the way. I had to admit, I was also pretty excited.

The door opened and the seamstress let us in. She had placed a short veil over Haven's dark hair, the edges embellished with lace hanging down to her shoulders. It was a perfect match for the dress. Not too long to hide the *wow* factor, but still enough to be considered bridely.

Looking at her reflection in the mirror, Haven's eyes were filled with tears. Ronnie placed the flats she brought just for this occasion. With the whole look put together, even I had to stop my eyes from welling up.

"You look absolutely stunning," Ronnie choked out around the emotion swirling in her throat. I could tell she wanted to cry with Haven but didn't want to weird the girl out.

I checked the alterations, making sure the dress fit with the shoes but didn't sweep the ground. "How does it feel?"

I asked. I really didn't want to touch her to make sure it was snug. "Make sure you have room to breathe, but also, we want to make sure it doesn't fall off half way down the aisle."

Haven laughed and the tears that had refused to fall earlier fell in streams down her cheeks. "It's perfect."

Ronnie and I left her to change back into her regular clothes. That was enough emotional interaction for today. I just wanted to get back to the office and maybe have time for dinner with Billy tonight.

Bellamy

W e made it back to the office without an issue. I shouldn't have been surprised. Aaron was good at what he did.

"Bellamy?" I snapped my head up from my computer screen. Aaron almost never used my name. "Are you okay?"

"Yeah." I had to blink a few times to clear the fog from my brain. "Why?"

"I've been calling your name." He tilted his head, a smirk tilting his lips. "What are you doing back here?"

Where was Ronnie? She wouldn't have left without saying goodbye. Although, if I hadn't heard Aaron, I probably missed her goodbye, too.

"Just focused," I lied. My parents contacting Georgie and Henry was really starting to eat away at me.

His lips curled up in a full blown smile, as if he knew I was full of shit. "I've got to head out. I'm on Haven and Adrian duty tonight." He leaned against the doorway, shoulder propped on the frame, legs crossed at his ankles. The man could look good just standing somewhere, it was unnatural.

"I'll be fine to lock up." I stood, crossing the room to wrap my arms around his neck, linking my fingers behind him and bringing his lips to mine. I still had to stand up on my tippy toes to even get close to his mouth.

He wrapped his hands around my waist, pulling me in closer so that all of me was pressed against all of him. "I'll call you when I drop them off tonight."

I nodded, walking past him to tell Haven goodnight. The happy couple sat on the chairs in our front room. Adrian had his hand on Haven's knee. Their chairs touched as if they had moved them so they could be closer.

They were adorable together, and they couldn't keep their hands off each other for one second. She beamed at him, and even though he was clearly already smitten, I would say Adrian fell just a little bit more in love with her right then.

"I didn't mean to interrupt," I said, wringing my hands together, completely unsure if I was intruding or not.

"Nonsense," Haven said, looking at Adrian. He nodded and turned his smile up at me. "I was just telling him about that diner you took me to on my first night in town."

"Oh, Billy's?"

"Yes!" She clapped her hands, and Adrian smiled. It melted my heart. Haven was adorable and fun. I suddenly felt bad that I had complained about working with a celebrity. She was nothing like what I thought she would be.

"I can call Billy and ask him to sit you in the same spot, so you can be alone," I offered. It was the least I could do. I felt like they didn't get enough alone time as it was. They were both successful business people.

"Would you?" she all but squealed.

I nodded and bid them farewell. Aaron pressed a quick kiss on my cheek before leading them toward the car. "Lock the door, Sunshine." Aaron hollered through the glass. He stopped Haven and Adrian to wait for me to flip the lock. Since I was alone, it was probably a good idea.

Plus, I knew Georgie would be around if I needed anything. He smiled before they crossed the street.

I walked back to the office, searching for my phone, I knew I had it earlier. Shuffling papers around, I found it under the stack of invoices for new brides. I still needed to go over Holly-Jay's books. *Ugh*, it was going to be a late night.

I pulled up Billy's contact. Although, looking at the time, I didn't think he'd answer. So I called the restaurant.

Marcie answered on the second ring, "Billy's. How can I help you?"

"Hey, Marcie. It's Bell, can you get Billy for me?"

"Sure thing, sweetness." I heard her yell for him through the phone. "He'll be right with y'all," she said to me. He must have been on the dining room floor because it took a couple minutes for him to pick up.

"Hey, Kitten," he said by way of greeting. It made me smile and instantly relax. Billy just had that way about him.

"Haven and her fiancé will be there in a few. Can you fix up the table in the kitchen so they can eat in peace?" I didn't want to bother him, especially since the dinner rush would be in full swing soon.

"Sure thing. Are you joining them?"

"Not tonight, old man." I heard his sigh. "I have a lot to catch up on here." I did, it wasn't an excuse. I really needed to get this together before the concert Friday.

"Alright, Kitten. I'll get it ready. Don't forget about tomorrow."

Shit. I had already forgotten that Billy wanted to have dinner with Aaron and I tomorrow night. Especially with all the stuff going on with Haven's concert and wedding.

"Of course," I said, hoping he wouldn't be able to scent the lie. If he did, he didn't call me out. Instead, he told me he would be ready for his high profile diners to arrive, and that he loved me.

I laid my phone down and ran my hands through my hair, taking a minute to process my thoughts. I took a few deep breaths, centering myself to get this done.

A few hours later, I had input everything into Holly-Jay's system. New brides confirmed and on the calendar, accounts balanced, and invoices paid. I double checked everything was turned off before heading outside.

I slid my key into the lock and twisted it, making sure to hear the click. The air was chilly, especially since the sun had set a while back. It felt good to have everything done. My next few nights would be work free. I started toward the house, taking my time, and enjoying the decorations through town. It was a beautiful night; the stars were out in full blaze, and candles in the street lamps burned bright, illuminating the quiet streets.

I tossed and turned on my bed. After learning my parents were now harassing people I genuinely liked, and that I hadn't spoken to Ronnie about the voicemail they left me,

I couldn't sleep. The only thing I could do was eat. I ate a whole pint of Ben & Jerry's. Did it help my feelings? Nope But it tasted good. At least there was that.

I didn't call Ronnie like I wanted to. I didn't want to burden her with it because she already knew how awful they were. She didn't need the reminder. Not like I apparently did.

I cried until I couldn't cry anymore. I cried for the girl who grew up hating herself. For the girl whose creativity suffered in silence. I cried for the girl who thought deep down she didn't deserve Aaron's affection.

So when he called, I didn't answer. I let it go to voicemail. Hopefully he would think I was asleep. I had already gotten into bed, so it was partly true.

He didn't leave a message, but he did text. He must've thought I didn't answer because I was already asleep. Oh how I wish that were the case.

> **Mr. Handsome ♥: You must be asleep, so good morning beautiful. Can't wait to see you.**

I shouldn't have opened it. I forgot it would tell him I did. Stupid read receipts. My phone screen lit up in my hand. *Shit.* He was calling again.

It finally quit ringing, going to voicemail. The second my screen went black, it lit up again.

"Hello?" I said, praying he couldn't hear the tears in my voice.

"What's wrong?" His deep rumble came through the speaker, his question clear. I could have cried again right there.

"Nothing. Just tired."

"Don't lie to me, Sunshine." I imagined he was running a hand through his hair, trying to figure out why I didn't answer his first two calls.

"I got a phone call a while back, and it's been messing with my head," I admitted. "Nothing you need to worry about." And really it wasn't. He didn't need to borrow my problems. Plus, there was nothing he could do about them anyway.

"From who?"

"Nobody important." I was being short, I knew it. But I really didn't want to go into details. Aaron knew that my parents and I didn't get along. He didn't need to know just how horrible they were.

"It was your parents wasn't it?" I could tell he struggled to ask because of the pause on his end. I almost choked on my breath.

"It's not a big deal." I tried to breathe around each word. I could ignore it like I should have originally. "How was dinner?"

"It was fine." Now he was being short. "Bell-" he started, but cut himself off, apparently reconsidering what he'd been about to say. We were both silent, waiting on the other to break.

"Well, I'll see you sometime," I said truthfully. I wasn't planning on working tomorrow or the next day. Thursday would be a running day, so I would take these two days for a rest.

"Hey, Sunshine?" He stalled my hang up. "How do you feel about hockey?"

I couldn't help the snort that came out. Hockey wasn't a typical topic of conversation for me. I knew nothing about the sport except that it was violent.

"I've never watched a game," I said, shrugging my shoulders as if he could see me.

"Come with me tomorrow night to watch the Carolina Hurricanes play."

"A date at a hockey game?" I asked, almost incredulous. I didn't know if I could handle the hostility and people.

"It's premiere seating. Just you, me, and a few of my friends."

"I guess I can try." I wanted to spend time with him. Really I did.

"I'll send you my address. Meet me here around lunch?"

After agreeing on the time and what I should wear, we hung up. I felt lighter than I had before he called, helping me to relax and enjoy the sleep taking me into dreamland.

Bellamy

I called Billy to let him know I needed to take a rain check on dinner. He was disappointed, but I would make it up to him. We had dinner at least once a week, since I'd moved here, and I didn't want to miss it. But once I told him what I was doing instead he chuckled and wished Aaron luck.

I made it to Aaron's house a little before lunch. The Uber I paid for was quiet the entire drive, and I gave a silent thank-you to the heavens for that. Unnecessarily chatty people made me anxious, and I really didn't need any more anxiety running through my system.

His truck was in the driveway of the cutest house. It was a white ranch style with black accents. The front door was painted a muted black that complemented the rest of the house.

Aaron threw open the door, standing there in a bright red jersey and a pair of ripped jeans. I assumed the jersey was for the Carolina Hurricanes—the colors matched what little I looked up online. I had never seen ripped jeans on a man, but he wore them well. He looked so handsome and carefree. I loved the little tint of pink on his cheeks from my stare. "You made it."

"I did," I said, walking up the sidewalk to his front door. He didn't have any plants in his front yard. Just grass and a sidewalk. It was a little depressing, but the house had a lot of character.

He wrapped me up in his arms as soon as my boots hit the porch. I sagged into his embrace and wrapped my arms around him, too. He smelled like leather and mint, a new combination I hadn't noticed before.

His arms were tight around my body. It felt nice and loving, especially after all of the awful things I'd had running through my head. The way this man broke down my walls so fast almost gave me whiplash. He was always saying what was on his mind, constantly praising me even though I had a hard time accepting it. But I knew he was sincere.

"Let me show you around." He pulled back, looking directly into my eyes. His excitement at me finally being at his house was apparent.

His place was all clean lines, and no mess. It put my place to shame. I suddenly felt a little less like a put together adult looking at all the pristine surfaces of his house. Nothing was out of place, not even a sock. Weren't men supposed to be messy?

The kitchen was all stainless steel and navy cabinets. A big window sat on the far left wall, letting in so much light he didn't even need to turn the overhead lights on.

An array of colors caught my attention—yellow, pink, purple, red. He had a small table pushed underneath the window with a vase of tulips sitting in the center. It was the only pop of color in the otherwise monochromatic space.

He crossed the room and picked up the vase. "These are for you."

My eyes snapped to his. Tulips were my favorite. Ever since I was a little girl, I had been obsessed. I even grew my own. Every spring, I had a whole area in my front yard that bloomed with the brightest buds. It was almost impossible to find them this early though. He would've had to have ordered them.

Which meant this date wasn't a spur of the moment thing like I had thought. My heart did a little flip in my chest at his clear affection.

"Thank you." I could feel the blush on my face, hot and furious. No one had bought me flowers before.

He shrugged as if it wasn't a big deal. But to me it was everything.

Glancing at the watch on his left hand, he asked, "You ready to head that way?"

I nodded. "You know I know nothing about hockey, right?" I teased, placing the vase on the kitchen counter. He laughed as he headed for the front door. I trailed after him as he swiped his keys from a hook behind the door, and pulled it shut behind me, locking the deadbolt. He grabbed my hand and hauled me toward his truck.

The laugh that left my chest surprised me. I liked playful Aaron, and I wondered if he was like this with his friends.

He opened the door for me to climb into his truck. It was chilly, so when he cranked the engine, he turned on the seat warmers. My butt definitely thanked him. I didn't think about the cold, and all I had chosen to wear was the gray sweater dress I had thought about for our first date and a pair of leggings. I was suddenly starting to rethink our destination.

We arrived at the stadium and Aaron led us through the colossal entrance.

"We're a little late, so stay close, okay?" he said over the deafening noise of the crowd. He held my hand the whole way to one of the many snack counters. The young woman behind the stand perked up at our approach. Her face fell when she saw Aaron's hand in mine.

That's right, hussy. This one's mine.

The attendant's baby blue eyes stayed glued to Aaron the whole time he ordered, even when he pulled me closer to nuzzle his face in my hair. He ordered barbecue nachos with so much cheese it could constipate a cow, a hot dog that looked like something you could get at a gas station, and a pitcher of beer.

He asked if I wanted anything, but with my anxiety already threatening to break the surface, I just shook my head.

My senses were overloaded. The walkways were packed with people, some standing in line to order food, others waiting around for their orders to be called. Most had on a jersey or at least the team colors.

I immediately felt out of place, and not for the first time. The adrenaline running through my system was keeping me upright along with Aaron's hand grounding me in the present.

The more people that pressed into the building, the higher my guard. I could feel the heat rising in the air, and the worst part was that the game hadn't even started and intoxication was clear on many flushed faces.

Aaron kept me tucked into his side, as if he knew what I was thinking. I didn't want any of these people to touch me. It wasn't that I thought they were dirty or unclean. It was mostly to protect myself. Thinking about strangers—someone I didn't even know touching my body...had my past pressing in around me. Doctors and nurses, weight loss gurus, all the strangers my parents forced me to undress for so they could prod and pluck at my insecurities.

Aaron's hand left mine when the girl from the stand called our number. He grabbed the items from the attendant with a small thank you, and I swear she swooned.

I carried the beer as we made our way toward a private section of seats located near one end of the rink. Finn and Benny from the club were already here with another man whose skin was like the smooth color of burnt umber. He wasn't as large as Benny or Finn, favoring Aaron's more subdued build, and looked only a few inches taller than me.

Finn spotted us first, reaching out to take the nachos from Aaron. "I didn't think you were gonna make it, man!" He fist bumped Aaron as we wiggled between the glass and seats.

"Had to get some nachos!" Aaron shrugged. It was odd to see him so relaxed and joking around with his friends.

Finn turned his dark eyes on me. "Hey, Bellamy." He didn't reach out a hand—not that I would take it anyway. With all the hubbub and hollering going on, my senses were on overdrive. I didn't know where to look, who was here for what team. And worse, one of the perks of anxiety because it wasn't already bad enough, I felt like I was going to throw up or shit myself.

Benny piped up, "So Bellamy, what are you doing with Aaron here?"

"Oh…" I stuttered, trying and failing to focus on his voice. "He invited me. I hope that's okay."

The four of them burst out in laughter. Aaron threw his head back, laughing like he did in his driveway. "He didn't mean *here*, Sunshine." Around breaths, he continued, "He meant with me in general."

If I could focus on anything other than my anxiety racing through my body, I would have probably been embarrassed. I looked toward the ice, trying to compose myself before attempting to answer Aaron's friends.

"She actually likes your ass?" The man with locs similar to my boss's wife asked, his voice teasing and light. Not at all what I expected from him. Tattoos of swirling black lines covered every visible inch of his rich brown skin.

"Yeah she does, Landon." Aaron slung an arm around my

shoulders and pulled me into his side. The armrest of the plastic chair dug into my side and I had to bite back a wince. Aaron seemed to notice my sharp intake of breath and pulled away. "You okay?"

"Yeah," I said, trying to get my lips to turn up into a smile. Instead, it felt more like a grimace.

"No, you aren't." He turned his body in the chair, fully facing me. "What can I do?"

Aaron's ability to read me, after such a short time knowing each other never failed to surprise me. In the best way.

"I'll be fine. Just a little embarrassed," I admitted, and I was, among other things.

The teams took to the ice right as Aaron thought to introduce me to the man with hair like Holly-Jay's wife's. His name was Landon, and he had known Aaron and Benny since their first deployment overseas.

The crowd roared as the ref dropped the puck. Off the players went, controlling the puck with what I googled and found was called a hockey stick—original, I know. I would most likely leave here tonight knowing no more than what I googled last night.

The players shoved each other, each push more violent than the last. It amazed me the speed in which the bulky players glided across the ice, it was hard to keep up with where the puck was.

Aaron drew little images on the back of my hand with his fingers, making sure to keep contact with me while he and his friends screamed about players and injustices. The first period ended with a loud buzzer. Landon and Benny offered to get more beer and whatever I wanted.

I shook my head, still not ready to eat anything. When they left, Finn and Aaron talked about the game so animatedly, you would think they had a personal stake in the fate of the game. I got lost people watching. Some rose to stretch or get snacks, while the ones left behind sat and talked.

"So, Bellamy," Finn says, his deep voice bringing my attention back.

"Yeah?" I turned my body to face him as much as I could. Aaron took the opportunity to put his arms around my waist. So much physical affection, and in a public place. It unnerved me as much as it pleased me.

"Your friend the other night," he started, and my instincts went on red alert. I knew he was talking about Ronnie. The way he had kept watch over her at my house the other night and the strong reaction he had to her had clued me in.t Aaron didn't think anything of it when I had brought it to his attention, so whenI leaned back making sure he caught my eye, He just chuckled and turned me back to Finn.

"Ronnie?" I asked.

"Yeah. Is she seeing anyone?" he asked with no fanfare, just his normal straight face.

"No," I said, not willing to give him anything further. If he wanted information, he'd have to go to the source.

He nodded, observing me in that cold calculated way I assumed a serial killer would look observing their next target. But he didn't scare me, not even with his bulk and those tattoos. Not anymore, because I knew his secret. He wanted Ronnie.

Landon and Benny returned with two pitchers of beer and a sundae that looked absolutely amazing. Benny handed me the ice cream. The bowl was plastic, which surprised me until I got a look at it. It was a hockey puck with the logo for the Carolina Hurricanes on it. A keepsake for kids, I'm sure. The ice cream was cold, and since the room was pretty much an ice box, it didn't melt easily.

I sat there with the bowl in my hands, looking between the four men drinking their beer, wondering why the hell I was holding it.

Aaron whispered in my ear so none of them could hear, "It's for you, Sunshine."

Surprised, I looked up into his green eyes. "Me?" I asked. I didn't remember asking for ice cream. Honestly, everything kind of felt like a fever dream at this point.

He nodded and scooped out a chunk of the vanilla ice cream covered in chocolate sauce, raising it to his lips and eating the whole bite. I laughed as his face registered the cold and he huffed a few times to obviously get the feeling back in his mouth.

"Brain freeze?" I asked, a little dopey that he would have his friends get me something.

I ate my ice cream as the next period took place. Again, the players were rough, even more so than the last period, and the fans were eating it up. Screaming for more.

A man carrying an empty pitcher of beer walked in front of our seats, probably on his way for a refill. Once or twice, the players had bumped into the plexiglass in front of us, causing me to flinch back.

Aaron continued to rub soothing patterns on my hand, going from the tips of my fingers to the top of my shoulder. Every time a player slammed into the wall, he used his whole hand to keep me steady.

I finished off my ice cream and Aaron placed the empty container on the empty seat beside him.

A fight broke out on the other side of the arena, causing the boys to stand up and shout at the players, or refs—I wasn't really sure. All I knew was it looked like blood on one of the players, and the other was sent to what Aaron told me is called the penalty box.

The game resumed not a minute later, sending the teams from one side of the rink to the other. I gave up on trying to understand the game other than getting the puck into the net. Three players ended up smashing into the wall right in front of us, causing people to erupt out of their seats again in hopes of another fight. One player hurriedly got back to his feet and skated off while the other two traded blows.

The scene unfolded in slow motion. I couldn't look away as they hit each other and shouted obscenities. All of the boys were on their feet, damn near getting up into the glass. The player in red got a good hit in on the player in the green, sending a chunk of bloody tissue straight into the glass.

Panic exploded all around me as the noise of the crowd reached deafening heights. I was taking in harsh labored breaths, sweat poured down my neck, and black spots coated my vision. Oh God, I was going to pass out.

Finn noticed and pointed toward me with his thumb trying to get Aaron's attention. Benny turned right as the guy from before strolled through with a now-full pitcher of fresh beer. Benny was so large, he sent the guy toppling over.

Golden liquid sloshed straight into my face as the pitcher

left his hand, careening toward my head. With a sickening crack, the heavy plastic nailed the side of my head and before I could echo a sound, everything went black.

Aaron

"Bellamy!" I was screaming her name, trying to get to her through the crowd that flocked toward the fight. Even though we had a private area, it didn't mean the walk way was clear.

I shouldn't have tried to get closer to the ice. I should have stayed by her side. I knew she was having a hard time with the violence, which was admittedly why I got her the ice cream. She loved the stuff, and I had hoped it would calm her nerves.

But when Finn had nodded in her direction and I saw her face was paler than I had ever seen it before, I knew something was very wrong. Benny had tried getting to her first—with three sisters and a fiancé, he knew better than anyone how to talk to a woman in crisis.

But now she was on the floor. The idiot with the beer was kneeling near her, screaming for help. When I finally pushed through the crowd, I found her on her side, blood pooling around her beautiful curls like a halo of death.

Logically, I knew she wasn't dead—head wounds bleed a lot—and if it were anyone but my sunshine, I would have ripped him a new asshole for being careless. But all I could focus on was getting Bellamy somewhere I could take a look at her head and determine if she needed stitches.

"Call the medic!" I shouted, knowing one of the guys was probably already on the phone. The game had stopped and it felt like the whole arena was holding its breath, waiting on the outcome of such a display. Some of the players were in front of the glass calling for the medic as well.

"Bellamy." I gently pulled her body up from the floor into my lap. She was still limp. I needed to get her awake before I had a full blown melt down. "Bellamy, baby."

I ran my hand down the side of her head that wasn't coated in blood, gently shaking her shoulders. "Come on, baby. Open those beautiful eyes," I pleaded with her. I would beg right here in front of an audience just to make sure she woke the fuck up.

Landon led the guy who'd had the pitcher away, knowing full well that if Bellemy didn't open her eyes soon, I might just beat the shit out of him. I'd seen my fair share of wounds in the marines. But nothing I felt then compared to what I was feeling now. The air in the arena had all been sucked out. I felt like I couldn't breathe.

Benny and Finn were moving the crowd back. It was a slow process, but eventually the medics skated across the ice and the crowd made a path for them. I placed some napkins on the gash in her head, hoping to staunch the bleeding so they could do what they needed to.

If only she would open her eyes.

The leader knelt down in front of us, eyes focused on Bellamy. "Head wound!" he shouted as the rest of them made their way closer, already pulling out supplies and gently nudging me out of the way.

The rational part of me knew I had to move; I needed to let them do their job, but the irrational part of me wanted to shout and rage that they couldn't make me leave her. Finn lay his hand on my shoulder, letting me know they weren't going anywhere with her alone.

The leader looked up at me. "Has she eaten today?"

I nodded, knowing she just ate that bowl of ice cream. But if she had eaten anything else, I wouldn't know.

"Is she on any medications?" he asked next, and I remembered she picked up two prescriptions, but not the names of them.

"Anxiety," I said. "But she takes something else too. Why?"

"Head wounds bleed a lot, but she isn't responsive." He

looked back down where his colleague was running a small pen-sized flashlight across her eyes.

Her chest still rose and fell, which calmed me, if only a little.

The lead guy turned, addressing his staff. "Let's get her back to the medic clinic."

"With all due respect, sir," Finn said, his voice firm. "We'll be accompanying her." Thank God Finn was thinking clearly, because it took all my focus to keep from being sick.

The medic told us where to go before two of his men went to lift her off the floor. I knew she would be humiliated if she woke up to find out all of this happened because of her, so I moved the men away and lifted her, being careful to cradle her head into the crook of my arm.

She looked peaceful, as if she were asleep, but I could feel the cold sweat running down her back and the warm blood caked in her hair.

"I'll follow you."

He nodded, understanding clear in his eyes. He led us to where the tunnels opened. Under the stands, it was a whole network of pathways and rooms. We rushed toward the locker room for the Hurricanes. The medic threw the doors open and we crossed to the area where the players got ready and called for the doctor.

I didn't take time to notice anything other than the padded table covered in white cloth that the leader had me lay her on. Once she was laid flat, the team doctor got to work stitching up her gash. None of the guys said anything as we waited.

When he finished wiping up all the excess blood from her face, he turned to us. "You may need to have her checked, just in case. But I think she'll be fine." He smiled at us all. "She'll have a nasty bruise for a while. I can write you a prescription for some pain management if you think she will need them." I nodded and he wrote it out, tore it off, and handed it to me. I'd have to get it filled.

With that he walked out of the room. I grabbed her hand, running soft circles over her skin, wishing she would just wake the fuck up so I could know for sure she was okay.

With just me and the guys left in the room, Bellamy's eyelids twitched before opening fully. Her face scrunched up in confusion at first, then what little color she gained while unconscious fled her cheeks as she seemed to remember what happened.

She lifted her hands to cover her face and groaned. A strained hiss left her as her hands hit her stitches. "Oh, God," she cried.

"It's okay," I said. Because it was. Now that she had

opened her eyes, I could take her home and keep her in bed for the next couple of days, making sure she didn't overwork herself. Really, her and Veronica had everything lined up already. What little details remained, Veronica could handle.

Once the medic cleared her to leave, he gave her meds for pain and drank a whole cup of water. Finn, Benny, and Landon all helped me get Bell to the truck

"Thank you." I clapped them all on the shoulder, hoping they would understand how much I meant that.

"You would do it for any of us," Landon said with a shrug.

"I'm gonna take Bellamy back to my place and let Billy know what happened," I said in place of goodbye. They all nodded and headed back inside for what was left of the game. Finn took the prescription and told me he'd get it filled and dropped off at my place after the game.

I drove in silence. I wanted to make sure I could hear her soft breaths as they came and went out of her chest. I couldn't stand the thought that she was seriously injured.

I almost drove straight to the hospital, but she had already been through enough, and she hadn't fallen asleep yet. We pulled up to my house, and much to her displeasure, I carried her into the house. I sat her down on the couch gently, placing a kiss on her lips. "I'll be right back."

I walked to the bathroom, filling the tub with luke warm water and epsom salt—the lavender kind that helped relieve sore muscles—before striding back into the living room where she lay exactly as I had placed her.

I took a minute to admire her; the way her shoulder curved into her neck, up to those springy dark curls, the voluptuous slope of her stomach, all the way down to her ruined suede boots.

She must have felt me staring. Her eyes landed on mine, and I couldn't help but smile. How did I get so lucky? She was fucking stunning, even with dried blood crusted in her hair and the bluish tint around her already swelling head. Just a bit lower and he would have hit her temple.

Things could have been so much fucking worse.

I strode to her side and gently pulled the boots off her feet. She didn't question me, which made my heart soar. She was trusting me, whether from the effects of the pain pills, or because she genuinely wanted to trust me. I wasn't sure, but I'd take it.

I peeled the gray dress from her body slowly, taking great care not to hit her stitches. It was soaked and reeked of beer. Her breasts were caged in by the sexiest bra I had ever seen.

The black lace was right in my face when I bent down to take her leggings off. Her matching thong made me groan.

But I kept it under control. She needed to be taken care of, not ravaged.

She didn't say a word the whole time I stripped her down in my living room. Not even when I lifted her up into my arms and guided her legs around my waist. She instinctively wrapped her arms around my neck and lay her head on my shoulder, letting me carry her toward the master bath.

I sat her on the edge of the tub, taking care to make sure she was stable enough that she wouldn't fall in. I lifted off my knees, intending to leave the room when she croaked, "Stay."

Her eyes were heavy with sleep, and I knew now if I left she would just fall asleep in the bath. I didn't want that, but the thought of her naked sent me into a frenzy. I couldn't imagine what I would do once she was naked and in my grasp.

I took a deep breath and solidified my strength. The Lord knew I was gonna need it. I helped her out of her bra and underwear, then I let her use me to help her get into the tub. She sank down into the water.

"Do you want me to wash your hair?" I asked. I didn't have the slightest clue how, but I was sure I could figure it out.

She mumbled something, but it wasn't enough that I could make out what she was saying, so I grabbed the shampoo and a cup from the counter. I wet her hair, trying my best to stay away from her stitches.

I lathered up some of the shampoo between my hands and ran them through her hair. She mumbled, but stayed still as I continued to massage her scalp. Then, rinsing the suds from her hair, I called her name, trying to keep her awake long enough to put her in my bed.

I drained the tub before lifting her up and out of it. Toweling her off was a lot harder than I anticipated with her drowsy state. I wrapped the towel around her sopping wet hair before walking her into the bedroom.

I had already pulled back the covers, so when I sat her down, all I had to do was move her feet under the sheets and pull the comforter up to her shoulders.

She was already asleep by the time I got the bathroom cleaned up, softly snoring into my pillows. I kissed her temple and walked into the living room to gather the rest of her clothes. Throwing them in the washer, I set the cycle and passed out on the couch.

The next morning, I made sure to make breakfast before

she got up. Bacon, eggs, sausage. I even made my mama's biscuits, and gravy from scratch. Biscuits were just coming out of the oven when I heard Bellamy's soft footsteps on my carpet.

She held a hand to the side of her head—it was probably throbbing by now. I laid out two of the pain pills with a glass of water. Finn had dropped off the prescription at some point last night like he said he would. She had found a shirt somewhere, but I could just make out the underside of her ass poking out from the bottom.

Biting the inside of my cheek to keep from launching myself at her, I nodded at the pills when her eyes met mine. "Take those for the pain." I had to clear the frog from my throat before speaking again. "I'm so sorry, Sunshine."

And I was. She got hurt on my watch. The guilt was eating away at me, so slowly I thought I might go insane.

She smiled as much as she could without hurting. "It's not your fault. It was an accident." She took a seat at the little table under the window. As the golden glow from the morning sun shimmered over her and light swarmed around her frame, my breath caught. It made her look even more beautiful, with no makeup and her hair a complete mess, this was my favorite version of her.

"Benny thought you were having a panic attack before the

pitcher hit you." I loaded up a plate of food for her— eggs, bacon, and sausage on one plate, and a biscuit cut in half and smothered in gravy on another. Her eyes were glassy when I got close enough the sun didn't blind me.

"Hey, it's okay." I sat the plates down and cradled her hands in mine. On my knees in front of her, I could see the leafy green of her eyes. It was stunning, probably my new favorite color.

"I know you've picked up on a few of my...issues," she started, and I had to stop her.

"First, you don't have issues. You have little quirks, and honestly most of them are cute as hell, Sunshine." I couldn't let her think that her hindrances made her any less human than anyone else.

She ate a few bites of her eggs, chewing slowly. She needed time to tell me all the things I didn't know yet. That was fine. I had all day, I could be patient.

"I know you know I have anxiety." Her hands were shaking, the silver fork glinting in the light. She placed it down on her plate, uncaring where it landed. "Everything was so loud. The fans started to press in on the space we had, and I just couldn't stomach the thought of strangers caging me in."

I nodded. I had underestimated her aversion to touch. I

wouldn't do that again. Not ever.

"I didn't see the pitcher. I just remember the sweat and the black dots in my eyes." Her eyes were focused on her lap, where I still held her hands. "I didn't mean to scare you."

I pulled her down out of the chair onto the floor with me, arranging my legs so I could have her in my lap. Putting my arms around her body, I just held her. I let her talk through all the horrendous things her parents had said to her over the years, how her grandmother left her one thing—her wedding ring—the only thing that mattered to her, and her parents refused to give it to her.

I learned that she had a trust fund that she didn't have access to because her parents held it over her head as punishment. I wrapped her as tight to my body as I could as she cried and told me all of the missing pieces of her life.

All the things I'd learned about her this far had me craving more, even if it made me angry. I wanted to keep her all to myself.

I wanted to protect this woman for the rest of my life.

Bellamy

Aaron had been stuck to my hip ever since the accident, even going as far as to rearrange his shifts with Greer so he would always be in the office with me. I couldn't blame him. I had given him quite the scare. Not that I meant to.

It had been a few days since the hockey game. Ronnie and Xavier visited while I healed at home. Both of them had gawked at the bruise that had formed around the stitches, but I assured them I was fine and that business would continue as usual.

It was the night of Haven's fundraiser, and as I caked on concealer and foundation to cover what was left of the faint bruise, Aaron slipped into the bathroom. "You don't need that."

I laughed. Of course I didn't need it. I wanted it. "No, but I really don't want to explain it if someone sees it."

I noticed the slight wince in his body. He thought the accident was his fault, that he could have prevented it somehow. Which we both knew he couldn't.

"It's not your fault," I said, turning to lift up on my toes and place a gentle kiss on the underside of his jaw.

The doorbell rang. We both paused. Ronnie and Xavier were meeting us there and I hadn't ordered anything recently to be delivered. Aaron strolled toward the front door with a groan.

"Wait..." I began as Aaron turned the knob. Everything felt like slow motion as my mind tried to cave in on itself.

Three people stood on the opposite side of my door. Aaron was speaking, calm and collected, a southern gentleman to his core. However, I couldn't hear the words tumbling from his lips. The two people I feared and detested most had finally found me—had finally left their gilded palace, for whatever reason. As much as I had tried to forget their faces, it was clear who they were.

My parents.

Still half inside the bathroom, I was stuck between crossing the room to close the door in their face, or hiding. Neither of which would garner any respect, and poor Aaron was standing in the middle of the uncomfortable silence.

"Well, daughter. Are you going to let us in?" My father's gruff voice filtered through my hazy thoughts.

Aaron's head swiveled toward me, his eyes alert. When I

didn't speak, he spoke for me, his words clipped, "We were just headed out. A work function."

"Who are *you* and what are you doing in our daughter's home?" My mother's shrill voice broke my further thoughts on the stranger.

"He's my boyfriend, and we were just leaving." My voice felt stronger than I did on the inside—far stronger than I thought I could muster the next time I saw my parents. "So you came all this way for no reason, because I have nothing to say to you, and I sure as shit won't be listening to anything you have to say."

I crossed the threshold of my home with Aaron on my heels, making the unwelcome duo retreat backward on my front stoop. By the look on my mother's face, I could tell she was unhappy.

Aaron lay a hand on my lower back after locking my door, guiding me toward his truck and without another word or glance in their direction we left.

Aaron drove us to the venue and parked in the designated area for security, making sure I could get back and forth to the truck in as little time as possible just in case I needed to rest.

I found Ronnie talking with Haven, practically buzzing with unshed energy. With a small smile at Haven, I pulled Ronnie away.

"Whoa, where's the fire?" she complained as I practically dragged her around the security tent where Aaron was checking in with the rest of the team. I waited for him to come to us, my hands vibrating with anxiety. He met us after what felt like hours.

"My parents, Ronnie." My voice cracked on her name and I had to take a breath to center myself once more. Aaron's hands smoothed over my back, running up and down my shoulders. "They're here. In the quarter."

"Excuse me?" Ronnie almost screeched.

"They showed up at my house before we left. Ronnie, I don't know what to do." I wanted to cry just to release some emotion, but I refused to give them one more tear.

Her arms wrapped around my shoulders carefully to avoid my head wound. "We'll figure it out. We always do. Do you know what they want?"

"No."

"Well, let's make a plan right after we check everything. I'll scoop Xavier up, too."

Aaron kissed the top of my head, and I tried to shake off the thoughts swirling. I had a job to do. My whole career stemmed around this event and the wedding.

I walked around the venue while Aaron slipped off into his position around the perimeter. Jeremy was setting up his table of assorted goodies. Plastic folding chairs had been set up a little ways from the stage for the historical society, leaving the rest of the lawn to be standing room only.

The weather had been perfect, if not a little cold, all week. The show would start after a few words from the mayor were said about the historical society and why we were all here—to raise money to save the precious landmarks around the quarter.

Haven nodded, placing in her ear monitors. She was about to join the band on stage for her sound check. Adrian stood by the edge of the stage, never taking his eyes off her.

I glanced to where I last saw Aaron, and found his eyes on me. He sent me a comforting wink and I blew him a kiss. We had talked about so much since our first meeting, and I couldn't help but feel my heart flutter every time I looked at him.

"Have y'all done it yet?" Xavier asked, clicking his camera for test shots. Even though he already followed Haven and Adrian around the town, he was here to capture a few pictures of the performance.

"No." I rolled my eyes.

"What exactly are you waiting for? Divine blessing?" he sounded annoyed, which threw me off.

"What's going on Xavier?" I wasn't playing this game with him. Aaron and I were solid, but my parents showing up already had me on edge and I wasn't in the mood for his attitude.

"Nothing," he snapped, walking away and leaving me alone. Ronnie and I still needed to get the silent auction items up and set out, so I headed in that direction.

Xavier could be moody for sure, and with only two weeks until Haven's wedding and still no assistant, he had to be feeling the stress. I could give him a few minutes to cool down. Maybe he would talk to Ronnie about whatever it was that was bothering him.

I got all of the auction items ready and in their spots under the tent behind the rows of chairs for the historical society members. It didn't take nearly as long as I wanted it to. I stood there with my hands on my hips glancing around to see if anything needed adjusting, making sure everything was in order.

Strong arms looped through mine and pulled me back into a chest I knew well. Aaron placed a kiss on the top of my head. He leaned back to look into my eyes, hands splayed across my back.

"You're beautiful," he whispered, and it took my breath away. No matter how many times he said it, I would never get tired of hearing the words from his lips. He looked at me like I was the only woman in the world. Like I hung the moon and the stars just for him.

The event went off without a hitch. Haven's set was wonderful. Even I had to admit she was a force on stage, all of the donated auction items had been claimed and we raised a good chunk of change tonight. All of the historical society members cheered as the tally went up on the leaderboard.

We hit just above our goal, and Holly-Jay pulled Ronnie and I aside after the cleaning crew had shown up.

"This was an amazing night, girls!" Holly-Jay exclaimed, practically jumping in her thin high heels. "I want to thank you both for going above and beyond for Haven. We don't normally coordinate the extra events, and I'm so glad that you two took the time to do it. If not, who knows if tonight would have gone as smoothly as it did." She took a breath to let that sink in. "I know we said the wedding would be the determining factor for the promotion, but I want to give y'all the official offer on Monday."

Ronnie's big goofy grin matched my own. She met me in an embrace as we laughed and jumped along with Holly-Jay.

"We'll discuss options in the next few weeks," she said as Kelly came to whisk her away. "Great job, ladies."

We squealed, but my heart did a little patter. Aaron and I hadn't talked about the possibility, and with my parent's presence heavily on my mind, I couldn't help but bring down our mood.

Was it possible for a heart to be so full and break at the same time?

Because that was exactly how I felt. Aaron was still leaned up against his truck, hands in his pockets, head tilted back against the glass.

"Hey," I said so he would know I was there. I didn't like sneaking up on him because I liked seeing the smile bloom across his face when he saw me. "We got the promotion!"

"That's incredible, Sunshine." His voice dipped low, much like his head did to nuzzle my neck.

My heart flipped and goose bumps bloomed on my skin. I wanted tonight to be about us, to finally feel exactly how much we cared for each other. I'd waited for him long enough, and even though I knew I would never recover if I had to give him up after I'd shared myself with Aaron, I wanted it.

I wanted *him*.

Aaron

Something was off with her. Most likely the fact that her estranged parents decided to show up unannounced.

The past couple of weeks had been the best I'd felt in years, and it was all because of Bellemy. The woman who had yelled at a perfect stranger, who was the most clumsy person I'd ever met, who I was pretty certain I was in love with. We had fallen into an easy way of life together fast, only two weeks into knowing each other. It just felt right. We both worked like crazy, but when we got home, we spent all the time we could touching each other. I memorized the way her lips felt against mine, the feeling of her soft flesh.

I was convinced she was made for me. Sent by God himself, and I didn't know what I had done to deserve her, but I wanted to keep her. I wanted her to know how much I loved her, even though neither of us had spoken the words.

I drove us back to her place where I had admittedly made myself comfortable. Even going as far as bringing a few things from my place so I wouldn't have to miss any time with her. She had cleaned out a part of her closet for my clothing, and even bought a lock box for the pistol I kept on me while I worked.

I took off my boots at her door where she flipped off her flats and sauntered into the bathroom. I heard the water turn on, but the shower never started. So she wanted to soak—I couldn't blame her. She barely had any time alone since we started dating, and I had to admit my selfishness in that act. I was just thankful her uninvited guests weren't here either.

After removing my harness and locking my pistol up, I walked past the bathroom. She was already in, bubbles covering the surface, her head leaned back against the lip of the tub. She looked peaceful, relaxed. As much as I wanted to walk in there and disturb her, I knew she needed this time.

I continued into her room and took off my pants, leaving one of my clean shirts on the bed for her to wear when she got out of the bath.

Tiptoeing through the house, I made myself toast and turned all the lights off in the main living area after checking to make sure the locks were engaged. I settled into her bed and waited for her. Not long into a random movie I'd picked off her Netflix list, I heard the tub drain and the shower turn on. I loved that she took a bath then rinsed off and washed her face in the shower. It was a quirky little routine that made her even more adorable.

After a few minutes, she strutted out in nothing. Her hair was still in the knot she had it in earlier, and I could see the hint of tears in her eyes.

"Sunshine?" I asked. I couldn't focus on anything but her face as I made my way to where she stood in the doorway completely naked.

"You're amazing." She whimpered. "You know that?" More tears gathered. Before they could fall, I pressed my lips to hers. I felt the wetness on her cheeks, but she kissed me back, pushing me toward the bed.

When the back of my legs hit the mattress, I sat down. She climbed on top of me, hungry, and deepened the kiss. As her tongue stroked mine, her hands went to the bottom of my shirt, tugging it up and over my head, leaving me bare except my boxers. She rocked her hips against my already hard cock, trying to gain friction. To find her release.

I wrapped one arm around her middle and spun us, placing her back on the mattress and her head on the pillows. Her curly hair slipped from the tie she had it in earlier, fanning out over the white sheets.

She bit her bottom lip, eyes still wet with tears. She had

never been more beautiful to me than in this moment.

The steel in her eyes cemented the fact that she wanted to be in this moment with me.

"Sunshine," I breathed against her neck and pressed my hips to her core, making her gasp. "Is this what you want?"

I lifted up onto my elbows, needing to see her face, hear her confirmation that this was what *she* wanted. Not what she thought I needed. I didn't need her body to be happy with her. I just needed her.

"I want you in any and all ways I can have you," she whispered. The words hit me like a ton of birds decided to take flight straight into my heart.

"You have me baby," I replied, sealing my lips over hers. Trailing kisses down her voluptuous body, I got a good look at her. Pussy glistening, already wet with desire.

"Goddamn, woman." I groaned. Her stomach heaved up and down with every breath she took, and her breasts had fallen to her sides.

I covered her with my body, taking her lips in a bruising kiss. I wanted her, but I also knew it had been a while for her, so I needed to work her body up to accommodate my girth. I wasn't bragging, but I had enough sense to know I could hurt her if I wasn't careful. And the last thing I wanted to do was cause her pain in any way.

Taking my time, I trailed kisses up and down her neck, sucking lightly on the place where her collarbone met her throat. Earning a little moan from her. That noise broke something in me as I made my way down to her perfect tits.

I watched the pretty peach skin of her nipple draw up in anticipation, making them into perfect little points before sucking one into my mouth. She arched her back and gasped as I bit down just enough to send a dart of pain to her nerves before flicking it with my tongue as I kneaded the other with my fingers.

I switched, taking care of each of her breasts, teasing her and eliciting sounds from deep in her throat. I was so fucking turned on, I could almost come in my boxers.

Her eyes followed every movement as I knelt between her legs and brought one up to my shoulder, then the other. I placed kisses on her knee and down her thigh until I made it to her bare cunt.

She shivered under my touch when I spread her with my thumbs, and lightly blew on her making her whimper. Flattening my tongue, I ran it from her entrance to her clit, and her hips bucked up into my mouth. I held her down with the palm of one hand and chuckled.

She moaned and squirmed against my mouth, but I wanted to hear her beg for it.

I notched a finger at her entrance, coating it with her arousal. "Tell me what you want, Sunshine," I rumbled into her soft flesh.

Her hips bucked, and she whimpered, "Please, make me come."

Her breathy plea mixed with the intoxicating smell of her made me feral. I didn't tease. I slipped my finger into her, relishing in the feel of her squeezing my finger. God, help me. She was tight, wet, and so fucking worked up, I couldn't contain myself.

I captured her clit with my mouth, working it over and adding another finger to her wet pussy. She groaned and lifted her hips, pushing into my face, and I loved every minute of it. I loved the way she rode my face as I brought her to the edge of her orgasm, and when I curled my finger to touch the soft pad of her g-spot, she shattered.

Her eyes rolled to the back of her head as her body shook and her pussy clamped down on my fingers. I eased them in and out, letting her ride the high as long as she could before pulling them out and licking them clean.

I knew I had her release coating my face, and I didn't give one goddamn fuck. I'd wear it like a badge of honor because it brought her pleasure.

I ran my hands up her body, over the swell of her soft

stomach and peaks of her breasts, placing soft kisses in their wake. Removing my boxers, I settled between her legs and lined up my cock at her entrance.

"Are you ready for me?" I asked before kissing her, swallowing her moans.

Bellamy

aron took his time kissing me. I could taste my release on his tongue and it only made me hotter, wetter, *hungrier.* He was mine and I was his, and in that moment, it was only us.

At some point, his boxers had come off, and I could feel the tip of him ready to make a mess of me. He was large. I knew it from the few times we had messed around, but having him that close sent a little flutter of panic through my system.

"I'll go slow," he said, as if he could read my mind. "Stop me if it's too much."

His kisses turned languid instead of frenzied, passionate instead of starved, and I gasped into his mouth as his cock pushed into me.

It stung for a second, mainly because I had never been with anyone as large as him, but also because I hadn't had any action in almost a year.

I winced and he stopped, pulling back to look at me. I hooked my legs around his hips, encouraging him deeper. He looked torn between stopping and ravaging me, his face pinched tight as if he was about to lose all control.

He continued pushing, watching my face for any sign of pain. His cheeks were flushed as he held his breath. I felt his hips sit flush with mine, and my body felt fuller than it ever had before. He gasped out and fell to his elbows, whispering in my ear, "God, Bellamy."

I never wanted to hear anything more in life than what he just said. It meant he was just as gone for me as I was for him, and I squirmed.

I felt the fleshy part of his stomach brush mine as I curled my hands around his biceps, feeling the hard muscles there.

"Just, give me a minute." Sweat had dotted his brow, and I pushed a wayward strand of hair out of his face. He kissed my palm and started to move inside me.

He was slow at first. Barely moving, short thrusts that rubbed the spot inside me he had hit earlier with his fingers. I needed more, so much more. I wanted him bare and completely unhinged for me. I wanted to make him feel as good as he made me feel.

I rolled us, using my full thighs to pin him to the bed. He was so large he didn't slip out, and at this angle, the burn felt incredibly delicious. I raised up and slammed down on him, loving the way his grunts turned to groans of pleasure as I rode him. Slick with sweat, he reached up to pinch my nipples. I let out a moan so much louder than any other time I could remember.

Grinding my clit down on his hips, I felt so fucking full of him. And watching him watch me? Pure unfiltered ecstasy. When he pulled my nipple into his mouth, I nearly came. "I'm going to come if you keep doing that." I cried.

My shaking muscles clamped down on him, and he took the opportunity to flip me back over. "Not yet, Sunshine. I'm really going to fuck you now," he whispered the promise in my ear. "Don't worry baby, you can take it."

I nodded with a moan and smiled at the challenge.

He set a brutal pace, our skin slapping together, building that delicious friction again, building and building, then he looked at me.

"Come with me." He changed our angle so his pelvic bone rubbed against my clit and covered my mouth with his when I came. I detonated, my orgasm coming out of nowhere and everywhere at the same time. He swallowed my screams of pleasure as he grunted out his own release.

We stayed like that, him still inside of me, kissing and groping each other, coming down from a high I swore I would never be able to come back from.

After a few lazy kisses, he pulled out of me, still semi hard. He disappeared into the bathroom. I heard the sink turn on and he returned with a warm rag. He wiped his release from me, taking care not to press too hard at my sore entrance, and it was the most tender thing he could have done. He disposed of the rag back in the bathroom before crawling into bed and pulling me into him.

"Not to ruin this magical moment," I squirmed. "But I really have to pee."

He threw his head back laughing, his chest vibrating under my palm. I rolled off the bed, looking like a newborn fawn learning to walk for the first time. He swatted at my ass as I walked to the bathroom to clean up.

Nobody likes a yeast infection.

Tiptoeing back into the room, I slid into bed beside him, letting myself embrace the warmth and affection he so freely gave. My feelings intensified, making my heart swell and patter a hard rhythm.

Aaron tipped my chin up with those talented fingers. "I got carried away earlier, I'm sorry I forgot protection."

I laughed, "That's the furthest thing from my mind, I'm on birth control, and I'm clean. I trust you."

He placed his hands on either side of my head as he

kissed me. "You're it for me, Bellamy." He twirled a stray curl around his finger. Looking me directly in the eyes, he said the words I so desperately wanted to hear, but broke my heart clean in two, "I love you."

We slept in, both of us spent from the night before. I didn't say those three little words back to him, opting instead to kiss him silly, hoping he could feel it without my having to say the words aloud. If I did, I was positive I would crack. I knew a break down was coming, my parents being the catalyst.

I would tell him soon. He didn't need to be around to see how bad it might get with my parents.

After wiggling out from his arms, I rose to get to the bathroom before I peed all over myself. So not a cute wake up call.

Returning to the bedroom, I found his discarded T-shirt on the floor and slipped it over my head, then padded softly to the kitchen. I put a bagel in the toaster and pulled out my peanut butter and chocolate chips, needing the carbs after last night. I was weak in the best way. Sore in all the right places and needy, ready to go again.

I was almost finished with my second bagel when Aaron scooped me up and took me back to bed. Clutching my food, I was thrown on the bed as he pretended to go back to sleep, his eyes popping open as I took a big bite.

"Now, this is how I wanted to wake up," he said, his breath already smelling minty. He must have brushed his teeth before coming to abduct me from my kitchen.

I laughed. "To me stuffing my face with a bagel?"

He took the bagel from my hand with his mouth and chewed slowly. He swallowed and I watched as his throat moved. "I don't care if you're eating, drinking, or sleeping, as long as you're beside me when I wake up."

I threw my head back and laughed so hard I snorted. He would think something like that up. But it was sweet, and a little romantic.

"Don't make it weird," I scolded playfully, to which he rolled on top of me and gave me the best wake up kiss I'd ever had. Everything with him was perfect, and I selfishly wanted it all.

"I have to go home to grab a few things, but I'll be back before dinner," he said, lifting up and dressing in a pair of gray sweatpants. I swear, I almost told him he wasn't allowed to leave, but that would have been a whole level of crazy I wasn't willing to admit.

"Keep looking at me like that, Sunshine," he rumbled, climbing back up my body, "and I'll have you spread open for me, and screaming my name again."

I let my legs fall open as he lifted off me, his kiss lingering on my lips. He glanced down where my legs were open and I swore I heard a growl low in his throat.

"Greedy little thing." He pulled on a shirt as I sat up. I wanted him to come back to bed, but I also needed him to leave so I could call Ronnie and tell her all about last night.

He kissed my temple as he walked out the door, to his truck. I waved as he drove off and stepped back inside.

Bellamy

I immediately checked my phone, reading the messages from Billy and Ronnie. Xavier hadn't texted, and I made a mental note to check in on him. Something was going on and he wasn't talking about it.

Ronnie was making sure we made it home safely after the event, and to tell me Haven and Adrian were up in their love nest waiting for Monday.

I hit the call button beside her name and she answered, sounding like she might have been jogging. "Hello, my little lovebird."

"Hey." I wasn't sure where to start so I blurted, "I slept with Aaron."

There was a pause on the other line before she damn near broke my eardrum with her squeal. "Tell me everything!" she demanded, and I laughed along with her.

Spilling everything, I told her how amazing last night was, and how he told me he loved me. She switched the call to video which confirmed she was out on a run. Her hair was up in a messy bun, and her ears were covered by wool ear muffs.

"You're glowing!" she sing-songed. "I can't believe you waited this long. But I guess it was worth it, right?"

It was. The way it happened was perfect, and I wouldn't take it back for anything. She read something in my face and let out a breath. "Are you having second thoughts?" There was no judgment in her tone. Just a simple question.

"No, no. Nothing like that." I didn't want to have to tell my best friend that I was unraveling, so I lied instead. "I'm debating on bringing him to game night."

"What about your..." she paused as if she didn't know how to bring it up.

"I haven't seen them since I left them on my doorstep." Hadn't heard a peep in almost twenty-four hours. Which I had decided was a good sign.

"How are you going to deal with that?" Her eyes burned holes into mine. She was so serious. "Because you have to deal with it, Bell."

I nodded, but I hadn't a clue how I would deal with my parents. How could I voice a plan I didn't have?

"Do you need me to meet you there?" she offered, and even though my first instinct was to hop onto that lifeline, I knew I had to do this on my own.

"No. I need to do this on my own." I said, not feeling at all confident in myself.

"I love you, Bellamy." Ronnie said, her face smoothing into the bright warmth I knew and loved.

I had a few hours before Aaron came home.

Home.

That was new, even for me. But it felt right. I couldn't imagine my life now without him. In the short amount of time we had known each other, it felt so intrinsic. Like somehow, we had always been meant to end up here, together..

Gathering up my curls, I wrapped them in a hair tie on top of my head. It probably looked kooky, but who cared? Pulling out my favorite vinyl record, I placed it under the needle of my new player. The scratchy tones began, and I felt more at peace than I had in a long time.

Gliding around my house, I cleaned a little and read a little, caught up on Ronnie and I's socials, and answered emails I had been pushing off.

A knock sounded at my door. I almost didn't hear it above the music, so before walking that way, I turned the knob to lower the volume.

Crossing over the hardwood floors in my socked feet, I slid to the door, opening it wide, expecting Aaron's handsome face to be shining back at me since it was close to dinner.

Instead, it was my parents. This time they marched right into my house, my mother looking around for anything and everything to complain about, and my father's disgusted face told me he didn't think my tiny home was up to his standards.

"What do you want?" I sighed, knowing this was coming sooner or later. "To belittle me in my own home that I bought with my own money? To pick apart my life that you know nothing about?" My chest was heaving, anxiety thick in my stomach. I needed to slow down before I worked myself into a spiral.

Naturally, my mother looked affronted by my accusations as if they weren't the truth, her eyes comically wide at my audacity to speak to her in such a way. I was done cowering from them, and I had an army of people who loved me at my back.

Seeing them again after all this time, I realized I wasn't

afraid anymore. I had more confidence than I had when I was a teenager. I worked hard and was recognized by a high profile magazine. They didn't get to take my wins from me.

Not anymore.

A sardonic laugh escaped. They didn't know me. They'd never known me. As far I was concerned, it was their loss.

"Why don't you get dressed into something more...appropriate, and we'll have dinner, " my father offered, trying to diffuse the situation before it devolved. "We have much to discuss."

I didn't want to eat dinner with them. "I'll meet you at Billy's Chicken Pit in an hour. That's the best you'll get." I wasn't going to bargain with them. If they wanted my time, it would be on my terms.

"That greasy hole in the wall we passed on our way in? You can't be serious!" my mother shrieked.

"That greasy hole in the wall gave me everything you two didn't."

With a twist on her heel, my mother strode out of my house without another word. My father glanced around once more, as if memorizing the place, before following her out.

The second my parents left my step, I raced to find my phone. Dialing Aaron's number, I waited for him to pick up. Two rings, and his voice filled my speakers. "Miss me already, Sunshine?"

A sob broke on my tongue as I started to laugh. I stood up to my parents for the first time, and I did it alone. Hearing his voice on the opposite end of my phone made me feel even more powerful.

"Bellamy." His voice turned to concern listening to me cry silent, happy tears. "Talk to me, baby. What's going on?"

"My parents. They came back," I replied, taking in shaky breaths. All I wanted to do was throw my arms around my man and tell him about how proud of myself I was knowing he would be proud of me, too.

"I'm on my way."

Aaron

Nerves competing between worry and exhilaration swirled in my gut. I made it to Bellamy's house in under thirty minutes. Enough time for her to rush out to meet me at my truck, looking stunning with her hair piled on top of her head. Tilted a little to the right, but she looked happy, so fucking happy. It was like all my worries melted, seeing her smiling and confident, made me damn near wild. I needed to marry this woman, there was no one else for me. The thought was like a bolt of lightning, sharp and unexpected. In my head, I started making plans.

I'd follow her anywhere she went. Private security was needed all over the place, and with my buddy Finn's sister expanding Dusk 'Til Dawn, I could possibly convince them to open a new location wherever we went.

She didn't wait for me to exit the truck, instead she yanked the door open and hopped up into the cab, launching herself across the console to pull my face to hers.

"I love you," she whispered, and if I could have fallen even more for this woman, I swear I would have, right there. Tears lined my eyes as I took in her freckles, her bright hazel irises that expressed so much, and I kissed her. I kissed her senseless, or maybe it was the other way around. Eventually, we parted our mouths long enough for her to fill me in on the interaction with her parents.

I was so proud of her for standing firm in her convictions. For standing up for herself on her own. She was the most inspiring woman I had ever met.

"So we're heading to Billy's?" I huffed a laugh. She nodded, her smile bright, and I stole another kiss. The drive was quick. When we pulled into the gravel parking lot, she sat waiting on me to open her door. I couldn't help the goofy grin on my face because I had forgotten to turn on the child locks, so she could've gotten out on her own.

Except she knew how much it meant to me to spoil her in any way I could.

After she jumped down from the truck, I tucked her under my arm. The weather was turning quickly, days getting colder in preparation for December. It gave me even more of an excuse to touch her. Not that I needed one anymore.

We walked into the teeming restaurant. Billy stood by the register speaking to customers. When his eye caught

Bellamy's, he smiled brightly and excused himself.

"Kitten!" he bellowed, wrapping her up in his arms and swinging her around as much as he could. "It's been too long. I thought we scheduled dinner for tomorrow?"

She nodded. "We did, but a complication came up. Looks like we'll be seeing you two nights in a row this week."

"Well, who am I to turn down a beautiful woman's company twice?" He gave me a wink and started toward the kitchen. Bellamy grabbed his hands to stop him.

"We're meeting some people," she said hesitantly as if Billy would be upset with her. "My parents decided to visit."

A flurry of emotions passed over his face. "Bellamy," he started, but she put her hands up in surrender.

"I want you to meet them because you're the best parent I've ever had." Her eyes glossed over, much like Billy's. He pulled her in for another hug and rested his head on her slipping bun of hair.

We all made our way to the back of the restaurant where no one was currently sitting, we pulled two tables together and Billy drew the partition to cut us off from the rest of the customers. It was secluded, and exactly what we would need once her parents got here.

Marcy knocked on the partition just as Billy stood to grab some homemade biscuits and honey.

Marcy and Billy whispered between themselves and Bellamy gripped my hand. I knew I'd never met her parents, but from the way they had acted when they showed up yesterday, I worried for her.

Billy turned around and nodded in confirmation. They were here.

Her mother entered first, followed by her father, whom she looked the most like. His skin was just this side of brushed copper, giving him a constant tan. But I knew Bellamy's glow was all her own, and tonight she sat up straighter in her seat, ready for whatever they threw at her.

A man I didn't recognize followed in after her parents. He wore a suit that screamed money, and was tall and thin with an air of arrogance that only someone who grew up having everything handed to them had. He unbuttoned his suit jacket before taking the seat beside Bellamy's father. His eyes hadn't left Bellamy and a part of me wanted to growl at him that she was mine.

Billy returned with a pitcher of tea and bread. No one spoke as he pulled out the seat at the head of the table.

"What is the meaning of this?" her father bellowed, gesturing to Billy who comically bowed over his large belly, and then sat down and turned to direct the conversation to Bellamy.

"Alice, Thadeous." She nodded at her mother and father. "This is Billy. He owns the restaurant you're sitting in, and he's the closest thing I have to a parent."

Incredulous eyes took him in. I watched as they surveyed him with an air of disgust. They didn't speak, didn't rebuke the fact that she had just called Billy her surrogate-father.

After a few tense moments of silence, Alice hissed, "We gave you everything, you ungrateful child." I could feel the energy in the room shift with her venomous words. "However." She smoothed down her blouse for the umpteenth time. "We have a plan for you."

No one spoke, so her father began,"This is Royce. You're betrothed."

I choked on the tea I was slowly sipping. Bellamy's mouth dropped open and Billy shoved himself free of the table.

"You will return to our home until the marriage is complete," Alice spat. "Really, Bellamy, did you honestly believe we would let you live like you are now for the rest of your life?"

Shock coated every face except Royce's, who looked way too fucking smug.

"The audacity," Bellamy began. It was whispered, but strong. "Who the hell do you think you are? Waltzing back into my *adult* life and telling me what I'm going to do? Am I also expected to lose half of my body weight before popping out babies for your Ken doll? Starve myself and become a shadow of the person I am today?"

All eyes were on her as she carried on.

"And what happens when my arranged marriage fails and my husband steps out on me with a newer model? Will that not cause you just as much shame as my body does now? Or will you turn a blind eye like you have with me for the last so many years? And all for what? Because I carry your last name?"

She was standing now, hovering over the table like a force of nature. "If that's all you care about, you can have it back. I don't need it. I also don't need the fortune I'm assuming you promised Royce here after he and I marry. Give it to him, it's only money.

I. Don't. Want. It.

I have *love* here, something neither of you would understand. I'm *happy*, forget me, just like you did when I left the first time. But this time, I'm not the one leaving. You are, with your fake lives and hate filled hearts."

"Really, Bellamy, the hysterics aren't necessary." Her father's tone sounded almost bored, and I wanted to rage.

"Hysterics? Do you hear yourself when you speak?" Her shoulders dropped as if all the fight just left her body.

Shaking her head slowly, she began again, "I—"

"I can assure you, I will not step out on you," Royce said, sending my already pounding pulse skyrocketing.

"No, you won't." Controlled anger bled from my pores. Through gritted teeth, I bit out another reply, "Because she won't be marrying you, *ever*."

Her chest was rising and falling when her head swiveled in my direction. Silver lined her eyes making the green stand out.

"Young man, I understand you're quite taken with my daughter." Thadious looked disgusted at having to say the words. "That will pass one day. I can make it worth your time to go ahead and part ways now." He calmly pulled a leather billfold from his breast pocket and clicked a pen open. As if money would solve everything.

Bellamy scoffed. "You think throwing money at him will just turn his feelings off? That his love for me can't possibly be genuine or true? Do you honestly find me so repulsive that no one could ever love me?"

My hand found hers and I wrapped my fingers gently around her wrist. Anchoring her, because once she went down this road, she could never go back.

"It's not about love, you insolent child," her father growled as he leaned in and slammed his meaty hands down on the table. "It's about your future. This diner in this town will not be your future. What about our legacy? Did you not think of that?"

Now she was laughing as tears streamed over her cheeks, rivulets of emotion running freely for everyone to see. "Legacy? What legacy, Dad? Lies, heartbreak, and *years* of abuse at the hands of the two people who are supposed to love you without boundaries?"

She used the back of her hand to wipe her tears away before continuing. She offered me her hand, and I didn't hesitate, sliding my fingers in between hers. "If I ever decide to have children, it will never be your legacy that lives in them. It will be *theirs*, and I will never be the parent you are. I hope you find peace someday, but I'm telling you right now, if you ever find it, don't look for me. Because I don't need either of you. I said goodbye to you both years ago, and now I've built my own family."

She kissed Billy on the cheek, slammed back the partition, and walked away from her parents for the last time.

Bellamy

Save the Date

The next week and a half after the showdown with my parents, Aaron and I both worked a lot in preparation for Haven and Adrian's wedding. But we also made time for *us*. We watched movies, made love, and just enjoyed our time.

We enjoyed meeting with Billy and his grandkids for Thanksgiving. I thought seeing him happy would be the highlight of it all until he made a toast. My heart had attempted to thump, thump, thump, right out of my chest as he'd declared his fatherly stamp of approval to Aaron, ending his speech with his eyes on the both of us. Everyone had cried, even the burly grandsons.

I hadn't spoken to Ronnie or Xavier about my parents after our dinner. I hadn't been ready. I would be tonight at Xavier's game night.

Aaron and I walked hand in hand toward Xavier's porch, which was still decorated for fall. Complete with corn stalks, scarecrows, and leaves in colors of gold, brown and red. He had a tall sign leaning against the blue siding of his house reading *welcome*. Arranged perfectly pleasing to the eye around his wrap-around porch was an autumnal scene of pumpkins, hay bales, and even a wagon. He had the space decked out for photoshoots, and had won the local front porch decor prize this season.

Surprise, surprise.

Xavier answered the door, obviously proud that we had taken the time to enjoy the fruits of his labor. His chest was pushed out as far as it could go, making his green shirt pull tight across his chest.

"You're here! Finally!" He flitted his arms around and waved us into the house. I glanced back at Aaron who was smiling at my friend's antics. "Well, come on. Penelope's here."

I hadn't seen Xavier's sister in years and was surprised she even came home. When she went off to college, she had disappeared, only talking to her brother a few times over the course of her schooling. We crossed from the kitchen to the living room. Ronnie and Penelope were already drinking little glasses of what I guessed were Xavier's famous "woo-woos", a drink he named after the reaction one would have after drinking a few and standing up.

Penelope had changed. I almost didn't believe she was the same person. Her long blonde hair was more golden than I remembered, and her physic had changed, but she was still one of the prettiest women I had ever met.

"Bellamy!" she exclaimed as Aaron and I made our way into the room. "And you must be Aaron! You two are a hot topic around here."

My face flushed as I sent a glare in the direction of my friends. Leave it to them to gossip about my relationship.

Aaron placed a gentle hand on my back and smiled down at me, letting me know in his own way that he was amused.

Xavier and Ronnie had cooked tonight. Normally, we each made something coordinating with each other, but they took mercy on me this time since I was otherwise occupied last night. The spread of homemade pizza and sliced potatoes fried to golden brown smelled heavenly.

We each dished up a plate. I placed an extra slice of pizza on Aaron's plate before joining the others in the living room to eat. After the time we had spent together, I knew the man could eat a whole cow by himself.

Penelope was just as funny as I remembered. She made us laugh throughout the whole meal. Even Aaron chuckled a few times.

After all our plates were clear, we brought out the games.

We laughed, drank, sometimes watched movies, other times we played games and giggled like the children we could be. Whatever was going on in the world could wait as we just relaxed. We had been doing this almost the whole two years since Ronnie and I moved here. It was our time to just relax and forget about all the things that bothered us.

As the night went on, I admired the way Aaron fit right in with my friends. Even Penelope seemed to be enjoying herself with us. I learned that she had just graduated and had moved in with Xavier to figure out her next chapter.

Xavier still refused to talk about his ex, though. Which I understood, I could admit it would bring the mood of the night down. I also knew I still had to fill them in on my parents.

I sighed heavily and Aaron placed a hand on my lower back.

"I met with my parents." Alcohol helped me blurt it out. And blurt I did. I rehashed the whole affair, every single detail I could remember. Ronnie jumped up and crossed the room to hug me as I let it all out. As the tears left me, I felt free, like the weight of worry just fell away. For years I had been terrified that one day my parents would just show up, tell me all the ways I was failing and then leave me broken and empty.

But they did show up.

They had told me all the ways they thought I was failing. And in spite of that, I was so far from broken.

I was thriving!

We all had a group hug with encouraging words before Aaron and I went home. The ride back was quiet, just us in companionable silence. He held my hand, thumb brushing over my knuckles in a soothing caress.

We pulled up to my gate, and as if we had been doing it for years, I waited in the passenger seat for him to open my door. I stepped down from his truck into his arms, wondering how in the hell I went from not wanting him to touch me to not being able to get enough.

We stood there, breathing in the cold night air and listening to each other breathe.

"Some day, Sunshine, I hope to rid you of your parents' last name."

I jerked back, tilting my head so I could look into his eyes. He didn't mean...no, he couldn't. We had only been dating for a few weeks.

"I want to be the one who cherishes you, who worships at your altar. I want to be the final piece in your life that makes you feel irrevocably whole."

Tears escape my eyes, warm against my cold cheeks. I

couldn't speak. The implication of his words sat heavily upon my heart and head. Instead, I lifted up on tippy toes and brushed my lips over his, savoring the way he kissed me like I was glass.

When his tongue teased the seam of my lips, I opened and hopped up into his strong arms. They wrapped around my thighs and ass, gripping me tightly as he led us into my house.

Our lips didn't separate as we crashed into the door, his hips pinning me against the wood. I made quick work of the lock, and once inside my house, he slowly set me down on my feet, only to push me against the back of the door. "I love you, Bellamy. I love you so fucking much."

Tears continued to fall as his words hit me like a freight train. He went to his knees before me, unbuttoning my jeans and slowly slipping them over my flesh and stomach that hung over my waist. As he kissed along the skin that had been dented in by the material, his eyes stayed locked with mine, shining with so much vulnerability, like he was afraid he had scared me.

As he rocked back on his heels, I bent down and kissed him like I was starved, letting my hands roam his shoulders and back.

He lifted back up, forcing me to stand again. Slipping his

fingers under the waistband of my lacy underwear, he slowly tugged them down, leaving them trapped around my ankles. He went straight to my pussy, tongue tracing up each side before slipping between, finding my clit just waiting to go off. He licked and swirled, coaxing my orgasm from the base of my belly.

Heat swarmed my body as he slicked his finger through my wetness and pressed it into my body, curling just enough to have me seeing stars and shuddering against the door.

He moved to stand, lifting my shirt up and over my head, leaving it to crumble on the floor. Our mouths came together, tongues tangling in a rhythm well learned at this point. He walked backwards as I slipped out of my shoes, padding after him on the way to my bed.

I spun us, shoving him back on the bed and crawling over his body, loving the friction of my skin on his jeans. My nipples grazed his soft henley, sending shivers down my back and arms. I sat back on his thighs, inching up his shirt to expose the little pudge of his belly before his body turned solid around his chest.

He lifted enough so I could remove his shirt completely and throw it across the room. Leaning down, I trailed my lips over his neck, the stubble a little longer than when we met but so fucking sexy.

As I worked to undo his pants, we were a heavy breathing mess, and I was loving every minute. When I got the button free and wiggled his jeans down over his hips, I lifted off his thighs, rearranging so I could get him completely naked.

Once his cock was free of his jeans and underwear, I couldn't help but admire him. His pale skin against my slight tan, the way my nails left imprints on his skin, how he flushed when I appraised him...

"I love you, Aaron Lark," I whispered, leaning down to give him a slow lick. He groaned, throwing his head back into the pillows.

"You're killing me, Sunshine."

I chuckled as I took him into my mouth slowly, moving up and down his shaft, gagging a little as he hit the back of my throat. He growled, gripping my head and gently pulling me up so he could place kisses on my lips.

He flipped us, and I squealed as he lined himself up and began to push into my body, eyes fixed on mine as he buried himself inside me. Panting, he covered my body, elbows by my head. With one hand, he caressed my face, cupping my cheek, and started to move in short, slow thrusts.

"You're perfect, Bellamy."

As his pace picked up and his thrusts became harder, he pressed on my clit with the heel of his hand, angling my hips up and over his thighs. I screamed out in pleasure.

"God, do that again for me baby," he crooned.

Bliss and agony ripped through me as he continued rubbing hard circles over my clit. Warmth spread over my limbs, tingles surging through me as another wave of pleasure resurfaced and a gush of heat flooded out of my body.

"*Fuck*, baby," he said as he grunted out his own release. He crashed on top of me, his weight like the best blanket on a winter day.

When our breaths slowed and our hearts beat in the same rhythm, he lifted up and gave me a cheeky grin. "That was the hottest thing I've ever seen."

I couldn't move, blissed out and so content, boneless, weightless, everything and nothing. I had never felt anything like that before. Sealing his lips over mine, he dragged me up, half-carrying me to the bathroom where he started the hot water and stepped into the tub.

We cuddled, my back to his front in the warm water, until the bubbles were gone and the water turned cool. Planting a kiss on my shoulder, he got out and toweled off, securing it just under his little pudge.

"I'm going to change the sheets. I'll be right back." he said as he leaned down to kiss my forehead. I heard the hall closet open and shut, then the tell tale shuffling of bed sheets being stripped and replaced.

It didn't take him long before he was back and opening drawers to offer me a rag. He had learned all my little routines. But tonight, I just wanted to fall asleep in his arms as soon as possible. So I whipped his towel from his hips and we laughed in unison as I dried off and sauntered off to bed.

Pulling the drain for the tub, he followed behind me, sliding into bed and pulling me into his side. We both drifted off into a stated slumber some time not long after.

Bellamy

avier called an emergency meeting at our local coffee shop early the next Monday. Ronnie and I needed to get the finalized wedding details to Holly-Jay this evening. Friday was the rehearsal, so Aaron was stuck hauling guests back and forth from the airport to Bedknobs & Broomsticks.

Ronnie and I met at the door, early as usual. We got our coffee from the young barista and found a table by the window. Snow had fallen last night, dusting the sidewalks in a thin layer of fluff. I took a sip from my hot chocolate, letting the warm goodness flow through my body, warming me up from the inside out.

Ronnie looked like she might be sick, but I didn't get the chance to ask. The bell above the door to the coffee shop opened and Xavier strolled in. He took one look at where Ronnie and I sat, scowled and walked to the counter.

"What was that about?" Ronnie whispered.

"I have no idea," I said honestly. "He was short with me at the benefit, too, but at game night, everything felt fine."

Ronnie pushed out of her seat and made her way to where he was standing waiting on his coffee. They spoke for a few minutes before she turned back toward me. A look of confusion settled over her features.

Xavier was shooting daggers at me though. What in the world had I done to make him upset?

"Hi, Xavier," I said politely.

"So, are you just going to pretend you didn't betray me?" His voice was like ice.

Betray him? What was he talking about? I wracked my brain, trying to piece together his contempt.

"You make new friends with the man who broke my heart and you don't think it's important to tell me?"

"Xavier, I don't know what you're talking about." I said, trying to think of who he might be speaking of. The only new people I had hung out with were Aaron's friends. We all knew Finn and Benny from the club.

He threw up his hands and slammed them on the table. "I saw the Facebook pictures, Bellamy."

I winced, trying to decipher his words, "What Facebook pictures?"

He hastily took out his phone, scrolling through to find

whatever it was that I did behind his back. "These." He flipped the phone around, and there were pictures from the hockey game. Landon had posted pictures of that whole night.

It hit me. Landon was Xavier's ex. I felt my eyes widen. Oh, God. "Xavier. I didn't know," I said. My pulse skyrocketed.

"Okay, Bellamy." His sarcastic tone made me shrink in my seat. Clearly he'd already made his assumptions, and it would take a lot of begging to change his mind.

I looked him in the eyes, praying silently that he would believe me. "I didn't know he was your ex. He was at the game with Finn, Benny, and Aaron. It didn't even occur to me that he could have been your ex."

He watched my face as I told him the truth. I had barely spoken two words to Landon. Just introductions and he had asked if I wanted anything when he went on a beer run. I hadn't thought much of him in those moments because I was already fighting off a panic attack.

He sighed, glancing down at his cup. "It hurts. You know?"

I quickly grabbed one of his hands. His eyes lifted to mine, tears and shock clear on his features. "I'm so, so sorry. I would have told you if I had known."

He smiled. It was faint, as if he was still trying to be mad, but I saw it. Relief swept through me. I could only have one melt down at a time, and I had met my quota for the year with my parents.

Ronnie sighed, glancing out of the coffee shop window. "I don't know if I want to leave."

Xavier and I turned to her. Ronnie was always down for an adventure, never putting permanent roots down for that reason.

"What? Why?" I knew why I didn't want to leave, but I also understood the reality if we did. We could have a business of our own, no one to answer to, only taking on what jobs we knew would be perfect for us.

"It's a huge opportunity, it's just..." she began, as if she could read my thoughts. With her head bowed, she looked toward her lap before quietly whispering, "I'm pregnant."

My heart swelled. Ronnie, pregnant? She would be an amazing mother. I had no doubts.

"Oh my gosh, Ronnie!" I gushed, launching out of my chair to pull her into a hug. "That's amazing news. Who's the father?" I was aware that was an abrupt question, but I really wanted to know..

Her cheeks deepened to a shade of red I had never seen on her.

"Oh no. Not Behemoth?" I mocked.

She pulled her bottom lip between her teeth and nodded

with a smile. I felt my lips tip in one to match. Xavier wrapped his arms around the two of us as we jumped around like children.

We paused, long enough for Xavier to ask, "Does he know?"

"Of course he knows!" She rolled her eyes as if he asked her something crazy. "Wait, did you just call Finn 'Behemoth'?"

"Am I wrong?" I asked, and we all laughed. "Seriously Ronnie, that's amazing news!" I added, but I was still unsure why we couldn't take the new store in Tennessee. Finn didn't have roots either, not that I knew of.

"When did this happen?" I asked, head spinning with a thousand questions. "How far along are you?"

She had to be at least six weeks, which meant she had been drinking while unknowingly pregnant.

"Eight weeks tomorrow," she said, and I caught her rubbing her lower abdomen as if she could already feel the life inside of her.

"Why didn't you tell me?" I asked. No wonder Finn came to check on her the other night. He was probably smitten, Hell, she looked about ready to burst from giddiness.

"I found out Friday before the benefit." Her eyes came back to mine, and they were full of tears. "We got the promotion from Holly-Jay, and you were so happy. I couldn't ruin your night. Then, well, your parents happened."

For a second, I pictured what it would be like. To have a family, a little niece or nephew running around my little house.

"I'm sorry," I said, hating myself for being so oblivious.

"Hey, don't be! I'm barely coming to terms with it myself." She laughed.

"Wait, are you supposed to have coffee?" I looked at her now empty cup and back to her.

She gripped her cup and playfully growled, "Alright, baby Finn. Why is everyone trying to take my coffee away from me?"

We spoke about all of the options we currently had before leaving the coffee shop, waving goodbye to Clay, the young barista, as we did. We all walked arm in arm into the shop, and I felt lighter than I had in days.

Ronnie was pregnant. With Aaron's best friend's baby. I was certain Aaron and I would be solid forever, and I had unburdened myself of my toxic parents. Life was starting to feel really, really good.

As we rounded the pharmacy, my steps faltered, my breathing erratic as I caught sight of Aaron. He never ceased to take my breath away when I saw him, the way his stony features softened just for me, the way he opened his arms for me to jump into. It was like coming home every time.

Bellamy

I couldn't believe November had flown by so fast. Haven and Adrian's wedding rehearsal went off without a hitch. The banquet hall was decorated perfectly. Gold and white banners had been twisted and hung up around the stone walls. Little fairy lights intertwined and twinkled to mimic the stars.

The tables were draped in burgundy cloth. White napkins lined the delicate china we only used for our A-list clients, and the silverware was polished to shine.

Haven looked stunning in a floor length cream dress. It was sleeveless, which was probably smart since all the sconces on the walls were lit with real flame and putting off a ton of heat. Adrian wore a cream suit to match with a burgundy pocket square. They looked absolutely amazing together, and they looked at each other with such love I almost cried.

I kept myself busy, checking on the guests to make sure

everything was to their liking. We had a few more celebrities arrive that morning for the wedding. They weren't too outlandish in their requests, which surprised me.

Every so often, I'd catch a glimpse of Aaron staring at me from where he was positioned near the entrance to the venue. Sparks kicked through my body every time. I hoped that never went away.

I was tired—exhausted, really. By the time all of the guests had retired back to Bedknobs & Broomsticks, it was past eleven. I was ready to crawl into bed with Aaron's arms weighing heavy around my waist as I went to sleep.

Ronnie bumped my hip as we helped clear the last of the tables. "Wanna have a sleepover tonight?"

We usually did the night before weddings. It was kind of our good luck ritual by now, and I had totally forgotten. I knew she would understand if I said no, but I really didn't want to since I knew with the baby, things would change eventually.

"Let me talk with Aaron first."

"Speak of the devil and he shall appear," Ronnie sang as

the two muscled arms I was just thinking about wrapped around my middle. Placing a kiss on my shoulder, he moved beside me, letting his arms drop.

"Handsome devil, you mean," Aaron said, his lips on the shell of my ear.

"Don't go getting a big head there."

He swatted my butt; a quick smack, but in the empty hall it cracked louder than thunder. Redness crept up my neck at the abrupt halt in the cleaning crew's steps.

Ronnie's snort of laughter broke the second her eyes found mine, and everything resumed, as if I had pressed play on a remote.

"Thanks for that!"

"Ah, it was just a little love tap, Bell." Ronnie snickered.

"Don't encourage him," I grumbled, but couldn't help the stupid grin from splitting my face once I looked back at Aaron. "Ronnie is staying the night, so you, mister, have to find other accommodations."

I fluttered my lashes at him, knowing full well he had his own house he could go to. He leaned down and pressed a quick kiss to my lips. "Only if you promise not to get into trouble."

"We'll be on our best behavior, sir."

"No, we won't!" Xavier called out from across the room

where he stood with his camera, bags all packed up and ready to go. "Don't let her lie to you like that."

Aaron led the way with my hand in his to Xavier's car. They loaded it down as Aaron and I said goodnight.

"I love you," he whispered across my lips. It still sent goosebumps all over my body and butterflies erupting in my belly every time he said those three little words.

"And I love you."

It was like being caught in our own little bubble. Hard to believe it had only been a little over a month that we had known each other. His kisses lingered as I got into the car, and Xavier sped off.

We ate our weight ice cream and binged movies before passing out in the living room, no trouble to be seen.

The next morning came fast, and with it, the big day had arrived. Our bride and groom would be Mr. and Mrs. Adrian Scott by sundown. Ronnie, Xavier and I made our way toward Misty's flower shop. We helped her load flowers into her van to drive them to the fountain. It was already blocked off last night to be cleaned. We arrived just as the maintenance crew turned the water on.

The cobbled streets had never looked better. The rented chairs were placed in neat rows, their coverings secured with navy blue sashes. Round tables were being set up on the other side of the fountain, bringing it to the center of tonight's festivities. They had put lights in the bottom of the fountain, casting a glow on the copper surface.

Everything was coming together while Ronnie and I helped Misty place vases of flowers on the tables. Xavier took a few pictures of the completed table scapes. Covered in white cloth, the tables boasted tall vases of deep red roses, tall eucalyptus, and a few delphinium stems dispersed between them. Golden chargers were laid at every place with a delicate white and gold veined plate on top. Tonight's dinner would be plated, so no guest would have to lift a finger. Wine glasses were turned over, waiting to be flipped and filled.

Haven arrived for makeup and hair, her two bridesmaids in tow. We met them last night, but I couldn't remember their names. It didn't matter. Ever since Ronnie and I arrived, everything felt like it was hurtling at full speed. "We're heading to Haven," Ronnie said as Xavier snapped a few pictures of the fountain. "Want to come and take some 'get ready' pictures now, or in a bit?"

He mumbled something about needing more photos, but followed us anyway. We traveled the stairs up the old church to the bridal suite. Haven was already in the chair, the makeup artist expertly crafting the same look from her bridal portraits.

Haven spotted us and waved the makeup artist away. "Ladies!" she cried "I'm getting married!"

I offered her a little smile. She was sweet, one of the easiest brides Ronnie and I had ever worked with.

"You are!" Ronnie shouted back as if we couldn't hear the excitement in her voice normally. "Is there anything we can get for you?"

Haven smiled. "Nothing I don't already have."

She wasn't kidding. People had sent her all kinds of arrangements and gifts, from big to small. She didn't seem like the type to want much of this flashy stuff, but I guess people bring what they want for you.

Her bridesmaids were dressed in the same deep red as the roses in their bouquets. The slight variation in colors paired nicely with Haven's dress, making her stand out amongst the sea of burgundy and navy.

Ronnie and I helped her into her dress, buttoning up the delicate lace-covered buttons all the way up to the small of her back. When she turned to look at her bridesmaids, they gasped. It was a beautiful moment and I was so happy Xavier was here flashing his camera.

Haven would remember this day forever, and I had a feeling Adrian would, too.

We got notification that everyone was ready. Glancing toward Haven, Ronnie and I asked if she was ready, to which she replied, "Hell yes!" making the whole room erupt in laughter.

Xavier went ahead of us to capture her first look with her father. The man was standing right inside the church doors, ready to give his only daughter away. He was crying, and it made me think of Billy. Would he walk me down the aisle to the man that captured my heart?

The bridesmaids made their way down the cobblestone aisle. We shut the church doors, getting Haven into position, fluffing the ends of her dress to sit perfectly so when the doors would open, Adrian and everyone waiting would see the perfection that Haven was.

The wedding march started, played by a quartet Haven insisted on. It was a haunting melody, a beautiful and entrancing sound. When the doors opened, I could see Adrian staring up at his soon to be wife, a vision in white shrouded by the dark stone of the old church. His eyes stayed glued to her in a soft, dream-like way. I even teared up a bit watching their love shimmer in the air over all the guests.

She walked with her father arm in arm toward her future. It was a wonderful ceremony, and the reception was filled with idle chatter and clinking drinkware.

The newlyweds took to the makeshift dance floor, swaying together to the string quartet in the corner. I felt the tears well up as couples joined them. It was a beautiful moment, suspended in time forever by the flashes of Xavier's camera.

I spotted Ronnie walking around the tables, encouraging the guests to join the happy couple on the dance floor. Her smile almost glowing. I couldn't be happier for her, and I knew deep in my bones, that her and I together could accomplish anything...even raising a baby.

Billy's hand reached across the table, closing around mine, sensing the emotions bubbling up. He gave me a small smile and squeezed my hand once more before pulling back and getting up to leave.

"You did great, Kitten." He said, leaning down to kiss the top of my head. A tear slipped out as I watched him walk toward the love of my life and give him a hearty shake.

Aaron spotted me instantly, as if my tears were a beacon, and gave me a heart-melting smile. I still couldn't believe that he was mine. But I thank my lucky stars every night that he is.

Epilouge
Aaron
(Five Months Later)

I glanced at my watch, noticing the time. Oh shit. Bellamy might actually kill me this time, and if she doesn't, Finn might. Our idea of fun wasn't exactly letting our women drag us to a gender neutral baby shower, but neither of us had much say in this event.

Of course Ronnie didn't want to know the sex of the baby. Bellamy and I both thought she did it to annoy Finn. Any chance she got, she made sure to grab that man by the balls and twist.

It would be funny if Bellamy wasn't the exact same way with me, twisting me up in different ways.

I took one last look at the realtor offer on my house. It was more than I paid, a solid offer. Since I basically lived at Bellamy's now, we both had decided it would be better if I sold my house. It was too far from her work, and ever since Haven and Adrian's wedding, Finn and I had started working on our own private security business close by.

It had been a labor of love. After acquiring a bank loan, Bellamy and I had carefully built a start-up plan with Finn's approval. All four of us, sometimes six when Xavier and Penelope joined in, had worked late nights and early mornings to get the building ready.

I signed the offer with a nod to the woman across the table from me.

Bellamy was standing just outside the backdoor, her hair swept up in a messy bun. A few tendrils had come loose, hanging like corkscrews on the sides of her face, her sharp makeup highlighting the contours of her cheeks.

When she turned toward the sound of my truck and smiled, it hit me again—how goddamn lucky I was. Her curves were on full display under an olive green dress that I couldn't wait to peel off of her when this was over.

She met me halfway to my truck, lips curling up in my favorite grin. She leapt into my waiting arms, and I crushed her against me, running my hands down her back to squeeze her plump ass.

We hadn't heard anything from her parents since their showdown a few months back, other than a lawyer contacting us to let Bellamy know she would be receiving the contents of her trust *in full* and her grandmother's ring.

"You're late," she scolded, pulling back to whack my chest.

"I'll make it up to you," I promised.

Her smile was wicked, and I could only guess what punishment she would reap from me. "I can think of a few things." Her lips ghosted mine as she spoke, sending a lick of heat straight to my groin.

"Oh, can you?" I asked before her lips covered mine, a little trill sounding up her throat as we kissed. "I love you, Sunshine."

She flashed her grandmother's gold ring we'd had reset on her finger in my face. "You better."

After everything, it had felt like the perfect piece of jewelry to use as a symbol of our engagement. We didn't have a date yet, but I couldn't wait for the day when my sunshine would finally say, "I do."

Acknowledgements

Please hold while I cry....buckets.

I published a book! A real, whole ass book.

My dream of becoming an author really came true, and it's all thanks to you, the reader, and my little cheer corner.

To my husband, who watched me pour my heart into this book night after night, thank you. Thank you for believing in me when others didn't. Thank you for always supporting my dreams even if you don't understand them. For all the snack runs, making sure that I drank enough water to move every few hours, and for making sure I take care of my mental health above all else.

To my littles, thank you for your playful hearts. You inspire me everyday to be a better person, and to remember life is only as bright as you make it. So use all the colors in your tool shed to build whatever dream you want.

Dearest Gurga, (aka my sister) your belief in me will forever be one of my favorite memories the moment I told you I wanted to publish a book. Thank you for being as excited, if not more, as I am.

Tina, good gravy, this dream wouldn't be a reality without you. Seriously, you're like half my brain. Your belief in me and my writing kept me in high spirits when I needed it most. Thank you for giving me feedback, and letting me use you as inspiration for Ronnie's character. Thank you for pushing me to write this story, to push my self doubt away and just *write*. Thank you for being the sounding board for all of my crazy plans, plots, and overall mayhem that my characters go through. But most importantly, thank you for being an ear for me to put a voice to all my crazy dreams.

Jessica, I can't believe you read this bad baby in two days. The excitement you have exuded throughout this whole process is much appreciated, I don't think I can put it into words. I can't imagine this process without your constant encouragement, and positivity, over everything, your belief in me, in my words, and in my hair brained ideas.

To my editor and fellow author, C.N. Maxwell. Thank you for your patience and guidance through all the edits and my many questions. You truly went over and beyond for me, and I will never be able to thank you enough. Through the whole process you were consistent in your critique and I think it made Sunshine a stronger book. (PS: You can totally disown me now bahaha)

To my proofreader, final pass editor, and gentle friend Trinity, you are so special. I don't have enough words in the world to express how grateful I am for you. Your editing is unmatched, you caught things I never would have. There isn't anyone else I could imagine taking a final look at my draft. You helped elevate this book past the potential I thought it had. Your keen eye for details, your commentary, it's gold, and I am honored you agreed to work with me. I can't imagine ever writing a book without you again. You're stuck with me....forever. (Now let's co-write that book.)

To Ashley, my very first beta reader that I had never met prior to sliding into your DM's to ask if you would read my book. You seriously gave me some of the best feedback I could have ever imagined. All of the sensitive topics you helped me navigate with a steady hand and compassionate heart.

To my beta readers who read the first draft, thank you for your encouragement and support. I don't think I would have continued to pursue my dream if not for y'all.

To Jon, my nonreader friend, your reactions and encouragement really gave me the leg up I needed to finish this book.

To my parents, I finally started, and finished something.

Can you believe it? I'll bet you thought this day would never come. But here it is, along with tangible proof. And to my bonus parent, thank you for everything you've ever done for me. I love y'all, always.

To all those who took time to read my debut novel, give me feedback, and send me messages, thank you! You will never know the joy you've brought me and my characters. Here's to many more!

Now turn the page for a super fun BONUS scene!

Bonus Scene

Ronnie and Xavier came over the morning before Billy's Christmas party; their peppy knocks on my door made me groan as Aaron let them in with a chuckle.

"They came to kidnap me!" I tell him, rolling my eyes and trying to get out of going shopping. I already had all the Christmas stuff I needed. Granted, Aaron suggested we get more than just a wreath of garland with berries for the front door and a Christmas tree. I had no idea he was such a Christmas die hard.

He crossed the room to haul me out of the comfy couch, placing a gentle kiss on my lips. "Maybe you need kidnapping." He teases while running his hands up and down my back.

"Why aren't they dragging you too?" I cut my eyes at the two fools I call friends, and Ronnie rolls hers mirroring my earlier action.

"Come on, Bell!" Xavier says, practically bouncing from

one foot to the other.

"Ugh!" I say as I step toward my room. Aaron swats my ass to get me moving faster, and I give a little yelp. Annoyed but changed into comfy clothes, I let Aaron walk us to the door and give him a kiss that lingers before we pile into Xavier's Red Rocket.

Xavier starts the car, and Christmas music blasts from the speakers as the pair of them belt lyrics as loud as they can.

"Friends night is a go!" Ronnie yells as if she's a secret agent with a precarious timeline. Xavier whipped the car in and out of traffic so fast I pretended not to notice as we made our way to the fake North Pole, which is the southern version of Christmas Shopping.

Kill me now.

Xavier parked in a spot pretty close to the exit, and we climbed out. Ronnie gripped my hands in hers once my door was shut and grinned like the cat that's got the cream.

She was practically vibrating with energy. She's so excited, like a kid at Walt Disney World. Her eyes were blown wide open as she took in the tunnel of lights we had to walk through to get to the shopping park.

The city converted its park into a Christmas Village, complete with Santa's workshop, and bakeries. They even had hot chocolate stands all throughout the mini village. To top it all off they had fake snow dusting the cobblestone pathways.

It doesn't snow much in the south.

Lights hung over each makeshift building in tasteful arrangements, like the elf statue near the entrance of Santa's workshop. Ronnie and Xavier hooked arms, making a quick dash towards the hot chocolate.

I followed them with a smile and shake of my head before catching up and linking my arm through Ronnie's. She squeezed me and ordered three hot chocolates, all with peppermint, and we sipped as we strolled through the village to get to the shops.

Ronnie, of course, had to have another ugly Christmas sweater to add to her collection. She demanded we pick one out too. As long as I've known Ronnie, Christmas has always been her favorite. She's a Christmas freak, decorating to the maximum, and I swore she now owned a Christmas sweater for every day in December.

She picked herself a bright green sweater with red tinsel sewn in odd patterns across the front and back. It had ornaments hung from the tinsel. I kid you not, real fucking *ornaments*. It was awful, but she insisted, so I indulged her and bought it as a gift. Besides, she could wear it when she got too big for her own clothes.

As we made our way around the village, the ornaments on her ugly sweater bounced every step we took. It made me smile; all the joy this created for the community. Children running around, oohing and aahing, screaming for more sugar, or at Santa.

Some whispered their wishes in his ear, looking like they were conspiring against their parents. The man they got to play Santa had painted blush on his cheeks and powder in his beard. He looked great in his red suit, with white fluff lining the coat and trousers.

I watched as couples mingled about, holding hands, sharing hot chocolate and other treats. I imagined Aaron here with me, and how he would hold me close as we walked the edges of the paths to make sure we never got caught in a crowd. He'd point out the odd Christmas light displays that caught his eye, and I would just smile at how happy *he* made me. There was a mermaid display over the fountain, flashing in time with low music played over invisible speakers, adding that extra element of wonder.

When Xavier and I managed to pull Ronnie away, we still had a few hours before Billy's Christmas shindig. Maybe I'd convince Aaron to give me an early Christmas present, like a nap.

My thoughts came to a screeching halt when Xavier didn't

take the exit back to my house.

"Where are we going?" I asked because we all had somewhere to be in a few hours, and I wanted to change before we went to Billy's.

"We're getting our nails done!" Ronnie screeched as if it was a surprise she had been holding in for a long time.

"Why?" I snorted. I didn't need my nails done, neither did Xavier. They just looked at each other and grinned. "What are you two up to?"

"Nothing! Sheesh, calm down back there." Xavier said, eyes catching mine in the rearview.

"I just want to spend more time with you," her eyes began to water, "I'm not used to sharing you with Aaron yet. Okay?"

Fucking hell, I hated when she cried. I was absolutely powerless against it, and she knew it.

"Please, Bell. Just-" she hiccuped and I blurted, "Okay! Just stop crying, please Ronnie." She did with a little smirk tipping up the corner of her lips. Xavier gave her a wink, thinking he's subtle.

I grumbled and sat back, crossing my arms and letting it happen. That was the best thing to do when these two got started.

He stopped at our favorite nail place. When we walked in,

the owner smiled and directed us to three awaiting chairs with deliciously hot water mixed with Epsom salt. I eyed my friends suspiciously. I know I didn't see either of them make a phone call for them to have this ready. So we must have had an appointment, and I just forgot.

After we got pampered, and a fresh polish and set of nails for all of us, we set back out into the cold December air. Ronnie stopped me before I could leave the nail salon and handed me a garment bag.

"We're heading to Billy's, but I already packed us all outfits!" Ronnie said, passing me to lift the trunk and pull out three black garment bags.

I glanced at the time, shocked by how much of it had gone by. "We're going to be late," I grumbled.
She just tilted her head and held out the black bag.

"And where do you expect us all to change?" I crossed my arms, fully aware of the bratty tone. "Why can't we just change at Billy's?"

Xavier rolled his eyes and took the bag with my name on it. He marched toward me, grabbed my elbow, and turned me around. I didn't argue as he squeezed my arm and pushed me into the bathroom, marked as employees only.

"Change!" He ordered through the door.

I stomped my foot as if he could see it.

"I heard that!" His voice was full of mirth.

"I don't care!" I shouted back.

I hung the garment bag up on the hook that was attached to the back of the door. I gasped when I unzipped it. A beautiful deep emerald velvet dress was hiding inside. It was way too formal for dinner with Billy and his family, and I contemplated not putting it on.

"Don't even think about it!" Ronnie shouted from the other side of the door.

"We still have to change, too, Bell! Get a move on gorgeous." Xavier said and I heard them both dissolve into giggles.

Have friends, they said, it will be fun, they said, *hmph.*

I stripped out of my clothes and placed them in the bag, carefully unhooking the dress from the hanger. The material was soft. It rippled like water over my skin, settling over my curves like a lover's caress.

The sleeves had delicate lace overlaid from cuff to shoulder in patterns of ivy. When I moved back and forth in front of the mirror, the velvet gave them an almost lifelike perception. It was a beautiful dress, and I felt like a goddess.

I unlocked the door, and it opened, most likely due to Xavier's impatience. My friends stood on the other side of the door, Ronnie's smile was a mile wide, and Xavier's jaw nearly hit the floor.

"I knew it!" Ronnie exclaimed, clapping her hands together. She swept into the bathroom and changed into a show-stopping red dress that complimented her milky skin and blonde hair. The sleeves were striped with white, reminding me of a candy cane.

Xavier was next. He took a little longer, and when he emerged, he had a triumphant grin and an utterly awful suit on. It was the tackiest Christmas suit I had ever seen. It had squares of yellow, blue, green, and white. Inlaid with Christmas images.

"Setting out for the ugliest Christmas sweater contest early?" I said, laughter evident in my tone.

He glared at me and said, "Let's get going, can't be late!"

Ronnie and I giggled the whole way out the door, tears sprang to her eyes. We laughed so hard.

Anxiety settled in my belly as we made our way to Billy's. Maybe it was the overall excitement in the car, or the dress I kept smoothing over my legs, drawing patterns into the fabric, but I couldn't shake my nerves.

We pulled into Billy's parking lot. Christmas lights were mounted across the roof line, casting a yellow glow over the gravel lot. Ronnie and Xavier smiled at each other, wide smiles that made them both glow with childlike wonder.

Ronnie gripped my hand as Xavier walked inside. We watched him disappear behind the door before looking at each other.

"Ready?" She asked, eyes watering slightly.

My brows kissed as I nodded slowly. She led the way; once we got to the door, she turned and asked me to wait a few seconds before following her in.

"Ooooookay?" I half said-half asked.

I waited a beat before pulling the door open, listening to the screech of the hinges that felt like a comfort.

Everything felt like it hit me at once. The smells of roasted ham, garlic, and cinnamon. The way the room had been cleared of the usual layout of tables, booths, and chairs. One long table ran down the center of the room, candles dotted the surface, and I spotted more around the room, actual candles lit with flame.

My eyes traveled over the decor that rested on the table. Long strands of green and red garland and gold ornaments adorned the tree in the corner.

My eyes scanned where everyone was standing across the room, staring at—I turned to look behind me—me.

"What's going on?" My voice was shaky, and I didn't like all the anxiety I felt rushing through my brain. I cleared my throat, ready to try again. I shouldn't be nervous. This was my family. I spotted Billy standing with his grandkids Josh and Cece, Ronnie and Finn, Xavier. Even Landon and Benny, Aaron's closest friends, had joined us.

The back door opened, and there he was, my man. Aaron was dressed in black dress pants, and a white button-down with the sleeves rolled up to reveal his corded forearms. He looked like a dream.

In the dim candlelight his green eyes were stuck on me, just like my hazel ones were glued to him. He smiled, and I swear my panties evaporated.

He slowly walked to where I still stood on the slight step up at the door, unable to move. When he was just an arm's length away he paused. I could tell his eyes were glassy, his smile the happiest I've ever seen him.

"Bellamy." He started, and it hit me. Aaron planned this—the elaborate trip around the city with my friends, the pampering, the dress.

"I've endured plenty of loneliness, grief, and loss throughout my life. That's how I knew, without a doubt, that the love I have for you surpasses even the waves that kiss the sand. I love you more than the sun that shines through dark clouds. More than the stars that freckle the night sky."

Tears trickled from my eyes, and everything else faded as I listened to this safe, handsome, and loving man pour his heart out to me.

"I've loved you from the moment our eyes locked in that club. And I knew then that you were meant to be mine, and I was meant to be yours."

Not taking his eyes from mine, he bends down on one knee and says the words I never dreamed I'd hear. "Bellamy Heidi Drummon. Will you do me the greatest honor and become my wife?"

He lifted the black box, and inside sat my grandmother's ring, nestled in blue velvet and polished to a shine—the cluster of diamonds glittered against the candles like the night sky.

I sank to the floor with him, uncaring how it looked, and nodded as the tears flowed harder and landed on my dress.

His hands bracketed my face as his thumbs swept away the tear tracks. "Words, baby." His smile lit up the whole room. More than the candles that dotted every surface, more than the twinkling Christmas lights. "Say I do, Sunshine."

"I do, fucker." I said through the hiccups and tears.

"I love you, Sunshine. I'd go to the ends of the earth to make you smile."

Now I'm full-on sobbing, wracked with so much emotion I can't contain it. His eyes were wet with tears as he slid the ring onto my finger.

Placing my hands on his cheeks, I see the diamonds sparkle, and tears threaten to flow again. I never thought I'd see this ring again, and yet Aaron found it and managed to get it fitted for me.

Ronnie squealed and launched toward where we were sitting on the floor, unable to hold herself back. She hauled me into her arms and jumped up and down.

Xavier was next, hugging us both as Ronnie's mouth started to run wild with colors and schemes. Plans on top of plans.

Out of the corner of my eye, I see Finn, Landon, and Benny slap Aaron on the back.

Dudes.

When Ronnie and Xavier scampered away, Aaron grabbed my arm and twirled me back into his body, kissing me breathless.

"I can't tell you how happy I am for you, Kitten," Billy says, wiping his cheeks with a hanky.

Aaron released me so I could hug the man who had been more a father to me than my own. He patted my back and ran soothing strokes over my hair while he congratulated me with words meant only for my ears.

I looked around the room in search of my man, and threw

myself back in Aaron's arms, fully content and happy—All of the people I loved in one place, and now with a *fiancé*.

About the Author

Taylor Wilson-West is a firm believer that the magic of words on a page can transport readers to new places, and finds comfort in making new, albeit fictional, friends. Currently residing in a small town in North Carolina with her husband and two perfect kiddos, she lives off Cheerwine, potatoes, and ranch dressing. When she's not reading or writing, she can be found shopping at bookstores, adding to her never ending bookshelves. Taylor finds it necessary to have a bookish candle that fits every genre and book character that she has ever fallen in love with. Her favorite moment in any consumable media is when confident, fat main characters get their happily ever after.

If you've made it this far, please leave a review! Reviews

are an author's best friend, and readers obviously! :P

GoodReads

Amazon

Find me here:

Instagram